BEAR AND RAVEN

JERRY AUTIERI

1

Gyna stepped from Prince Kalim's palace into Licata. The stone-paved street swept downhill to a jumble of white buildings with bizarre tile roofs. Moonlight draped silver outlines over the rectangular angles spread out below. A dog barked in the distance, but for such a crowded city she heard no other sound except for the mumbles of the escorts standing behind her. She glanced back.

The Arab girl who had guided her through the palace now stood with her thin hands clasped over her lap. She regarded Gyna with hooded eyes. Two guards in blue tunics and shouldering spears flanked her. One shooed Gyna away with a sweep of his hand while the other began to draw the heavy doors shut in the gate tunnel.

She clicked her tongue at the Arabs. They were no more use to her, not that she could communicate with them. Without Jamil the Moor to speak for her, she had no voice. Not that she could speak to Jamil in anything but rudimentary Frankish. In this place called Sicily, she was mute.

"Go see to our treasure in the tower," she muttered, repeating what Bjorn had just told her. "Send me off while you all get to plough foreign women. Did you remember I can't talk to them. You one-eyed bear."

The door thumped shut behind her, and the grate screeched and rattled as it lowered into place. She was cut off from all the rewards and celebration simply because she was a woman. The Arabs would not think of awarding her a man for the night. She had done as much to burn the Byzantine ships as anyone else. But her reward was a lonely walk through a foreign city.

Bastards.

The Arabs had at least returned her weapons. Being a woman, they had only asked her to surrender the weapons they could see. She kept a dagger hidden at her back that no one had ever noticed. She could have skewered their precious prince—that prancing fawn—at any time. As fun as that might have been, she kept the dagger for more practical defense. Her fellow crew understood she was no man's prize. The Arabs might not have the same understanding, and lopping off a few fingers would teach them respect.

And start a fight—which she would enjoy.

She took off up the road, in no hurry with the whole night ahead. The sweet scent that pervaded the city by daylight was now cloying by moonlight. As she proceeded downhill from the palace with its impossible golden domes, she was grateful for fouler odors flowing from trash-filled alleys. She could endure a stench better than the sweetness that plugged her nose and set her eyes tearing. Perhaps it was poison winnowed into the air against foreigners like her. Made perfect sense. Who could raid this place with eyes blinded and noses flowing with snot?

She continued along the street. The dockside tower that overlooked the main road into Licata poked its square crown above the flat roofs of the city. Her reward of gold waited there. The captain of that guard tower had seemed friendly enough. Not that she trusted many, least of all the Arabs. Trust was what got you killed. She trusted Bjorn, Yngvar, Alasdair—Thorfast sometimes. He was so quick with his tongue that she couldn't distinguish his praise from insult. It made her uneasy around him.

To think all of them would soon be rolling around with these foreign women. What was the fuss? They were all covered up and the few whose faces she had glimpsed were frowning and suspicious. She imagined Bjorn, his pants bunched at his feet and a stupid grin on his wide face.

"You're a fool," she said, but was not sure if she meant Bjorn or herself. She should have stood up for a reward of her own. "Now I'm running errands like a servant."

Glancing back at the palace, its domes shined like three miniature moons. The humidity of the night air imparted a silver halo over everything. The street remained empty behind her.

Would not a city as big as this have some people out at night, she thought. Certainly everyone kept the sun's cycle. But a guard patrol or a drunk should be out.

Her hand slipped to the longsword at her hip. Its comforting weight rubbed against her side. She was grateful to Bjorn for insisting she build the strength to wield it. It was a beautiful weapon that no man expected her capable of using. Combined with the deerskin pants she wore, most men glanced past her as if she were no more than an undersized warrior.

The road led to a turn around a blind corner. From behind she heard the scrape of boots on stone. She hesitated and resisted the urge to turn. She knew the other ambusher waited around the blind corner. The thief behind her would rush her ahead into the trap like a hound flushing out a hare.

She continued ahead as if she had heard nothing. But she was smiling. She would have some fun tonight after all.

A cart filled with the remains of rotting hay leaned against the building opposite the corner. A door set into the white walls of the building leaked faint yellow light around the jamb. As she approached the corner, she reached for the hilt of her sword.

In a single, explosive stroke she sped around the corner and drew her sword. It rang free from its leather sheath, striking moonlight off its carefully polished length.

Empty street lay before her. A cat leapt off a broken barrel set against a blank wall and sped across the street into shadow. The paved street flowed down toward the tower like a fluttering gray ribbon.

She held the sword in both hands, nonplussed. The weight of it in her loosening grip caused it to sag.

She whirled behind, sword readied again.

"Nothing," she said. Her voice echoed off the vacant streets. She spoke louder. "You're back there. I know it. Come after me if you dare."

Her face heated and she let the sword sink beside her leg. At least no one had witnessed her foolishness. She waited another breath, hoping someone would materialize. But after all she was alone. She clicked the sword back into its sheath.

"The tower," she said, pinching the bridge of her nose. "Will anyone receive me at this hour? Can't believe I'm jumping at shadows."

She shook her head then brushed her hair from her face. The tower could wait until tomorrow. She would pass beneath it, but not draw attention. Besides, she had eaten and drunk so much at Prince Kalim's feast she preferred to curl up on the deck and sleep. Perhaps she owed her imaginings to an over-stuffed belly. She rarely ate so much. It must affect her mind somehow.

So she followed the street downhill into the shadow of the tower.

Two men rushed her out of the darkness of a side alley.

Before she understood the threat, she was leaping free of them with speed like the cat she had just witnessed up the road.

She landed on her feet, facing them.

Two dark men with thick beards and shadowed faces lurched at her. They had long, curving blades in each of their square fists. Their shadowy bulk suggested heavy clothing or armor.

No time to observe more.

They ran at her. She skipped back.

Gyna delighted in battle and was fascinated with death. She had once glimpsed the Valkyries stalking the battlefield, picking the worthy dead for a seat in Valhalla. She had never spoken of this to anyone. Yet ever since she sought to find them again.

The deaths of these two scum would not summon the Valkyries.

They would summon guards. So despite her lust for fighting, she had enough sense to back away from the street toward the shadows where no Arab would witness her work.

The two grunted as she slipped out of their arms. She scrabbled into an alley on the opposite side of the street. Her sword was too long for the narrow quarters. Behind her, a shaft of moonlight revealed she had chosen a dead end. A gray wall sealed off the end, where a mass of formless trash had gathered into the corners to fill the alley with the reek of decay.

The two Arabs plugged the exit with their mass. Their smiles were as bright as the blades readied before them. They spoke in guttural threats.

She offered them a smile, raising her right hand in surrender while slipping her left behind her waist.

"Well, you've caught me. Mercy, I beg you. I'm just a poor woman with a sword too big for my own good."

Neither party understood the other, but the Arabs seemed to accept her feigned surrender. The lead Arab chuckled as he stepped into the alley. His companion was fast behind him.

"So what will it be? Rape then robbery? Robbery only? Maybe you just want to talk? You boys lonely?"

Yet they wanted only murder. The moment the lead drew within arm's length he struck.

Gyna struck as well.

She had drilled this strike every available day she had for years. Drilled until her arms felt as if they would fall from her shoulders. All the while Bjorn or Yngvar cajoled her to draw faster, to strike truer, to mask her intent better.

The strike never failed her.

She reached to her back, finding the hilt of the dagger with practiced ease.

It flashed out of its sheath in a reverse grip. She twisted to the side.

The blade sliced up into the startled Arab's throat, driving through soft flesh to judder into bone.

She shoved him backward onto the other attacker. The whites of his eyes flashed in the dark as his companion staggered into him.

Gyna grunted as she plowed harder into the enemy, spilling them both back into the street.

The lead Arab slid down his companion's body. The companion grabbed him under arm as if to set him upright, babbling in his foreign tongue as if begging him.

Gyna had tried to withdraw her dagger but she had lodged it in bone. She twisted the blade, drawing more blood and a garbled wail from her dying enemy. Then she released the dagger.

She had another in her boot. She had replaced them after her weapons had been returned. Prince Kalim had places where he demanded his subjects walk barefoot. Jamil the Moor had warned all of them of this. So she had prudently surrendered the daggers to her hosts.

Now she was going to bury them in the flesh of her hosts' brothers.

The other Arab let his companion flop to the ground, bloody hands pawing at his throat and one leg kicking. Gyna thought he looked like a crushed spider with its legs spasming in death. Yet she had no breath to laugh.

She drew her other dagger from her boot. This was shorter but no less sharp than her main dagger. The remaining Arab screamed and swiped at her with his own curved blade.

The air snapped before her as the wicked slash skimmed past her nose. He struck again, pressing her back into the alley. She was on her back foot as the hulking shadow of her attacker blotted out the exit. His curses flowed in time with his strikes.

Gyna stabbed her shorter knife at him, but he had reach. She would become stuck on his blade before she could draw close enough for her short blade.

In such a situation, she knew only one recourse.

She screamed, throwing her life at the feet of the gods and not caring what they did with it.

Though the Arab had no cause to do so, he skittered back as Gyna sprang. The ferocious shift in her stance had startled him. Even with his companion dead, he had likely expected a woman to be easy work. Yet Gyna defied simple expectations. She twisted them to her own benefit. His moment of shock was all she required to tear open his neck.

She was like a cat with iron claws launching at the face of her enemy. Her shorter blade sliced away the tip of his nose in one blow. As she crashed into him, she punched the blade into his gut. It slipped between whatever armor he wore, if any, and he doubled over with a moan.

Her knee crunched into his face, and before even she understood what had happened she had ridden him to the ground. His blood was hot and salty on her lips by the time she realized she had killed him. His neck and chest filled with dark blood and his startled eyes stared up at the moon above the alley.

She heaved while staring at the corpse straddled beneath her legs. She shook her head, then stepped off the body. She kicked the dead man then pulled her short dagger from his chest. The other corpse sprawled half in the street, her best dagger protruding from under his chin. She wrested it free with care. If the blade bent she would be doubly angered at these fools.

Standing between the two bodies, she wondered what to do next. The guard tower was nearby, perhaps too near. Had these two been guards just surprised at her approach? Her hands went cold at the possibility. Yet they had ambushed her. Guards would have at least attempted to force her to stand down.

But who knew what the customs were in this place? Maybe it was a crime to be out at night.

She ran her hands along the body of the man lying half in the street. He wore heavy clothes that she peeled back. Fleas leapt about the folds of his poor clothing. She leapt away with a shout. Fleas and lice were constant burdens, but she was currently free of both.

So they were thieves or other scum. They had chosen what they had thought an easy target. She would have to explain their deaths if anyone caught her standing here. But the night remained eerily silent despite what must be thousands of people all around her.

Using her dagger, she flipped aside the Arab's shirt at the waist to reveal a tattered leather belt and a small pouch tied to it. She cut this away and used her dagger blade to sweep it into her palm. Hard coins pressed through the cloth pouch. She smiled as she slid the gold and silver coins into her palm.

"You weren't a waste of time," she said. "No one has to know where I got these."

She fed them to her own purse, then started back toward the ship. She wiped the blood from her face with the back of her arm. She would have to clean up somewhere. For now, in the moonlight no one would see the signs of violence all over her. By morning Bjorn and the others would return and she would be saved from explaining her night to the prince's guardsmen. Besides, would anyone care about the death of two thugs?

The docks were guarded, however, and she knew better than to saunter through this area with blood splattered all over her body. As always, her kills had not been clean. She liked it that way, though now it proved an inconvenience. She slipped off the main road and hugged the shadows for the final distance.

After a circuitous path through stacks of emptied crates and barrels or tarp-covered stalls, she arrived at the pier where the ship was docked.

She drew up short.

A dozen men stood around or aboard her ship.

These were not thugs, either. They wore heavy armor and carried long spears. Their ballooning pants were the blue of Prince Kalim's men.

"Guards?" she whispered in disbelief, ducking behind two barrels that smelled of fish. She peeked out, straining to see more of the scene unfolding at the ship.

Two men had drawn lots to remain behind and guard the ship against thieves. They were now both held between two guards each. Shouting echoed back across the docks, but Gyna could not understand what was said. The crewmen struggled and protested, earning nothing but return shouts. The Arabs aboard the ship were sifting through the deck, tossing whatever they found into a pile in the prow.

"My sea chest," she said, pressing against the barrels as if ready to burst through them. "I'll gut you if you touch my things."

But she could not make good on the threat and realized it. At least a dozen guards surrounded the ship with half of them holding flaming torches aloft.

At last one of the crew broke free and punched his captor in the face. The guard staggered with both hands over his nose.

One of the other guards speared the crewman with no more care than if he had been spearing fish in a barrel. The crewman screamed and collapsed to the dock. The Arab put his foot to his chest as he worked the spear free, then thrust it into the crewman's neck to end the screaming.

The other crewman hung limp between his captors as he watched the guard roll his friend's corpse into the water.

"Gods, curse them." Gyna pulled back. This was no search of the ship. This was theft and murder.

Something had happened tonight. Bjorn and the others were in grave danger. She had to warn them.

But she did not know where they were or how to find them.

And she could speak no language anyone understood.

She slipped away into the night, the echoes of the pillaging guards chasing her from the docks.

2

Two days of skulking along the waterfront had driven Gyna to the brink of madness. Her hands itched to grip sword and dagger and hack through the mass of people that flowed across the docks each day. She huddled inside the door of an abandoned building that must have once stored piles of shit, for the reek within its dark and humid confines stung Gyna's eyes and nose with bitterness. Truly, there was no pleasing scent on the air of this place called Sicily. It was an island of rot.

The dirt floor of the single room was covered in debris and decaying planks. It was no bigger than ten paces long and wide. The roof had collapsed into a corner and the wreckage was wreathed in spiderwebs. She determined from the heavy dust the only use this building had seen in a long time was as a haven for rats. The fat vermin crawled out of their holes at night. One had even nipped at her feet through her boots.

At night she surrendered the space to the rats, for she used the darkness to search for Bjorn and the others. During the day, she dozed in her hiding place after stealing bread from any one of the poor local families that suffered life at the waterfront. This cycle could not last long, she knew, before being discovered.

If she could speak the local language she might have learned much from just sitting in her hiding place. It seemed none of the workers at the docks were capable of speaking in normal voices. She had never seen a people so enamored of their own voices that they had to shout every trivial thought. But they surrounded her now. She just did not know what they said.

Yet she had a guess. The morning after the prince's guards had seized her ship she returned to find more of them questioning the locals. They pointed at the ship, at the city, at the sea, at the sky. Apparently the locals believed Gyna either flew like a gull or swam like a seal. They pointed everywhere except the obvious places she might hide. Perhaps these bolt holes were not so obvious after all. To her mind, standing in the doorframe of a decaying building seemed the first place to check. Yet no one had.

The ship remained tied to the dock, always surrounded by a dozen guards in heavy leather jerkins and blue pants. They each bore swords, spears, and a dagger. Not men to treat easily. She observed a night and day rotation of guards.

What had Bjorn and those other fools gotten into? She could guess the women they had gone to lay with were the source of the troubles. These Arabs seemed touchy about their women, and a bear like Bjorn was not a gentle lover. At least not to other women. Something had offended the prince enough to seize the ship.

She had spent the morning staring at the mast slowly wobbling on the tide. Her eyelids were heavy and she felt dozy. Tonight she would try the tower again. She had approached last night, but the sight of the guards there made her pause. Besides, whom could she speak to? Without Jamil the Moor she could only hope someone spoke Norse, an impossibility as far as she could tell. Jamil had likely become embroiled in whatever mess Bjorn had created.

When she did get ahold of Bjorn, she was going to teach him to leave her stranded like this. She slipped back into the reeking building.

Something caught her eye.

The guards surrounding her ship all turned as one to a small group approaching them down the dock.

"Norsemen," she said, hugging the doorframe as she stared out in surprise.

In truth she could not be certain they were true Norse. But they were all golden haired, tall, and broad shouldered. There were those among the Arab guards who were a match for their strength. But the fair skin of the three arrivals contrasted with the Arab guards. Their trimmed beards and combed hair along with gray cloaks pinned at their left shoulder marked them as men of the North. They also carried straight swords and round shields at their backs.

The Arabs took no exception to their arms. Two came forward and gestured the Norsemen halt halfway to the ship. An exchange took place and no one seemed to interpret between them. Perhaps the Norsemen had learned the local speech? That was as marvelous to Gyna as their very presence in this place.

She waited and watched. The two Arabs returned to their companions while the three Norsemen turned to each other in conversation. They all seemed to be waiting for something.

A cart filled with stacked barrels rolled into Gyna's view. The driver stood up and began speaking to someone she could not see. Hoping the driver would continue on, Gyna cursed when he instead jumped off his cart. He walked around his mule to tie it off to a post.

As much as she twisted or stood on her toes, she could no longer observe the docks. Something was about to happen to her ship. She had to discover what.

Alasdair had once told Gyna a key to remaining unseen was to appear as if you belonged to the place where you wished to hide. In shadow, seem as a shadow. In a crowd, seem as one of the crowd. As a lone woman standing among foreign men in blood-stained clothing wearing pants and a sword—well, she had no answer for that. It was not a problem Alasdair would ever face.

Yet confidence went a long way toward selling anything, she had learned. After slipping free of her hiding place, she stood tall and resisted any urge to duck behind a bale or slip into a crowd of bare-backed laborers. Sweat already flowed into her eyes from the intense humidity. Her nerves produced sweat twice as fast. Still, she walked around the cart as if she had business with it. She wished to pull her cloak hood overhead, but it would only draw attention.

She stood behind the cart, leaning casually on the barrels as if she were only waiting to unload them. The Norsemen and the Arabs now both looked down the docks at another approaching party.

Her stomach churned and eyes narrowed.

A wiry man in a gray robe and white head cover swept down the docks as if he were Prince Kalim himself. His pointed face reminded Gyna of a rat. He stood as if he were three times taller than any other man, yet he was the shortest among the pack of guards accompanying him.

She recalled his name, Saleet, the bastard who had harassed them at the palace. Yet what fouled her guts was the man at his left.

Jamil the Moor was hardly recognizable in his new robes. Yet his proud gait and regal head were unmistakable. He wore the same robes and head cover as Saleet, though his gray hair and fair eyes lent him a softness unlike his companion. He walked a step behind Saleet as if in deference. The old moor's eyes were focused and lively, and directed at the ship. He licked his lips as if about to devour a succulent hunk of meat.

This could only mean trouble with Jamil at the heart of it. She had never trusted him. His back may have been bent and his head lowered, but she had seen the hatred in his eyes. She had seen what Yngvar could not. The glares and curled lips from the old Moor whenever Yngvar turned away. He was not a dog but a wolf. Yngvar had treated with him too lightly, as if a man who's only weapon was his words could be no threat.

But words could bite as deep as a sword and take off a man's head with equal efficacy. Had she not learned as much from her dear sister and brother-in-law, Waldhar?

Now it would seem Jamil had his freedom and undoubtedly that came at a cost to Yngvar and the rest.

Saleet and Jamil had five palace guards with them, probably the same she had seen seizing her ship. They wore ballooning blue pants and carried heavy swords at their hips. They were a dark wall of muscle behind Saleet as he greeted the three Norsemen.

Trite and ingratiating greetings were shared from both parties. Gyna spit in disgust. Especially for Norsemen bowing their heads to a foreign rat who could not hold a toy sword in battle, never mind a true weapon. Whatever language they spoke, Gyna only heard thin and scrambled words. Too many of the locals were screaming at each other closer to her. Though it sounded to her as if they all must be spoiling for a fight, they merely conducted business.

The cart driver appeared from around the corner and pulled up short. He let out a shocked yelp and pressed a hand over his heart.

She saw the recognition spark. Guards had been asking after her. She could not be hard to describe, she thought. A beautiful and dazzling woman wearing pants and carrying a sword like a man. None of the local women would rate as beautiful much less carry swords.

She reached for a dagger, then reconsidered. The hesitation cost her.

The driver backed away, pointing and shouting. The conversation around her died and she felt a dozen eyes turn to her.

She plowed into the driver, who tripped as he was already stepping back. She needed a distraction. As her hand was already on one of her daggers, she drew it and ran to the front of the cart. The mule swung its heavy head toward her with a look of indifference. Bjorn loved animals. Perhaps because he was half-bear himself. But she appreciated them either for their labor or their meat.

The dagger, lovingly sharpened by her own hand, sliced through the mule's bindings. She then flipped it in her grip and rammed it into the mule's rump.

She was already fleeing as the mule screamed and bucked. His hooves slammed into the cart and its painful braying drowned out the shouts of the driver, who now had to calm his animal rather than follow her.

Running was another sure way to draw attention. Once she had fled the chaos she slowed and resisted the temptation to glance behind. Some men stared at her with their dark eyes deadened from a life of bitter labor. Most gave slow blinks then turned aside. Two or three watched her scurry between bales and crates stacked along the dockside. No one gave chase.

She smiled. She was good at this.

As she puffed a lock of hair off her eye, a lean man with sad eyes and an owlish face stepped into her path. He lowered a spear in both his gnarled hands and called out to her.

She darted to the side behind a wall of stacked barrels. She grabbed the lip of one to topple it, but the barrels were filled and unbudging. The guard chased her, shouting in his garbled language.

Abandoning the barrels, she sped toward a dockside market that had sprung up overnight. Locals had set out stalls and tables with various goods sailors might desire after a sea journey. Every kind of good lined these rows from spools of rope and new scales to vegetables and pigeons in wicker cages. Old men and women argued for attention from the scant customers who bumped through the avenues of their goods.

Gyna plunged into their midst with the spearman chasing.

She slammed into a table stacked with small blocks of salt. The table and its contents sprayed back on the old man behind it. He screamed as Gyna leapt both the table and his prone body. A younger man, either a guard or a son of the merchant's, grabbed her arm.

The younger man's grip was sweaty and strong. His curses battered her ears as he yanked her around. The spearman shouted from behind. Another answered him from Gyna's left.

The young man squared up to her, his face red and twisted in anger. But his eyes widened in shock when he realized he had snagged a woman. She flashed a smile.

Her knuckles crunched bone in the young man's fine cheeks. Her fists had been hardened to fighting and flesh there formed a thick cushion. She no longer had delicate hands like her precious sister. But she did have a formidable weapon always available.

The young man released her in shock, slipped in the shattered blocks of salt, and landed atop the older merchant.

Now two spearmen converged on her. She slipped away into the crowded rows of tables. The merchants were already carrying away goods in their arms. Gyna's hip bumped another table where rows of wooden mugs splashed onto the ground.

She hurdled this table, then the next, each time scattering goods and sowing chaos. At last, some of the merchants chose to block her rather than let her run loose. The first man wore only a brown vest over his body and his stomach swelled like a pregnant sow's. He seemed intent on bouncing her off its girth, but as she ran, she drew a second dagger.

The fat merchant barely escaped an eviscerating slash. Instead he suffered a deep score across his belly as Gyna shoved past.

That was the last of the merchants to block her. She threw whatever came to hand behind her. The guards doggedly pursued. She was running out of market and the main road into Licata now loomed ahead. Regular guards were posted there, also leaning on spears. They seemed unaware of the madness she was weaving in the market.

Then she tripped.

She did not know what had caused her fall. She was now a noselength from the ground, her dagger dropped out of reach, both palms and knees burning from the skid over hard-packed earth.

A shadow spread over her. She rolled to the side, reaching for her dagger. Her fingers brushed the hilt, but it slipped away. At the same time, a spear point slammed into the ground where she had been.

"You want to kill me?" She staggered to her feet and continued to pitch forward. Her sword dragged heavy at her hip and she had a single dagger remaining. She looked back at the heaving, sweating spearmen. "What did Yngvar do that you'll kill me on sight?"

But she received no answer. Instead, she evaded the second spearman's thrust. Yet he was unskilled and Gyna found herself grabbing the shaft of his spear. Both shared a look of surprise.

Then she tore it out of the guard's grip and batted the shaft against the side of the head. He cursed and staggered back.

The other guard stood only to meet the butt of the same spear. It hammered into his face, breaking his nose. Gyna laughed, but dropped the spear and fled. It was too big to be of any use to her.

She slid sideways into a shadowed alley. Behind her, angry

shouting and protests echoed from the makeshift market. The shadow cooled her, but sweat now stung her eyes. Her breath came hard and gasping.

A foot-chase was no good. She was light and nimble and had to rely on this against her bulkier foes. She leapt up to the eaves of the low buildings providing shade. She pulled up and hooked her foot onto the tile roof. One faded red tile threatened to slip free, but she hauled onto the roof before it did. Scrabbling up higher along the gentle pitch, she heard someone follow into the alley.

But whoever gave chase, continued past.

She lay flat and still on the roof, the sun prickling at the back of her neck and exposed flesh. It took all her effort not to pant. It felt as if she waited half a day for calm to return. But in truth, judging from the unchanging sun, she had not even lain still for an hour.

At last confident, she slid off the roof back into the alley. Two tiles chased her down, crashing to the alley floor. Her hands went cold, but no one investigated. She had slipped her enemies.

For now.

She had to return to the ship. Something was happening that she could not miss. Norsemen conversing with Saleet and Jamil before her ship could only be treachery at work. She followed the alley out the opposite end, to find a short road with only a black-robed elderly woman tottering along it. Speeding past the woman, she gained another alley that let her double back toward the market.

Peeking out at the scene, the market was already righting itself. More guards had joined. Apparently the confusion had drawn opportunistic thieves and the local guards had lined up three that squatted in a line with hands behind their heads. The merchants she had injured shouted and gesticulated at the guards. The fat merchant with a slashed belly now had a white wrap about his gut.

She slinked past this toward the dock. Crouching low and head swiveling toward every sound, she arrived at the end of the dock where her ship was still tied.

"Gods, I missed it."

The Arab guards were gone. But she understood what had happened nonetheless.

Norsemen were now aboard her ship. The crew were loading casks and chests in a long line from the end of the dock to the deck.

Saleet and Jamil had sold her ship to the Norsemen.

Whatever caution she had assumed to this point burned away in red flames that filled her vision. She stalked toward the crewmen handing their goods down the line. Her nostrils flared.

"Hey, dog-shit, who is your leader?"

The Norseman put his cask down and faced her with a frown. The man next in line held his hands out expecting the cask. But he also stared at Gyna in shock.

"You two lovers forget how to speak? Who is your fucking leader? I'm not asking a third time."

The astounded men pointed down the docks to one of the same cloaked men she had seen dealing with Saleet. He stood at the top of the gangplank, his rank identified by the gold armbands on both biceps.

Gyna sneered at the two crewmen and strode down the line of men who had all stopped to watch her pass.

She reached the bottom of the gangplank and pointed at the man standing by the rails. The ship was not high-sided and reached only to her hip. But the Norseman looked like a giant from this vantage.

"What are you doing on my ship?"

Her hands itched to draw her sword. Its weight tugged against her leg as if begging to be released. The Norseman gave her a bemused grin.

"Your ship? I was told the last owners are all awaiting execution."

The words hit her harder than if the Norseman had flung a hammer. She stepped back, stomach tight and eyes blinking.

Before she could add more, she heard a familiar voice from behind.

She turned back along the dock.

Saleet and his guards were rushing down the length. The burly Arabs had their spears lowered.

Rushing alongside Saleet, Jamil waved as if he were greeting an old friend.

Her Frankish was not strong, but she understood him well enough.

"Hold," he shouted. "Your friends are waiting for you."

Gyna glanced behind. The Norse chief and two of his men had their hands upon their sword hilts.

The Arabs drew closer.

Gyna looked between the dock and ship at the green sea slapping the hull.

"I should've learned to swim like the others."

3

The chaos swirling around Bjorn was like a salve. After so long in the dark, languishing in his own filth and inhaling the stench of death, even the bottom of a doomed slave ship seemed a paradise. He had been chained to a bench and commanded to man an oar. He was so big he sat alone on his bench. Sweat from his frantic rowing pricked his face and his palms burned with the friction of the oar he had let fall away.

A ringing bell from above had sounded a retreat. All the Arab crewmen had scrambled up the ladder to reach the top deck. The throbbing drums had ceased, but his ears still pulsed with that hideous beat. The chains about his legs looped through rusty iron shackles clasping his ankles. These were then bound to the deck by an iron loop. He pulled at them, tight and biting against his skin.

Slaves, both Norsemen and other races, cried out for rescue. He did not. What was death, after all? He never feared it. If he had not earned his seat in Valhalla then neither had any other man. He would not die with a weapon in hand. So he grabbed the chain binding him to the floor. It was cold and hard in his huge fist. A chain could be a weapon, especially if he wielded it. So let Odin see it in his hands and welcome him into his feasting hall. After a day of fighting in Valhalla, he would have a new sword picked from his defeated foemen.

He did not worry.

The ship groaned and rocked. With such a huge ship, he wondered at the size of wave that could shift it. Men screamed and begged their gods.

He stood. On the next bench over, Thorfast stood as well. His jaw was set and eyes resolute. Bjorn nodded to his oldest friend. Thorfast did not look like Thorfast without his brilliantly white hair. Long weeks of imprisonment had wasted him to mere bones. His cheeks stood out like sharp rocks. Scabs showed where the knife had grazed his scalp. Bjorn was confident he looked no better himself. But they would both be restored in Valhalla.

Across the deck in the fleeting candlelight he nodded to Alasdair and Yngvar. Both were standing as well. Both squared their shoulders with pride, though they too were shackled to the deck. Bjorn's one eye normally viewed half the world. After losing it he never saw the whole world at once unless battle madness overtook him. Then he could see everything for he looked through the eyes of the bear god and not his own.

Now, as he faced death, he saw the world with both eyes again.

He was glad to die with Yngvar, his only kin. True he had his father, Aren Ulfriksson. Yet he was an old lord hiding behind the high walls of Rouen in Frankia. It felt strange to think of him now with death at hand. He believed his father would die in his bed and go to Freya's hall, not Odin's. Bjorn would never see his father again. But he would see Yngvar soon, restored to the fullness of his strength and glory. Not like this wasted, pale man in chains before him.

Bjorn raised his chin. Let death come.

And it did.

A massive iron ram's head shattered the hull. The deafening crack of wood shocked his ears. The spray of warm water lashed his face. The force of the blow sent him reeling back.

Water exploded through the breach as the massive shaft of the ram groaned and shuddered through the hull. Bjorn crashed to his back. The candles extinguished, casting him into darkness, abandoning him to the piercing screams of terrified men. The salty, cold hand of the sea rushed across his face, pushed into his nose, and hauled him under.

Ran, the whore goddess who ruled from the sea floor, seized him in a tight cold grip. His mouth opened out of instinct. Water rushed in, shooting burning streams into his chest.

The chains at his legs snapped taut and yanked him back. He had no sense of direction in the cold blackness. Bass echoes thundered through the water surrounding him. Another loud crack and the heavy pull of Ran's grip dragged him once more toward the sea floor.

He had lost his grip on the chains. Now he scrabbled to find them again, even opening his eyes to be burned by the salt water.

But his chest burned and panic seized him. He could not control his flailing limbs. He fought the urge to scream.

More thunderous crashes and he was spinning through the cold darkness.

A heavy object collided with his head. His vision flashed white then faded to darkness.

Then silence.

Where was this place? Where were the Valkyries? He had not died in battle so perhaps they had not seen him. Had Ran pulled him to the sea bottom? If she had, then the goddess should appear to him.

But there was only soundless black.

Hands ran along his body. Cold hands of dead sailors eager for the fleeting warmth of his dying flesh. Would they eat him, he wondered. Would their rotted, brine-crusted teeth tear his throat open?

But the dead released him.

Sounds. Words. These were words. But they were dull thumps against his eardrums. No meaning. No form. Just words falling from unseen lips.

He felt as if he had slumbered a long, dreamless sleep. Now he awakened to shapeless darkness again.

Or did he see? At times he thought he saw dim lights. At last, the hearth fire of Valhalla must be rising in his vision. He had not gone to Ran's Bed as he had feared. Odin had remembered him and lifted him from the muck of the sea floor.

Had the others reached this place? He would clasp Yngvar and the others in mighty bear hugs. They would laugh and raise drinking horns of the sweetest mead to their great fortunes. Together they would feast and fight until the last battle in the time of Ragnarok.

Why could he have these thoughts? Who was thinking? Bjorn was not Bjorn. He was no more than thoughts in darkness. But what body again felt the brush of hands? What ears heard hushed words spoken as if keeping desperate secrets? What eyes—or eye—blinked away leaking tears?

What light shed warmth over his bare chest?

A voice like chiming silver spoke to him from a flickering, shadowy form hovering over him. A woman. A Valkyrie? He could not see, but the words were as clear as ice on a still pond.

"Live, child of the bear god. Take up your ax once more. Kill your enemies. March across their backs to victory. Let the world fear your coming. Live."

He yearned to answer, to stretch out his hand and touch the source of the voice. Such beautiful sounds he had never heard before. Would he ever hear such a voice again?

No.

The voice continued to speak, but it slurred and quavered. It grew harsh, violent. The shadow over him rippled like a banner in the wind. Heat seeped across his body, reaching into his neck, his face, his head.

A light hand touched his naked shoulder. It was the shadow.

But it was not shadow.

It was a woman. She was dark-eyed and dark-skinned. He thought Gyna leaned over him. But this woman's eyes were not as big as Gyna's nor as fierce. These eyes were hesitant. Fearful.

These eyes were Arab.

The reality of the world slammed over him like a rockslide.

He lay on his back, naked but for gray pants torn away at the knees. Humidity, foul with the scent of sweat and tallow, slapped his face. Beads of sweat rolled from his body as he shifted with his new awareness. But he was otherwise dry.

The Arab woman, dressed in plain, dark blue robes, recoiled with a squeal. She was a girl, no more than twelve. Her hair was long and tightly curled. Her small hands blocked her face as if Bjorn had flung sand at her.

He was in a tent big enough for himself only. The girl was already half out the flap, and now completely fell out of it. Only her candle remained behind.

Bjorn coughed uncontrollably. But he fought to sit up.

He had suffered no injury for his ordeal, though his head swam as he rose. His lone eye gathered all he needed to know. He was in a tent pitched with a single post. Sitting up, his shaved head skimmed the rough cloth of the tent roof. The candle was the only item here besides a pile of dirty rags tossed into the corner.

Kill.

That was the word that echoed through his mind.

Kill these fucking Arabs. Kill all of them. Don't stop until I am dead once more. Send me back to Valhalla. Send me to my friends.

The shackles were gone, but fierce welts showed where they had snapped tight. He flipped onto hands and knees, his body fueled with hatred and killing lust.

More voices came from outside the tent. The girl shouted—a horrible voice that had stolen sterling tones of the Valkyrie's sweet words—and men answered.

Bjorn found his roar.

He lumbered to his feet. Fresh from the world of the dead. Reborn with a terrible purpose to kill and never stop killing. He punched away the tent that fell around him, batting it with meaty paws that had idled too long in Prince Kalim's lightless prison.

The tent pole came to hand.

He charged forward, the tent falling from his shoulders like a cast-off cloak. He saw the world with both eyes. He saw all around him. Anything that he might kill was as clear as a lone star in a midnight sky.

Arabs were everywhere. Men with swords and spears, or bows and quivers. They were stretched across—land. He could not tell where he was.

He had eyes and heart only for death.

"Valhalla!"

The Arab girl screeched and fled with her hands over her ears. The nearest Arab was a vague shape of black against red. An enemy. Someone to kill.

Bjorn charged this man, who had only just drawn his sword.

He brought the tent pole down on the Arab's head with force enough to shatter the wood. The Arab's head bent sideways at the neck and he crumpled in death.

Flinging the broken post away, his mighty head swiveled around seeking a new opponent.

A spearman charged at him from his blind side. Though the fool did not realize Bjorn had no blind side in battle.

He caught the spear in both hands, tearing it away as if snatching it from a child. The horrified Arab watched his weapon spin away. Bjorn bellowed, rejoicing in its reverberations through his chest and throat. He slapped both hands around the Arab's neck.

His thumbs dug into the enemy's windpipe. The Arab's eyes opened white and horrified. He scratched at Bjorn's iron grip. But he began to sink.

This was Bjorn's strength after the depravations of slavery. Had he been stronger, he could have twisted the Arab's head around and been onto his next victim. The Arab gasped and choked as he collapsed to his knees, held up only by Bjorn's might.

The fast pulsing under his hands began to slow. The Arab's face had grown so dark that all Bjorn saw was the whites of his eyes.

Shouts came all around. He was aware of surrendering his advantage as the others drew near. But like a snake constricting its prey, Bjorn was helpless to release. Once he had determined to choke this Arab, he would not release until he was slumped in death.

Rather than face the pointed ends of the Arabs' spears, the butts slammed around his head and shoulders. The heavy wood thumped against his skull and the thick muscle of his shoulder. Nothing slowed him. He continued to glare down at the Arab dying in his hands.

The other enemies battered him until blood mixed with sweat began to roll down his chin. The Arab in his hands had gone limp but

Bjorn still felt the weak pulse in his neck. He poured all his rage of his misfortune into the hapless Arab. He would suffer the agonizing, slow death Bjorn wished for every person on this island.

A heavy cloth draped over his head. He was cast back into darkness, the heavy scent of dirt and smoke rubbing off the cloth onto his face. The cloth cinched tight around his neck as the spear shafts continued to batter about his neck and shoulders.

Yet he persisted in throttling his foe. He roared defiance when the pulse clasped between his hands ended. Only then did he relent, shoving the Arab back to thump to the earth.

Enemies tackled him. He struggled to rise, but they had pinned his arms by weight of their numbers. His head had been stuffed into a bag, disorienting him. He guessed a half-dozen men held him down. In better days he could slough them off and keep fighting.

Today, he slumped in defeat.

Once the shouting Arabs squirming over his prone body realized he was no longer resisting, they too went still. Bjorn awaited their judgement, breathless and weary. He felt on the verge of falling into sleep once more. Would he hear the voice again? He longed for that silvery, feminine voice. But she had commanded him to live. To fight would be to die, and to die would defy the voice's command. If he did, he would not hear it again.

So at last he was forced upright and his arms wrestled behind his back. Heavy chains wrapped him. Bjorn, too spent from the flash of rage and too weak to recover soon enough, slouched forward and let the Arabs bind him.

His mind wandered as the Arabs shouted at each other, randomly prodding him with a spear point whenever one wanted to emphasize his words.

He remembered Gyna.

How could he have forgotten her? She was his great love. She was a beauty unlike any he had ever known. She was his song. But he had forgotten her.

She alone escaped the fate that had killed Yngvar and all the others. Where had she gone through all these long days of his captivity? Would he ever find her again?

If he died, he might not see her again. He was not sure if shield maidens went to Valhalla or Freya's hall in Folkvangr. Perhaps he would also go to Folkvangr when he died. Half of those chosen by the Valkyries did. But he was always assured a true warrior such as he would go to Odin's hall. His friends would all be there. But his great love might be elsewhere.

Such were his thoughts while the Arabs argued over his head.

At last the cloth sack tore away. The humid air was no relief, but at least the stench of the cloth abated.

He looked into the dark eyes of a fair-skinned man with a ragged scar in his beard. Smile creases were heavy around his sleepy eyes. He was smiling now. Crouched on his haunches, he was eye level with Bjorn.

"Norseman?" His captor's accented Norse was difficult to understand. He waited with a calm smile for Bjorn to nod. He extended two fingers by his face. "Two choices. Live or die."

Bjorn turned his head so his one eye fixed on the smiling man. The bear god had left him, for his vision was again a narrow cone. He growled and spit on the man's face.

He laughed and wiped the spittle from his nose.

"Die, then."

"No," Bjorn shouted. "I'll live long enough to rip a permanent smile on your face. Then I'll tear off your arms and beat you to death with them."

The threat was beyond this Arab's comprehension. Bjorn saw his brows furrow and head cock at the words. But at last his captor sat back.

"Good choice. You live. God loves you."

"How am I alive?"

The fair-skinned Arab gestured like he was scooping his hands through water.

"Pulled you from the sea. Don't remember? You killed my friend like you killed this friend."

The Arab pointed at his dead companion. The corpse hung between two others who carried him away. His head lolled, skin blue and mouth frozen in a gasp.

"I don't remember," Bjorn said, shaking his head. "I should've killed more. Didn't I sink?"

The Arab shrugged, either because he did not understand the question or did not have an answer. He stood now and pointed across the camp.

"You go into the cage, and you live. My slave. I will sell you, yes. And you are a strong man. You make me rich, yes."

Bjorn looked across the field to where a small cage of black iron bars waited for him. He looked back at the smiling Arab.

"I've been in cages before," he said. "You're going to learn how little that cage will protect you from me."

The Arab laughed, clapping his hands. Maybe he did understand. Bjorn could not tell. Two men grabbed him by the shoulders and hefted him off the ground. They marched him the short distance and forced him into the cage.

Bjorn slumped against the cold, rough bars as they locked the door shut. His arms still remained chained behind his back. He settled his one eye on his captor and marked him well.

Another Arab to kill before he went to Valhalla.

4

Gyna could not swim. She stared down at the water splashing between the hull of her old ship and the dock. Even if she could swim, her enemies would spear her like a fish. Blinded with rage, she had placed herself in a trap. Aboard her ship, the new owners gathered to the rails like black crows awaiting a feast of dead flesh. The captain, a golden-haired Norseman with a pockmarked face and flattened nose, smirked at her. His scarred hands rested on the hilt of his sword, and his thumb flipped away the peace strap. Two of his crewmen did the same.

Jamil the Moor and Saleet thumped down the docks, passing the bemused Norsemen that formed a delivery line to load their newly acquired ship. They stared after the Arab warriors with lowered spears escorting the pair.

Despite the unfolding danger, the rest of the dock hummed with ordinary business. The chaos she had sowed at the market had died away. Shirtless workers on docks beside hers shouldered wares with little more than a glance at the threat of violence. Men shouted and laughed in the distance. A group of merchants on one ship had gathered to watch, leaning together as if betting on the outcome of Gyna's plight.

She thought of drawing her sword. Her hand burned to wrap

around its hilt. The thick smell of the sea filled her nose, and she wished to wash it out with the scent of spilled blood. But if she dared, then that blood would be her own.

Once the Arabs were in speaking distance, Saleet began chastising the Norse captain in his irritatingly high voice. His first words made Gyna long to shatter his brilliant teeth.

The Norseman did not answer, but one of his companions took up Saleet.

"Well, you have given everyone quite the chase," Jamil said while his master shouted at the Norsemen.

"You are doing well," Gyna said in Frankish. "Though that will soon change."

Jamil laughed which drew Saleet back to her. His rat eyes flashed with rage. Lines pulling his brows together marred his delicate face and clear skin. He pointed at her and began to spew curses, or that was what Gyna assumed.

She had never paid mind to the bastard before, and admitted he possessed a mild beauty. It was not to her taste, of course, and he was shorter than her. Height and size were her key standards. He could barely grow a beard, either. It occurred to her that he was an Arab Alasdair. This thought caused her to laugh.

The laughter stopped Saleet's stream of invective. Jamil's laughter also subsided.

"You are mad," Jamil said. "You are captured yet you laugh."

"Well, not captured yet," Gyna said, again glancing wistfully at the green sea sloshing below the dock. "You may have snared my dumb lover and his dumber friends. But I'm not as easy."

"Dumb friends," Jamil said. "I will agree to that. They desecrated a holy place. And—"

"What does that word mean? Frankish isn't my language."

Jamil paused and rolled his eyes. "They did bad things in a holy place. And—"

"All your holy places are bad places."

"This was a mosque built by Prince Kalim himself. And—"

"Built it himself? That little shit can't lift a cup without three women to help him."

"He paid for it to be built. Would you let me finish?"

They stared at each other. Saleet, his guards, and the Norsemen watched with a mixture of impatience and fascination. Gyna suppressed a smile. They probably expected a woman to fall apart and beg for mercy. She was about to revise their expectations.

"Well, finish. Gods, my hair turns gray while your mouth hangs open."

Jamil rubbed his face. "Yngvar and all his crew have been arrested for their crimes and—"

"You mean they've been taken prisoners as part of your trap."

"Yes," Jamil said with a wicked smile. "Your stupid friends are now awaiting execution in Prince Kalim's prison and—"

"Now I'm going to join them," she said. She smiled and shook her head. "This is the worst threat I've ever heard."

Jamil nodded in satisfaction.

"No, I mean, this is everything I already knew. You can't scare me with what I already knew. A threat should scare me, Jamil."

"I care not if you are scared," he shouted, straightening his back and his hazel eyes brightening with ire. "I—"

"But you should care," Gyna said. "Can't control me if I'm not scared."

Jamil gnashed his teeth. Saleet, finally regaining himself, inhaled to renew his screaming.

Gyna struck.

She sprang at Jamil, both hands planting on his chest to knock him back. He stumbled to the edge of the dock and fell. His scream cut short with a splash.

Wasting no time, she slapped down the spear of the guard behind him. His grip had slackened from the mind-numbing exchange between her and Jamil. The spear now pointed to the deck, and Gyna slid up the length to grab the naked dagger in the guard's belt.

Saleet started shouting. The remaining three guards raised spears, but learned too late what Gyna already counted upon. From the side, the dock was not wide enough to make those spears useful. They jostled each other as they tracked her. As one spun, he hit

Saleet with his spear butt, sending the little clerk skittering to the side. He fell across the gangplank with a cry.

Holding the curving dagger in a reverse grip, she slammed it into her enemy's side. But it turned on the thick leather jerkin he wore. She shoved past him, and now the dock was like an open road to her.

She sprinted, laughing as she evaded the inept guards. The Norsemen still lined up, stood back in amazement as she sped past them. They were as pale fence posts to Gyna as she fled.

"Stop her!"

That was Norse, and shouted from the deck of her former ship.

That bastard captain commanded his crewmen. She was three strides to the end of the dock.

A wall of a man lumbered out in front of her. For an instant she thought him Bjorn from his size alone. But his hair was thinner and greasier, sticking to his head to make it appear too small for his body. He held his arms wide as if Gyna was his little girl running up for a hug.

But at the end of the dock, the water was not so deep. She decided to leap off and circumvent the slab of a man seeking to capture her. With a haughty laugh she leapt off the dock into the water.

She was never the one to leap off a ship into shallow water. Truth was she was terrified of the water and never told anyone. So unless the ship was aflame, she would wait until it was beached before jumping into anything deeper than ankle-height water.

This was knee high to start.

Her feet stuck in the mud. The impact from the leap plowed her deeper so that even with calf-high boots the mud threatened to flow inside. She stumbled forward, arms wheeling to keep herself upright.

The sword at her hip yanked her sideways. Fearing that it would fall into the water and be ruined, she snatched it overhead.

Collapsing to her knees, she now knelt in water up to her chest, holding her sword high as if surrendering it. She screamed in frustration as the warm water shoved against her back, pushing her toward the shore where the giant Norseman now waited. He started laughing.

"You fell!" he said, holding his sides as if he could not bear his laughter.

"Smart for such a big boy," she said. "I'm stuck here. Come get this sword and help me out. I am your captive."

The giant man laughed as he waded into the water. His crewmates stood overhead on the docks and joined in the laughter, clapping and pointing at Gyna. In the distance she was aware of Saleet's hysterical shrieking. She waited for the giant to wade out to her.

"Little girls shouldn't play with swords," he said as he plucked Gyna's blade away with one meaty hand.

"Sorry," she said. "My father left it out and I couldn't help myself. Am I a foolish little girl?"

"You are," he said, still laughing. He wrapped his other massive hand around her right arm and hauled her up.

The mud sucked at her legs and threatened to yank off her pants as she rose. Wouldn't these bastards love to see that, she thought. Water drizzled off her as she staggered out of the rolling waves onto the shore. The Norse crew ambled toward them, but Saleet and three of his four guards shoved past them in a greater hurry.

Saleet's fury was like that of a princess whose white linen dress had been splashed with mud. His head rocked with every word he snapped from his pretty mouth. His guards trailed along, spears ready. Yet from the way they looked over their shoulders it seemed they were more eager to be away than continue with this farce.

Gyna smiled. She was not done yet.

The mirthful wall of flesh that had dragged her to shore now stood over her, still clasping her wrist as if this would be enough to keep her down. He threw her sword on the pebble-covered beach and wagged his finger at her. He had four yellow teeth in the gap of his smile.

"Now, I think I'm going to teach you a lesson, little girl. You shouldn't be wasting a man's time like this."

"Oh yes, I'd enjoy a lesson," Gyna said. "Will you be my master?"

The suggestive look she offered hit the giant better than if she had slapped him. His companions also paused, but some broke into riotous laughter.

"Let me show the lesson I want to learn most."

She pushed against him and drove her cupped left hand into his crotch.

The giant's small eyes widened in shock as she crushed his testicles into his hip bone. She shoved him forward, twisting and clawing to find a better grip.

The giant howled and fell forward. She rode him down and began to twist her left hand.

"You want to give a lesson?" she hissed in his ear. "Well, here's one for you. Learn what life is like without your nuts."

She twisted and pulled. The giant bucked and roared in agony.

Laughing, she slipped off him and rolled to her sword. Her arm landed over it and grabbed it to her side. Covered in muck and wet clothes, her mobility suffered. Rather than gracefully leap to her feet and draw her sword with a flourish, she instead staggered to her feet and tripped forward.

Most of the Norse crew were on their hands and knees with laughter. Some fell over each other, breathless. The poor giant curled like washed-up seaweed on the beach and held his crotch.

Unfortunately, Gyna now stood in a semicircle of three Arab spearmen who were ready this time. Tiny Saleet jumped up and down behind them, screaming commands like the angry princess he was.

Behind her was an overturned rowboat and piles of sacks where dock workers had paused to watch the spectacle. Her belt had loosened and now her pants were dragging down under the weight of water and mud. She could never run fast enough.

"I thought this would work out better," she said to the guards glaring at her.

Saleet finally pushed forward, his finger pointing like one of the spears arrayed at her.

Whatever he said, the guards did not obey. But they did not back away.

Gyna looked past them for any hope of escape. Jamil was hobbling along the dock, aided by the last of the Arab guards. His soaked robes clung to him, revealing his frail body. The Norse captain and the remainder of his crew followed.

"I can't believe we're waiting for someone who can speak a language I understand." She slipped the baldric of her sword over her shoulder. She would not risk it dragging through the water a second time. "The gods must be laughing at me."

The captain paused by the giant. He knelt beside him a moment to whisper, then clapped the giant's shoulder before approaching Gyna.

Saleet paced back and forth in a tight line, waiting for Jamil who now joined his side.

"At last," she said. "Can we get back to threatening me with my life and such? This poor bastard's head is turning purple."

She spoke Frankish to address Jamil, but the Norse captain spoke first.

"You've done my crew harm."

"Your crew got in my way," she said. "And your little man mistook me for a play-thing. None of that's my fault."

The Norse crew continued to snicker and laugh. Two of them had leapt off the docks to help their giant companion writhing on the beach.

Saleet pushed before his guards now, emboldened by the numbers on his side. He pointed at her and continued to order his men. Jamil, still blinking salt water out of his hazel eyes, offered a translation Gyna did not need.

"You are going to wish for death before the day is done. Your skin will be peeled from your face. Your every bone will be crushed."

Gyna waved off the threat and looked to the Norseman.

He was ugly. Pockmarks and the sun had ruined his square face. He was not young, perhaps thirty years. But his hair was still fair and he was taller than her. What choice did she have?

"Take me on your crew," she said. "And I will be your woman."

The captain's eyes widened in appreciation. He slid his gaze down her body, stopping at her legs.

"I'm not sure I want a woman who wears pants like me."

"I won't be wearing pants for what we will do together."

She drew closer, and the captain reached for the short sword hanging at his side. The Arabs threatened her with spears. But she summoned the sweetest smile she could and held her hands up.

"You don't know what to do with a real woman?" She spoke louder, so that the crew could hear. They had, for a dozen of them began to cheer their captain.

"The question is if you're a real woman. You fight like a man."

"You'll never know if you let these Arab bastards take me."

She smiled again, then as quick as if she were striking to kill, she wrapped herself around the captain and kissed him.

His lips were dry and rough. He smelled of sour sweat and mead. He had once vomited on his shirt and had not yet cleaned it. That stinging scent still clung to him. Yet she pressed herself to his strong body. He resisted, to the delight and laughter of his crew.

Saleet began shrieking again and hands grabbed at her hair.

She pulled back to find Saleet pulling her hair.

The captain, standing with a bemused smile, offered no help.

"You are to come with us," Jamil said. "And face your punishment."

Saleet yanked again and the pain scrambled Gyna's mind. No one does this to her and lives. She reached for a dagger.

But it was not where she had expected. Her hand snatched at air.

The captain finally intervened, batting Saleet aside.

"Do violence to my crew, you rat, and you will pay with your life."

Saleet wailed and fell back. He crashed to his butt on the pebble beach. His guards might not have understood the captain's Norse, but understood they were four against thirty hardened warriors. They pulled back their spears rather than attack, which had to be what Saleet was shouting for them to do.

Another of the captain's crew began to speak the Arab's language. After a terse exchange, Saleet struggled to his feet with no help from his guards. Jamil glared at Gyna and offered a reptilian smile.

"God will send you back to us, I am sure. We have your friends. Would you leave them so easily? They will be tortured to the edge of madness. Then they will all die as pigs. You would sail away without helping them?"

Gyna sneered and took the captain's arm in hers.

"I go where the power is," she said. "And it's not with you or them. So get fucked, old man."

Jamil inclined his head. "Hell awaits you, whore. No matter how far you sail."

Her chest tightened. Looking at the ugly captain and his lecherous crew, she clasped hell in her arms.

5

The ship rocked on the waves as Sicily fell away. Overwhelming melancholy seized Gyna, bending her back and weighing down her shoulders. As the towers and roofs of Licata faded to blue-gray smears in the hazy horizon, she leaned against the mast and fought tears. Her neck pulsed with anger. Her head swam with rage. Her legs trembled with fear.

I will be back for you, my love. She repeated the thought all the time the Norsemen had launched the ship—her ship, Yngvar's ship—into the Midgard Sea. She repeated the thought as the sail lowered and snapped full with the wind. She repeated the thought and swore to never stop repeating it.

For Bjorn. For Yngvar. For all the others, even Thorfast. They were her family, more than Waldhar, her sister, or Adalhard had ever been. The Saxons were lost to her. Her father, Lopt Stone-Eye, had long rotted back into the soil of Denmark. Who else had let her carry a sword into the shield wall? None. Who understood her rage like Bjorn? None. There would never be another to understand and accept her.

So she would return long before her soul found hell, Nifleheim, or any other place the unwanted dead spent their days waiting for the end times.

Her fist tightened to a ball and she thumped the mast.

She would return sooner than Jamil or Saleet thought.

And they would beg her for mercy that she would never grant.

The dazzling blue of the sparkling water matched the sky filled with clouds like wool. The waves sprayed cool mist over the rails. The crew had settled now that the sails had been set. The steersman began a song, a familiar tune but with different words from what Gyna knew. The others joined it.

The singing was alien and weird. This was her ship, the ship she sailed with her companions and lover. But who were these men? They did not know the history of this ship. They did not know that dark stain on the boards showed where Hrothgar had spilled his guts to a Danish warrior that had gained the deck. They did not know the hull had been patched where an unseen rock had torn it open within sight of the enemy coast. None of them had scrambled to bring the ship ashore and repair it while the Danes sought them. They thought they owned the ship. But it did not own them.

Nor would it for long. Another vow she made to herself as she leaned on the mast, adjusting to the rolling waves once more.

She realized she was making vows and had no plan to bring any of them to fruition. A bitter smile escaped to her lips, and the captain, conferring with his steersman, took it for a smile at him.

Gyna's stomach tightened again. Well, she had promised to fuck him, hadn't she. There was a mistake, but it had made sense to her in the moment. Her bitter smile widened. So much makes sense in the moment that later proves to be foolish. She appreciated how Yngvar could dream up a way out of the noose at the moment he was about to swing from the tree. He did it so often it seemed he courted those troubles just to show how he could get out of them.

But she was not him. She was not even equal to Thorfast, who was probably the next best of their band in slipping trouble. She was like Bjorn. She would charge at trouble and hack a way through it.

Stick with what you know, she thought.

She smiled again at the captain, this time deliberately. If she was going to have any chance of getting back to Bjorn and the rest she had to teach these fools she was not their woman. They might not obey her, but they would fear her.

When she was a child, one of the boys in her father's hall had found what he thought was a lost puppy. He took it for himself, raised it in secret, later to discover he had carried off a wolf cub. It nearly killed the boy when it escaped.

Same situation now, but she was the wolf pup.

The captain swaggered up to her, his gait rocking with the waves. He too had been on land long enough that he had to readjust to the sea. His yellow smile nearly matched his hair color. The greasy locks blew across his face as he squinted at her through the glare of the sun at her back.

Leaning on the mast, she folded her arms beneath her breasts to emphasize them through her shirt. Would that the captain be perceptive enough to notice the dried blood splatter there, he might have more caution in approaching her. But he had not even strapped on his swords and carried only a dagger in his belt.

"Fargrim Varinsson," he said. "I lead this crew, if you have not guessed as much. Now that we are well underway, it is time we are properly introduced."

"Gyna," she said, raising her chin as if to challenge him to ask more of her family. "And this was once my ship."

Fargrim raised a brow. Under the pockmarks and lines of his face, he was not truly ugly. His eyes brightened with delight at her claim.

"I heard this ship belonged to Yngvar Hakonsson. A man every Dane can agree to hate. Are you claiming he borrowed the ship from you?"

Heat rose to her cheeks. To hear him speak Yngvar's name with such contempt made her knuckles crawl with the anticipation of smashing his nose flat. Instead, she smiled.

"So you know you will never keep this ship. Yngvar is not a man to surrender what is his without a fight."

Fargrim laughed, rough and gusty.

"Yngvar Hakonsson is a prisoner of Prince Kalim. We might have met the same fate if we were as dumb as him. No one leaves those dungeons alive. The only shame is that I cannot bring his head back to King Erik Bloodaxe. His bounty would make me a king as well."

"King Erik Bloodaxe?" Gyna asked. "Last I knew he played at being the Jarl of Orkney."

"Then you have been long out of news, Gyna No-Man's Daughter."

She smirked at the name. Somehow it fit her.

"Then give me news."

"I will give you that and more." Fargrim stepped closer. Gyna checked her instinct to punch and let him draw close as if she welcomed him. "Erik Bloodaxe is king of Jorvik in Northumbria. He strikes his own coins, too. He would pay many of them for Yngvar Hakonsson's head. So would his son, Gamle. But Yngvar's head will instead sit on the walls of an Arab palace. A pity. But perhaps you might be worth something, eh? You are one of his so-called Wolves?"

He reached out a hand to brush her hair off her shoulder. She stiffened and feared her anger showed in her expression. Nearby crew paused to watch and laugh.

Not yet, she thought. The lesson must be swift and terrifying.

"What value could a king find in the head of one little girl? It would shame him to fight with me."

"You fear for your life." Fargrim moved his rough, warm hand over her shoulder to rub the side of her neck. "But I have heard a shield maiden sailed with Yngvar. And now you claim to be her. Is it true?"

Gyna let her eyes flutter then looked away as Fargrim's hand caressed her cheek. It smelled of dirt and salt.

"To be such a famed woman," she said with false wistfulness. "I too have heard of her. A woman as beautiful as she is fierce. A queen with a sword who cuts down men like wheat. There are no women like her, not in this world or in the songs of heroes. I only wish I could match her."

"Then who are you really?"

Fargrim's fingers lightly shifted to her chin, gently pulling her gaze back to him. He drew closer still and more of the crew drew around and leered. She ignored them, and instead let his body softly push her against the mast.

She spoke breathlessly, as if abandoning her hope and her body to Fargrim's magical touch. Beneath all the acting, her heart throbbed for blood and murder.

"I am whoever you want me to be, Fargrim Varinsson."

He smiled and gave a throaty grunt.

"Well, there is what you promised me when I took you aboard my ship."

That claim again. His ship?

She slipped her arms around his neck and looked into his eyes.

"Your ship? Well, about that."

She cupped her hands behind Fargrim's neck, then bent her arms while tucking her head down into her shoulders.

Then she yanked Fargrim's head toward hers as she slammed the crown of her head into him.

She impacted him under the chin, snapping his head back with sudden violence. He crumpled with a low grunt, slipping through her arms to thump to the deck. He was as limp as a pile of rope dropped at her feet.

The crew watched, astounded, their mouths gaping. She was surrounded at the moment, but would not yield that advantage for long. She leapt over Fargrim's crumpled body and sprang for the prow. It was the traditional spot to make a last stand. Bjorn and she had fought their way out of this position a dozen times or more. Today she would do it alone.

Her sword cleared the sheath, bright silver in the light of the day. Its clear chime echoed over the hiss of waves breaking across the hull as the ship sped toward the open sea. The sail snapped overhead and the crew gave a collective gasp.

The giant Norseman whose balls Gyna had recently destroyed waddled forward, gathering a two-handed ax from where it had rested on the deck.

He reminded her of Bjorn and for an instant she felt a tug of nostalgia.

But enough of that. Some bastards needed a lesson written in their own blood. She clasped both hands on the grip of her sword.

"Not one of you gets closer or you'll be stuffing your guts back in your worthless bellies." One thin man with eyes so narrow they might have been shut reached for a spear that rolled between two sea chests. Gyna ranged her blade at him. "You want to die first?"

He paused, then looked to his companions. No one moved. He stood back.

"That's right. Now listen to me. You've stolen my ship. I know you paid for it. But it's not yours no matter what you think. And I see you all looking at each other. You're thinking how can you take down this crazy bitch and get her sword. Well, you fucking can't. No one has yet and none of you walruses are better than the men who've tried before. So quit inching toward me. You'll lose a hand at best."

She rotated her sword across the crew lined up before her. She actually did not know what they thought or if they had moved toward her. The rocking of the ship made it hard to tell. But now several of them stepped back. She stuffed down her smile. It was as Yngvar had always said. Tell a man what he believes, and be certain to never ask him the same. Then you may always be sure he will think as you demand.

She had told them to fear her and so they did. This was easy.

The massive wall of ball-less flesh—she was not going to grant this fucker a name; he was meat—was the only one to raise his ax and defy her.

"What are you all afraid of? She's one girl. Look what she did to our chief."

"And remember what I did to you, Broken-Balls. So I have bested your chief and the lump of shit you all hide behind during a fight. That earns me a place among you. By rights, I should become your new chief."

It seemed some would have cheered her deeds, but claiming leadership shut their mouths. Well, shit, that was the wrong thing to say. She smiled, chagrined at herself. Almost had them for a moment.

"You cheated both times," Broken-Balls shouted.

"You mean I played you both for the brainless fools you are? Well, what do you do on the battlefield? When an enemy's sword is bent, do you offer him a weapon to continue the fight? Do you ask for permission before you stab him through the eye? You're a strange lot if you do. No, you use every trick to your advantage. Don't snort at me for doing the same. If all of you got together to count ten sheep in a pen you'd have to start over every time you reached three. You're all stupid."

Fargrim moaned as he recovered from the blow. He held his face with both hands. The muscles of his arms strained against the gold bands clasping both biceps. Yet no one moved to help him. He rolled to his side as if to rise, but remained still.

She had only looked aside for an instant, but the crew she had accused of being stupid had found her weakness and exploited it.

Three men had grabbed the long oars off the rack and now shoved the oar blades toward her. Others were joining, including Broken-Balls.

"Crack her skull," he said gleefully. "Let's see if this pile of shit floats."

Gyna lunged forward, but now a half-dozen oar blades plowed into her face. She crashed back against the neck of the prow. One hit her square to the teeth and filled her mouth with blood as it gashed her gums. Now a dozen oars pummeled her, knocking her back to the rails. She hacked with her sword, fury growing with each blow.

An oar slammed across the back of her sword hand. It opened her grip and the sword clanged to the deck. Before she could retrieve it, the jeering crew slammed her back.

She now leaned over the side, feet barely planted on the deck. Her longsword was out of reach, but the crewmen were still wary of her. They prodded and battered her until she lifted off the deck and onto the rails.

The glittering green sea flashed beneath her. The heavy scent of salt and cool spray of the foamy wake covered her. An oar caught under her hip and levered her up.

The crew cheered and men laughed. She could not see them.

She looked at the water. She grabbed the rails, though her hand throbbed with pain.

Even if she could swim, she could never reach land before her strength failed.

What does the goddess Ran do with drowned women, she wondered. I'll soon find out.

6

Bjorn's arms had gone numb from the chains binding them behind his back. The iron bars he leaned against were rough with rust. Had his hands been free he might have broken through them. Perhaps when he was stronger. Even seated his arms trembled with weakness. He needed to eat. Though he had accustomed himself to a single meal of slop each day, he could not endure less.

And it seemed the meal of slop would soon be his again.

His cage had been loaded onto an ox cart. The driver had stared at him as if he were some sort of magical beast. But now he had turned his eyes back to the road and goaded the ox along the rutted dirt. Bjorn's teeth clacked at each jolt through a ditch.

Licata rose in the distance. Though he had only seen it a few times from the sea and never from land, he recognized its shape. Distant things were hard to perceive ever since Erik Bloodaxe had plucked his eye out. Everything far away seemed to slide and mesh together. Right after losing the eye he would get headaches whenever he tried to focus too far. Now he had adapted and learned how long he could stare at something before his head became heavy. He distinguished the forms of Licata's domes and towers, then looked away.

Prince Kalim's cells awaited him along with all the suffering that entailed. The slop. The odor of decay. The endless black. But now worse, for he had no companions to endure it with. They were all dead. All but Gyna, and it would not surprise him to find her a slave to the prince. He had stared after her too much for Bjorn's liking.

"You're really sending me back here?" He addressed the driver, who was a wretched old man with gray hair that made his dark skin seem almost black. He was shirtless now, hunched over so that every bone of his spine showed. He did not answer.

A column of armed Arabs followed the cart. These were his captors, who did not appear to be of the prince's army. Bjorn did not care who they were. Anyone who was not part of his crew was an enemy. And with all his fellow crew dead, he was left with a world of enemies.

Made his decisions easier. Just kill. Like the voice had commanded him.

At last the cart trundled through a side gate into Licata. People arrived to gawk at him. A group of children followed the cart up a narrow street that was paved with stone. The violent shuddering of the cart rattled the cage door and set Bjorn's teeth on edge. The children chased a short distance then abandoned him, laughing and singing as they fled into the side alleys.

The domed shapes of the palace were unmistakable. Bjorn sighed and adjusted his seating against the iron cage. Once the chains were off his arms, they would be useless for a short time. He imagined the painful tingling as they returned to his body. But then he would be able to strangle some of these bastards. He was glad to have done so once before he was bound. He would do so again until someone killed him.

The cart rolled to a stop inside the walls of the palace, wheels squeaking and crunching on the ground. There seemed to be much confusion and worry for this arrival. Servants ran in every direction and guards shouted at the column that had escorted him here. Bjorn hopped to the side on his hip to see, but his captors and the guards were obscured by the cart and palace servants crowding it.

With a grunt, he fell back against the bars and waited.

He heard a familiar voice among the jumble of speakers. Again he strained to see, but found the group breaking up to different tasks. Laborers, leathery and shirtless men who had long forgotten any expression but resignation, fitted heavy wood beams through his cage. Four men lifted him out of the cart. The ordeal rolled him about the cramped interior and caused one of the laborers to mutter a curse as they sought to stabilize him. At last they set him on the ground and withdrew the beams.

A dozen palace guards with spears formed around the cage door. Bjorn struggled to stand, though denied his arms he instead crashed against the bars. His captor, the one who could fumble through Norse conversation, arrived. He rapped the iron bars with his knuckles for Bjorn's attention.

"I have gold now," he said. "You are worth less than I hoped. But not much work to take you here. So I am happy to be a little richer."

"You better run when this cage is opened. I'm going to tear you apart like rotten sailcloth."

The fair-skinned Arab smiled with the kindness of a favorite uncle. "Ah, but you won't. Not today. Many spears face you, my friend. Your arms are bound. Be smart. Maybe you will escape? I cannot know. I pray you will. I do not hate you. I just love gold more. God bless you, wild one."

"I'll tear your eyes out of your head!" Bjorn crashed into the iron bars. His heart raced and his face heated. He knew rage wasted his strength, but anger ruled him.

The Arab unlocked the cage with a heavy iron key. He pulled the lock open and turned away. He did not look back, but left with his men while the driver of the ox cart struggled to turn it in the palace courtyard.

The remaining guards braced for Bjorn's charge, setting their spears. Someone, that irritatingly familiar voice, shouted at them out of sight. One used his spear to swing open the cage door and shouted at Bjorn, gesturing him out.

If he was ever going to escape, this would be the time. Once he was locked in the cells again, he could not think of a way out.

They watched him struggle to his feet, pushing against the bars and sliding up the cold iron until he was upright. But when he stood he found the bear god would not visit him. He had to cock his head to fit the Arab ordering him into his field of vision. He had no strength, no will to fight. He would have to survive long enough for another chance at freedom. A rampage now would only get him killed.

The guard shouted and motioned with his spear for him to exit. Bjorn stepped out of the cage with feigned indifference. He glanced around for a way out, finding nothing but high walls with bowmen smiling down at him while fingering the fletching of their arrows. Ladders were placed around the perimeter for easy access.

The Arab prodded him with his spear. The sharp sting on his arm made him growl. The others spread around him with their own spears lowered. He was proud they understood the threat he posed, but this had worked against him. If they underestimated him, he might have a chance to exploit. That was always Gyna's advantage. Enemies saw a woman before them and thought they had an easy fight. Those fools always died first.

In the end, he was marched through the courtyard into the halls he had left a short time ago. He kept his head lowered, uninterested in anything around him. Spears at his back ensured he would not survive any attempt to flee. Happy voices echoed through stone halls around him. Cream-colored walls faded to gray as his captors marched toward the prison cells.

Once within the gloom of the guard room, his stomach began to burn. He caught the whiff of filth from beyond the heavy wood door they pushed him toward. He had not expected to feel such terror. Fear was not known to him, or so he chose to believe.

But as the door swung wide and his guards shoved him into the darkness, he was overwhelmed.

"Not this again," he whispered to himself.

A rough hand pushed at his shoulder and emphasized it with a spear point.

Though his arms were still bound behind him, he roared with rage and fear. He twisted on the man, slamming him aside with his shoulder.

Even weakened as he was, his bulk was enough to force away his smaller captor. His guards were setting their spears against the walls of the square chamber. Others sat with naked swords resting against a table.

Bjorn barreled into them. He had to get out. That darkness would swallow him. He would die forgotten in filth. Better to die now, even with his hands bound.

He plowed into the mass of guards. Some tried to regain their spears. Others held their arms out to block him. Bjorn had no thought of what came next. Like a caged boar, he simply wanted to charge away to safety.

Slamming about, thrashing through the shouting, confused mob of Arab jailers, he nearly breached to the other side. But the Arabs had the weight of numbers against him. They piled atop him until he collapsed to the dirt floor. His face pressed into something pungent and wet. Mugs and plates from the table rained around him. Hands found the back of his head and shoved him deeper into the dirt. His nose bent and felt as if it would break.

The Arabs jabbered at each other while Bjorn bucked and wailed. But his strength was now spent. Without the bear god to bless him, worn as he was from his trials, he surrendered.

His captors were not pleased. Once they realized he had stopped resisting, they hauled him off the ground as a group. They cursed him and each other. The room was hot with hatred. Bjorn watched the floor glide beneath him. A trail of spit hung from his lips. They took him to the edge of the shadowed doorway.

The odor of death reached up and locked over Bjorn's head. It renewed his fight, and he began to wriggle like a fish in a net. But his jailers heaved him forward into the darkness.

His head slammed into something hard. Then he began tumbling down the wooden stairs. Each step thumped against his body, sending flashes of white through his mind's eye. In the total darkness he saw nothing. With his arms behind his back, each roll threatened to break them.

When he flopped to a halt halfway down, he simply rested and struggled against the pain that throbbed all over his body. The darkness fled as Arabs descended after him. They pried him off the stairs and flipped him down the final distance until he was facing the stone floor he remembered so well.

They dragged him up. Salty blood filled his mouth. His one eye pounded as if it might explode. In the guttering torchlight, he saw the iron-bound door before him. Carried by the chains binding his arms, he felt as if his shoulders would snap.

At last, the guards plunged him into the cell. He landed on his side against the cold and rough floor. How he remembered this coldness. The stench of mold, rot, and feces made him want to vomit. But his stomach was empty and he simply gasped and spit blood.

He realized he had been lying in the cell a long time. His ears still rang from all the shouting, but the Arab voices were now distant mumbles. No one had closed the door behind him. Why should they? His arms were still bound in chains. He had no strength to stand.

At last the golden light and tarry scent of a torch reached him. He rolled over to see who had come.

"By God, what a miracle this is."

Bjorn recognized the accented Frankish. He twisted his head to fit the speaker into his sight. His eye strained in the low light to focus. He saw a gray robe and white head cover. The man speaking had a neatly trimmed gray beard. Behind this one was a smaller man in the same clothing, but he covered his nose and mouth with a square of white cloth. He rattled on in Arabic, shaking his companion's shoulder as he did.

Now he remembered. The small rat was Saleet. The other hated man was Jamil the Moor.

"You recognize me now?" Jamil stepped inside, revealing the torch-carrying guard in the hall. Saleet seemed suddenly fearful to have lost his shield. He stopped chattering and fell back with wide eyes.

"I never trusted you," Bjorn said. "And I was right."

"Strange that the dumbest one among all your number was right. Your master, Yngvar, should have known better than to trust all communication to me. I was able to make plans right under your noses and no one knew otherwise."

"You're going to pay," Bjorn said. He let his head fall back, too exhausted to continue to hold it up to face Jamil. He realized it made him seem weak. But he intended to make good on the threat.

Somehow the gods would grant him this revenge. Or else why did they bring him back?

Jamil laughed. "You are in no position to do anything."

Saleet found his courage and now stepped inside. He grabbed Jamil's shoulder and began firing off commands. Bjorn closed his eye to rest it. Besides, he could not bear to see either of these two. Not under these conditions.

"Tell us what happened," Jamil said. "How many of the others survived."

Bjorn kept his silence.

More words flew back and forth between Jamil and Saleet. Then Jamil cleared his throat.

"You will tell us what happened, or we will remove your other eye. We have men who can do it in the most painful way and ensure you still survive. Would that please you? We take your sight in trade for your silence."

Bjorn rolled his head back to Jamil and fixed his lone eye on him.

"Why wouldn't you do it anyway?"

Jamil smiled. "Because we have another plan for you. Yet if you will not obey, we will change our plans and torture you to death."

What good was his silence? Bjorn protected dead men.

"They all died. And before you ask if that's true, it is fucking true. Saw 'em all myself. We were in the lowest deck. Huge ram head split our ship. Thorfast drowned. Ain't no way he could've survived all that water hitting him. Yngvar and Alasdair probably got smashed by the ram. I never saw. Rest of the crew got the same fate. We were all chained to the deck. No one was getting out alive."

"But you did," Jamil said. "How did you survive?"

Bjorn shrugged. "I was drowning. A Valkyrie pulled me out of the sea and told me I'd live to kill my enemies. She picked me out of the sea so I can twist your head around your skinny neck. You and that baby you call your master. I'm going to fucking kill you because the gods promised me."

Jamil probed his hollow cheek with his tongue. He offered a

translation to Saleet, who laughed and clapped his hands. After a short exchange, Jamil crouched down closer to Bjorn.

"You were picked up by Arab sailors who survived the attack. You were floating on some wreckage. There was no Valkyrie, no gods flying around your head. You were just lucky."

"Ain't what I saw. You're afraid. That's good. You better be."

Jamil lowered his head and laughed. "I have to admire your spirit. But here's what will happen. You are a big, strong man. A madman. We're going to put you on the front line of Prince Kalim's army. You will serve the prince with your life. See? We are merciful. You will die as a warrior, just like your kind desire. And you will die no matter how well you fight."

Bjorn stared at him. It was probably a lie to give him false hope.

"I can see from your face you doubt me. It is not truly our desire to let you fight. But the guard captain claims you are as a giant in battle and that you held off five of his best men alone. So your reputation has preserved you. For now."

"Give me an ax and I will kill. I'll kill anything I see. And I'll go looking for you."

Jamil chuckled then stood.

"And here's another mercy," he said. "Your little whore sailed off with your ship weeks ago. Left with another Norseman, saying something about sticking with a man in power. So she alone survived, and by now must be far away to the north. I'm certain she is riding her new lover's prick all night long. Think on that while you wait to die."

7

Gyna dangled over the ship rails, the spray of wake soaking her hair and sticking it to her face. The crewmen shouted like excited boys as they used their oars to lever her off the deck and onto the rail. The oar blades prodded her legs and back. The only refuge from the attack would be to flip over the side and hang onto the rails. But the ship was not high-sided. She would drag in the water and be torn away.

Damn this good sailing wind, she thought. Yet hanging over the side would avail nothing. The men wanted to kill her.

Despite the danger, the rage she expected to explode through her limbs did not come. Instead, faced with a choice of drowning or being bludgeoned to death, she felt nothing but indifference. She was not going to die now. She did not know how she knew.

But she was certain.

"Hold your oars! Stop, you stupid dogs!"

Their captain, Fargrim Varinsson, had recovered, and his strong, commanding voice boomed out over the growl of the waves breaking across the prow, the shouting of the crew, and the crack and snap of both sail and deck. It was the voice of a war leader, and even Gyna felt the pull of command.

The oars withdrew. Gyna hugged the rails as if she were clinging to the neck of an unbroken horse galloping for open fields. Her face throbbed from where she had been struck. Her legs and hips stung from the blows of the oar blades. She stared at the white foam spray beneath her, then slid to the deck. Despite the shakiness of her legs, she stood and feigned indifference to the pain enveloping her.

The crew sulked as they threw the long oars back onto the racks. Most had not participated but had watched with interest while sitting on their sea chests. These men teased their companions for failing to up-end a woman with all their numbers.

Fargrim held a hand to his head as he extended another for balance. The ship rocked as it sped over the waves. Yet Gyna had head-butted him hard enough to steal his consciousness. He would be unsteady on his feet for a good while. That thought made Gyna's cold heart warm.

"Come here," he said. "And don't pick up that sword. In fact, drop your daggers on the deck."

She had only looked at her sword. Its clean, sleek length flashed the blue of the sky at her. Her sword hand still ached from the blow across her knuckles. But it also itched to take up the blade again.

"If you don't drop all your weapons," Fargrim said, "you'll go over the side. Make your choice."

Though she could not swim, she still wondered if it would be better to risk the sea. The salty air and cheery waves made it seem so welcoming. Of course, she would either drown or be shredded by sharks. Not so cheery after all. She flicked her dagger to the deck. It thumped to the wood and she toed it aside to ensure Fargrim she could not snatch it back.

In her imagination she had instead thrown it at the giant slab of meat, Broken Balls. The dagger caught him by the collar of his vomit-stained gray shirt and somehow pinned him to the mast. Gyna laughed in his face—in her fantasies. In truth, he stood aside leering at her stupidly. She ignored him as she meekly obeyed Fargrim's command.

"Be a good lass for your master," Broken Balls said as she passed. "I'm sure he'll share you with the rest of us."

She left his laughter behind as if she had no care for the threat.

Though she wondered exactly what her plan had been when she joined this lot. Escaping Jamil and Saleet had been top of mind. But this had become something like running into a bear den to escape a mad dog.

Fargrim's eyes seemed to struggle to focus on her. The satisfaction his suffering gave Gyna her smile.

"You weren't taking me seriously," she said.

"Aye, I'll agree with you there," Fargrim said, rubbing his hand across his greasy golden hair. "But I do now. And I am sure you're that shield maiden who sailed with Yngvar Hakonsson."

"Am I as fierce as the skalds say I am?"

Fargrim frowned. "I would not claim to have heard any skald mention your name. Nor am I sure if you're fierce or foolish. A good measure of both, I expect. No matter. You are an unexpected prize at the end of a long and frustrating journey."

"I am not a prize," she said. The rage that had eluded her earlier now began to shake through her limbs. "I bested both you and your biggest warrior. I am part of your crew."

"When my crew disagrees with me, none of them lull me into a trap then head-butt me."

"Ah, but now you know how strong I am. And you called off your men. I think you are taken with me."

Fargrim smiled, though it shifted to a painful grimace as the ship rocked hard.

"I called them off because your head might make me some extra gold in King Gorm's hall. His daughter is King Erik's wife and Gamle is his grandson. You and the others have done him much injury over the years. He'll pay gold for you, I'm certain. And if not, it's not a far journey to Jorvik. I need gold to make up for having to buy a new ship."

Gyna narrowed her eyes. "It's not your ship and I am not your prize. Now, as a life boon you owe me, send me back to Sicily. There are a few Arabs I plan to geld before I fetch my men out of prison."

Fargrim blinked, his eyes rolling with each heavy press of his lids. "Life boon?"

"I should have opened you crotch to crown while you were laid out," she said, demonstrating how she would have slit his torso with an extended finger. "Then I should've finished Broken Balls while he stood around with his mouth open. Anyone else who challenged me would've died. Then I would have led this ship."

Fargrim blinked again, backing up from her finger as if it had been a real blade.

"But I didn't," Gyna said. "So you owe me your life. Now you know how to repay me. Turn back now."

Fargrim stared.

"Do you have something in your eyes? Don't just blink at me."

Not only Fargrim, but the entire crew burst into laughter.

"You only laugh now because I was merciful a moment ago." Yet Fargrim did not stop laughing. He doubled over and wiped at his eye with the back of his wrist. The others leaned back on their sea chests, nearly falling to the deck in laughter.

"You want to laugh?" Gyna's vision began to cloud. Her hands started to burn. No man mocked her like this.

She sprung at Fargrim, again taking him off guard. As he was bent over, his face caught her knee easily. He flopped back, his already rocked skull now at its limit.

Gyna followed up with a roundhouse punch to his temple. The shock of the blow rippled up her arm. He groaned and collapsed again to the deck. She had no weapons of her own, but Fargrim had his dagger in his belt.

Yet as she reached for it, something plucked her back.

Broken Balls roared. "Not again you, stupid bitch. Now you get what you deserve."

No doubt, Broken Balls was as strong as a bear. His hand had caught her shirt collar, but his other massive hand palmed the back of her head like an apple. He swung her around as easily as a child would fling a cloth doll.

Her head slammed into the mast. Her vision disappeared in a cloud of white. Her head struck the mast again. Pain bloomed so bright and white that she went blind. A third time her head crushed against the hard wood of the mast. Her ears rang with a shrill wail. Beneath it, she was aware of men calling out.

She bounced off the deck, face down to the boards. The scent of wood and water was thick here. The whiteness was only fading from her vision when she felt something land atop her back.

Hands tore away her boots, then her pants. Other scratchy and dirty hands pulled her shirt over her head.

So here it was at last. It was not the first time she had been raped. Even as daughter of the mighty Lopt Stone-Eye, she had once been taken by his Saxon allies. It did not make it any easier to endure. Yet at least she did not panic. She instead braced for the inevitable. Her ears were still screaming and her head throbbed.

Her naked body felt the wind rush over her. But the stench and heat of the crew muffled her to the boards. Broken Balls laughed and shoved her face into the deck. He was the first to penetrate her.

She surrendered. Why fight when she would only injure herself? She tried to squeeze her legs shut but otherwise offered no fight. She had to preserve herself for what might be a fight for her life when they were through.

Man after man violated her until the pain between her legs matched the pain in her head. Her fists clenched and her eyes pressed shut. Even warrior women had to endure trials like this. If she got with child from this disaster, she would drink poison to kill it, or if it was born she would personally smash its head on a rock.

If she had known hatred before, then nothing could describe what she felt now.

When she thought the ordeal over, she made to roll over onto her back. But another body leapt atop her and knocked her head to the deck again. Fargrim's breath smelled sour as he whispered beside her ear.

"Forget taking you to King Erik. If King Gorm will not pay for you, then I'll keep you for myself. This was just a taste of what you'll do for me and the crew."

When he was done with her, he crawled to the side on hands and knees. He vomited on the deck, sending the stinking, hot mess sliding toward her.

Despite all she had endured, she recoiled from it. She scrabbled left until she hit the gunwales. Men laughed at her or else sneered.

She pressed into the side, feeling the cold wood against her back. She covered her nakedness with both arms.

Hatred seethed through her as she watched Fargrim helped to his feet by the slab of meat, Broken Balls. Some of the crew still fastened their belts after their turn at her body. Most paid her no more mind than if she were a cornered rat.

That enraged her even more than the rape. Had they not seen her pull their two best warriors apart like plucking legs off crickets? Had she not twice beaten their leader? More appalling, her sword and dagger remained where she had dropped them on the deck. Did they not believe she could be any threat with them?

Fargrim dusted himself off, wobbled as the ship crested a swell, then kicked Gyna's clothes at her.

"Get yourself dressed," he said. "And if you can't behave on the journey to Denmark, I'll tie you to the mast day and night. I want you fresh for the king. I'm sure he'll pay better for a pretty face than some worn out bitch. That swelling better go down before we reach Denmark."

Fargrim glared at Broken Balls, who smiled sheepishly. Broken Balls then looked to Gyna and leered.

"So, little girl, hope you learned who your betters are. Too bad we gotta keep you nice for King Gorm. Though you're a fair bit looser now. Wonder if he'll still want you."

The crew and he guffawed. Her face throbbed both with injury and fury.

She gathered her clothes and crushed them against her body. She lay still, imagining all the ways she might destroy these men. That was even more important now than Bjorn and the rest. They would at least stay put in their cells.

But these bastards had to die to a man, and it could not happen too soon.

The ship rocked on the waves and the crew settled back into their routines. They skirted around her as she watched them at their work.

And the ship sped away from Sicily and back to the north, leaving Bjorn behind and sailing ahead to pain and death.

8

"How will I ever get back to Sicily and save those fools? Will I even find them again?"

Gyna asked herself these questions as she sat on Fargrim's sea chest. He and the crew prepared to pull ashore for the night.

Dark clouds hung in the pale orange sky. Denmark's southern shoreline ahead was thick with the serried tops of dark pines. Ancient boulders studded the beach. This was a good landing spot. The beach was smooth and clear of nearby trees. The water here was calm and deep. It might have made a good harbor but was not large enough to hold more than a few ships. Gyna had not been back to this part of Denmark since she left with Yngvar years ago.

She had come home to the lands of her father, Lopt Stone-Eye.

When she had left, all was in chaos. King Gorm had claimed her father's lands. His Saxon son-in-law, Waldhar, had retreated to his ancestral home. But he swore to return. Had he? Would he be in the fortress now? Was Fargrim and his crew of fools preparing to beach their ship in the shadow of enemies?

Gyna hoped they were. She needed their aid to kill all of Fargrim's men. Thirty men would be too much even for a blood-mad woman.

In truth, she had not been raped by all thirty men. A handful of these crewmen seemed good companions. What could they have done, in any case? She had seen as much done on Yngvar's ship many times. He held himself above violating captured women, but some of his crew—Gyna's sword brothers—held different ideas. No one stopped them, not even God-loving Alasdair. How was Fargrim's crew any different?

She leaned forward and watched the gulls circling around the shoreline rocks as Fargrim's ship approached the beach.

Of course Fargrim's crew were not different. It is the raider's way. The strong dominate the weak.

And they were all going to die anyway. She swore it.

Broken Balls, who had an actual name she refused to hear, slid over the side along with three of his companions. They waded through the waves to help guide the ship as it glided onto the beach.

Gyna held onto Fargrim's sea chest as the deck shifted to the port side. A short pole rolled into her foot as the ship juddered into the sand. She checked her dagger and sword and appreciated their weight. These were the only tools she needed. Her clothing was stiff with sea spray after a week of sailing. The blood splatter now was part of the fabric. A pant leg had been torn at the knee. Otherwise, she owned nothing.

The crew gathered sleeping sacks and gear needed for making camp. They packed their goods into hastily tied bales and threw these over the side to their fellows who had gone ashore. They raised weapons overhead as they sloshed through the shallow water. Even an errant splash could form rust on the blade.

"Come on, little girl," Broken Balls shouted up to her. "Get the cooking fire started."

She stretched and stood. No one on this crew believed she was a threat. They allowed her weapons. They even laughed when she drew her dagger against a crewman who had grabbed her leg. They denied she had ever beaten their best warriors. Fargrim's only concession to his beating by her hands was his grabbing at his head in what seemed dizziness.

She followed the rest of the crew ashore. She had been their cook over the last week. Several of the crew were expert hunters who could flush out game along the coast they had followed north. When they failed, a quick raid had yielded all they needed to feed thirty men. No one's belly was ever full, but no one suffered. Gyna always had a shift at the cooking pot.

The air was cooler and sweeter here. It felt like home. It had been home once. As she hauled the heavy iron pot onto the black iron trestle, she stared west. The trees blocked the view of the fortress that had been her home. Though Fargrim and his crew were Danes, they did not appear familiar with these lands. In fact, these lands were in constant disputes with the Saxons. King Gorm had always to look over his shoulder to the southeast, though according to what Yngvar said, King Gorm really wanted to look to Norway. Waldhar and Adalhard and the chiefs of other Saxon clans held him back.

For sea wolves, Fargrim and his men seemed woefully unaware of the state of their own homes. Even Gyna, whose eyes glazed at talk of jarls and their grudges with each other, knew the Saxons were always a threat. Yet they were beached across the water narrow straits from them. Perhaps Fargrim counted on the speed of Yngvar's ship to carry them away in case of danger.

Danger was coming soon enough, she thought as she let the iron pot drop into the hook.

After serving up a gruel of boiled rabbit meat and blood, Fargrim and his crew settled for the night. Broken Balls, who still held some interest in Gyna despite the others' indifference to her, lumbered across the sand to stand over her.

She clutched her small wood bowl to her chest, enjoying the warmth of the bowl more than the taste of its contents. She refused to look up at him.

"Tomorrow we go to Jelling and King Gorm. Your easy time will be done."

She nodded.

"If you plan to run, I will be watching you. Don't try anything so foolish."

"Why don't you tie me up, then?"

"That's a good idea."

She looked up and smiled at Broken Balls. His four-toothed smile enhanced his stupidity.

"Tie me to the mast," she said. "It's easiest."

"I will!"

He strode off to find rope. She watched him go speak to Fargrim, and he nodded as he cast a dark glance at her. She smiled back.

"You two are really so dumb that this is not even a challenge."

She spoke to herself, but Fargrim had not yet turned away. Seeing her speak, he waved off Broken Balls and approached her.

"You've something to say?"

"I was just wondering if I'll have to bargain for my own sale to King Gorm as well. You are not smart enough to even tie me up for the night."

"I was going to order that anyway." He prodded her left leg with his toe. "Now rinse the bowls and clean out the pot. After that, you'll be bound for the rest of the journey. So enjoy your freedom. It's the last of it."

"The hardest thing is knowing we'll never be together again after tomorrow."

He stared at her, seeming to wonder if she was serious. Then he shook his head.

"Get to work."

She did not doubt he would tie her up. He would likely do it well. However, if he entrusted the job to the eager and dumber-than-a-dead-walrus Broken Balls, she was confident she could keep her advantage. For now, she had to let these fools continue to believe she was completely defeated. If she were tied up for the night, no one would need to guard her.

After washing out wood bowls then rinsing, drying, and oiling the cooking pot, she returned everything to the ship then dutifully reported to Broken Balls.

"Fargrim said you'd tie me to the mast."

He was seated around one of three campfires with his friends. His eyes lit up at her appearance. He lumbered to his feet and snatched her arm.

"That's right, little girl. Let's go."

He pulled her through the camp. Night had fallen now and men looked up as she stumbled past. Their faces were orange and black with strange shadows cast from the firelight below. Fargrim stared after her.

The fires might do all her work for her. Though her father's old fortress was not visible from this vantage, they might notice light in the night sky. Fargrim was exceedingly confident of his welcome in Denmark. Through their journey north, he had extinguished fires as soon as they had cooked their meals. Now he seemed complacent enough to leave them burning all night.

Broken Balls threw her against the mast. One of his cronies followed him aboard to help bind her.

She held out her arms crossed at the wrists. "Tie my hands first."

"No," he said. Gyna's heartbeat sped up. Did he actually know what he was doing? Big men like him usually killed their enemies and did not bother tying them for later. "First I take your sword and dagger. They're mine now."

Gyna tried to not let the relief show on her face. She lowered her arms and let him remove her dagger, which he shoved into his belt. Then he lifted off her sword, which he slung by the baldric across his shoulder.

"Now give me your hands."

She held them out, again crossed at the wrists. As he wound the rough, thin rope about her she cried out and writhed.

"Not so tight! I'll lose my fucking hands by morning."

Broken Balls laughed. His friend joined him, unspooling a length of rope to bind her to the mast. He pulled the knot tight.

Gyna moaned and struggled. She had faked her suffering, of course. The knot was hardly tight enough to do its job. And that he had tied her wrists crossed would make the binding even looser when she straightened them later.

What a fool.

She repeated the same act as Broken Balls and his friend wrapped her to the mast. She flexed her muscles in her arms and inhaled the deepest breath she could without revealing her intent. Yet Broken

Balls was so enamored with her fake moaning that he seemed lost in his imaginings.

He yanked hard at the rope, and Gyna spread her arms wider against them. Yet she groaned as if the rope were slicing her in half. Once he was finished, he stepped back to admire his work. She offered her best glare. That was not false.

Broken Balls laughed, clapping his friend on his shoulder.

"That'll keep her good until the king sees her tomorrow." He moved in closer, setting his thick hand on her cheek. "And the swelling is gone. A prefect little face that'll fetch us all a purse of gold."

"You should demand more for me," she said. "A purse of gold cannot replace your smashed balls."

The slab of meat that was Broken Balls curled his lip. He hacked up a mouth of phlegm then spat in her face. The hot and thick spit blinded her left eye. Her instinctive twist of revulsion set Broken Balls laughing once more.

"I'll be glad to never see your face again," Broken Balls said as he straddled the rails of the ship. "Hope you suffer all night."

She glared at him as he left with his friend following behind. The spit slid down her face, dangled from her chin before settling on her ragged collar.

"You'll see me sooner than you think," she said under her breath.

For the rest of the night, no one visited her. Fargrim had gone as far to peek over the rails before returning to the fires which were now smoldering red embers.

When at last the sounds of snoring prevailed over the soft purr of the tide, Gyna stirred again.

She straightened her hands again, creating slack in the rope. She rubbed them together, working them through the rope bindings. Broken Balls had tied the knot tighter than she expected, but not tight enough. The bindings fell to the deck with a light thump.

Next she released her breath and pulled her arms tight to the side. She wriggled in her bindings, which slacked when she sucked in her gut. The challenge would be to get the bindings over her hips. After that point, she would be free.

Patience was her tool for this task, but her heart throbbed with excitement. While she could not see the majority of the crew, she knew a sentry would be set. Given Fargrim's careless approach to the coast, she doubted he would set more than two. Yet even so, she feared one checking on her. To be caught now would shatter all her plans.

Not that she had elaborate plans. She would get free of these fools and with the blessing of the gods she would summon the Saxons to their mortal enemies.

She hoped they were mortal enemies. Gods, what if they had bargained a peace in the years she was away? That thought sent ice into her hands as she struggled to bring them through the coil of ropes around her waist.

In fact, she began to consider the dozens of ways her plans could end with her under a pile of lusty men once more. Did Yngvar doubt himself when he dreamed up his impossible plans? He never seemed to. But he had to.

"Focus," she whispered to herself. Her arms burned from the ropes dragging across them. She thought the struggle would continue all night, but then her right arm popped free.

The slack this granted her made removal of the other arm easier. Before long, she was working the ropes over her hips. Sooner still, she was stepping up from a pile of rope still tied around the mast.

"That succeeded," she said under her breath. "So why won't the rest of this? Come on, woman. Don't be afraid now."

Despite her self-patter, her limbs trembled as she sank to the deck. The moon hid behind clouds and the stars shed no light of any help. Still, she would not risk her profile being spotted on the deck. She crawled to the rails, pulled up high enough to study the camp, then began to climb over.

Yet she felt a hand on her shoulder. Not a real hand, but the sense was the same. It was as if Alasdair were with her, cautioning her to have more caution.

"Don't move until you are doubly sure the way is clear." Those words in Alasdair's voice echoed through her head. He had so often warned her of this whenever they worked together that she heard him still.

It proved excellent advice. For the lone sentry watching the camp was awake and patrolling the shore to her left. Had she leapt into the water now, she would have drawn his attention. Unarmed, she would have no chance against him in a fair fight.

With silent thanks to Alasdair's wisdom, she pulled back behind the gunwales. Now she had to pray he was just running a circuit rather than climbing aboard the ship.

She closed her eyes as she strained to hear. But his soft boots crunched past on the beach sand. He did not slow or look to her. It was as if he walked in his sleep. Gyna waited a moment longer before peering over the rails again.

The sentry's cloaked shape faded away to the darkness where only the white of gentle sea foam showed. She let her breath escape, then slid over the rails to hang over the side. She let herself down onto the beach and sped away in the opposite direction of the sentry.

Had she any sense, she would flee under the cover of night back to her father's old fortress. But Broken Balls was still alive.

She counted his sins as she picked her way across the scattered sleeping sacks. These seemed like lungs rising and falling in time with the bodies of the men asleep within.

Broken Balls had smashed her head against the mast, had raped her, had spit in her face. But worse than anything else, he had stolen her sword and dagger. After Bjorn, she loved nothing more than these weapons. She cared for them like children. She honed their edges to cut a blade of grass lengthwise in three.

She found him easily enough. He was the lump of meat on his side, snoring like thunder. The similarity to Bjorn was startling as he slept beside weak campfire light. The dull red bathed him in strange shadows. Her collected weapons were stacked beside him as if he might embrace them as close as his lovers.

And during her pause his eyes fluttered open.

He shot upright and his thick hand reached for her sword.

9

Bjorn backed against the iron cage. The camp of Arab warriors surrounded him, brightly lit with a hundred campfires and three times as many warriors to surround them. Blacksmiths worked at temporary forges. Their beating at anvils lasted into the night, ringing out over the constant hum of a hundred different conversations.

The evening air was humid and carried black flies to his face. These danced over the half-dried blood that oozed from his scalp and down his face. Their light dance tickled his skin but he did not wave these off. Yet whenever he shifted they blasted away in a spinning flock around him. The wounds had not been from his handlers. He had struck his head a dozen times on the iron bars as he resisted being moved to his cage.

Weeks had passed in the prince's dark dungeon. Or had it been only a day. Or a month. A year. Time meant nothing to Bjorn anymore. The Arabs had robbed him of any sense of place or time. Constant darkness ruled him. The loneliness had been unbearable. Unlike his previous imprisonment, this time he had no companions in his cell. He struggled to speak to anyone who came near. He spoke through the small window in the door barely large enough for his eyes. Someone across the way answered him. But neither spoke the other's language. It was all he could to do to stave off madness.

Also unlike his last stay in the prince's dungeon, he was fed better food and with greater frequency. True to Jamil's promise, they were strengthening him. They wanted to use his strength in battle against the Byzantines. He appreciated this. And for his time in prison, he offered no resistance or fight whenever his door opened for meals. The guards did not abuse him. Neither did they comfort him. He was a prisoner, after all. But once in a great while an Arab different from the guards would come to prod his body and test his strength. He would stare into his eyes and open his mouth. At last, one day the Arab grunted out some words in his strange language and it changed everything.

He was led out in chains with four men of his own size and strength to watch him. He was given a heavy log and told to exercise with it. He had tried to strike his captors, but an arrow shot into the dirt between his feet warned him off the idea. He dared no more attempts. That time would come another day.

Once he was strong again and ready to fight, the cage arrived. Expecting to be herded into the courtyard for more practice, he instead found the cage hanging open. The four giants boxing him into the center of their formation held long, heavy spears. They had learned his disposition well enough to plant their spears against his back before he resisted.

Yet they considered him stupid. Bjorn knew he was not as clever as Yngvar or as witty as Thorfast. But he was not stupid. They had not invested so much time and effort into him that they would maim or kill him at that moment. Perhaps after the day of battle, but not on that day.

He grabbed the spear and wrenched it from his captor's grip. It was no small feat. The four Arabs were as tall and strong as he. But they were not children of the bear god. Bjorn felt the madness descending on him, and once he held a spear in hand, he was willing to embrace it.

The fight was short. He reversed the spear in his grip, but one of his captors swept his feet from behind. He crashed to his side with a roar. The spear remained in his grip, but the other two Arabs pinned him back at the shoulders with theirs.

He learned they were not unwilling to hurt him. The points drew blood and threatened to drive down to the bone. Too late, Bjorn realized he meant nothing to these four brutes. They were paid to herd him around and keep him contained. If they killed him in a supposed accident, would they care?

Rather than discover the answer to his own question, he relented. Yet as they recovered him from the ground and then guided him at the open cage, he felt the burn of shame. He was a child of the bear god. The Valkyrie had spared him not to turn meekly in the hands of his enemies.

So he had struck his head repeatedly against the bars as he wrestled with four men of his own size. They had prevailed but not without their own faces bloodied and bruised. Bjorn had laughed at them, even when he tasted his own blood dribbling into his mouth. They had only glares for answers.

Now he sat amid their war camp. He had travelled like a caged animal, loaded into a cart and delivered to his Arab captors. They had treated his arrival with spectacle and celebration. Despite his situation, it brought a certain flush of pride to Bjorn. They knew he would be a monstrous foe in battle and knew he would help deliver them victory.

Maybe he would. But he would kill as many Arabs as he could before he died himself. Arab or Byzantine made no difference to him.

Now as he rested against the bars of his cage, a group emerged from between the bobbing tents. Night had settled and torches and campfires brightened the sprawling camp. Twisting shadows spread everywhere. Five men flickered between these shadows and the golden light.

Jamil and Saleet.

Bjorn shoved himself against the bars. He stretched out a hand as if he could pluck them into his cage. But the two Arabs and their three guards halted out of range.

The wiry little Saleet folded his arms and smirked. Jamil the Moor also smiled at him, scanning him from head to foot.

"You look your old self," he said, stroking his neatly pointed beard. "Are you ready for your day of battle?"

Bjorn cocked his head to fit Jamil fully into his sight. The bars were cold and rough as they pressed against his temples. He still stretched his arms out, if only to feel as though he had a chance to crush his foes.

"Get closer. I'll show you how strong I've grown. Ain't got the guts for it, though."

Jamil smiled. "I am not so easily goaded, unlike the soft-minded fools you deal with. I have nothing to prove to an animal in a cage."

"Let me out!" Bjorn slammed against the bars, feeling his rage as a fiery aster in his chest. "I'll tear that beard off your fucking face!"

"So well spoken." Jamil frowned as if a filled piss pot has been shoved under his nose. It made Bjorn roar in anger.

"I'm ready to kill," Bjorn said, pulling back his hands. "Give me an ax and I'll leave you a trail of heads to follow. But you must let me out of this cage."

"We will," he said. "And you will have an ax and all the enemies you can kill. The Byzantines will come by the hundreds."

"That's not enough to tire me," Bjorn said. "I'll need to take some of you fucking Arabs as well."

Jamil gave a patient smile. His hazel eyes glittered as he regarded Bjorn.

"We have considered you might be more inclined to fight for the Byzantines. Realize that turning on us will be suicide. No Arab will draw near you. Should you ever face the Arab lines except to kill a Byzantine behind you, you will die. I've assigned an archer to you. If you die a coward, your gods will forsake you."

Bjorn stared hard at him. The fool had never been in battle before. An archer would have to stand high above the fray to keep a constant watch. And while the Arabs might wish to avoid him, the dictates of the battlefield would funnel their movement. They might have no choice but to come within the arc of his strike.

"Your archer better have the eyes of a hawk to keep up with me." Bjorn sat back in his cage.

Jamil gave a satisfactory nod. He drew closer now that Bjorn had retreated, yet still not close enough to risk being seized.

"Remember what I told you," he said. "You are being shown uncommon mercy. You may die in battle, fighting for our dearest Prince Kalim. But no amount of your brave fighting will carry you off this battlefield. You are to die here and be gone from my sight. The last of your miserable lot to leave this world. I have prayed for this day. I will praise God night and day when I find your corpse on the battlefield."

"Got to catch me first," Bjorn said. "And I don't die easy. You want to kill me? Better do it here while I'm in this cage. Otherwise, I'll be plucking your eyes out and eating them like—what was that thing I ate at the prince's feast? Tasted like pickled rat turds. Olives! Yes, eating your eyeballs like olives. Wouldn't that be a fucking treat?"

Jamil's dusky color blanched at the thought. Bjorn chuckled.

This exchange seemed to incense Saleet, who had been watching in brooding silence. Now he began his womanly screeching, shouting orders at everyone around him. At last he grabbed a spear from one of his guards with an imperious huff.

Bjorn stood as Saleet drove at him with the spear lowered. Jamil shouted for Saleet to stop. Bjorn kept laughing.

The wiry little man plunged his spear into the cage. Bjorn grabbed the shaft and tore it from Saleet's grip. Its long shaft caught in the square of the cage bars. Bjorn could not draw in its full length nor turn it. But he could break it and make a short dagger out of its blade.

Saleet fought to regain the spear, but his exertions were that of a child. If Bjorn could ever get his hands on the little bastard, he would flatten him with no more thought than killing a roach.

The shaft snapped easily in the cage. Bjorn was at his full strength and the leverage the tight bars offered made for easy work.

"Thanks for the weapon," Bjorn said, flipping the short spear blade in his hand. "Want to learn how to use one?"

Jamil gathered Saleet away from the cage. Bjorn wished for a chance to hurl the broken blade into one of them, but he lacked the accuracy to feed it through the tight bars. He contented himself with laughter and brandishing his spear at the Arabs looking on.

His victorious laughter was short lived. Both Jamil and Saleet left. But they were incompetent fools. Their replacements were hardened warriors who knew how to deal with him. One shirtless Arab with a black beard thick as wire that brushed his chest gave him a wicked smile. He mumbled a threat at Bjorn, who showed his broken spear.

"Come to test me? Open the cage door. I'll give you a challenge."

Another Arab arrived with a long torch. Bjorn knew the threat and backed up to the opposite side of the cage. The Arab shoved his brand inside, flaming bits breaking off as it passed the iron bars. He drove it at Bjorn's face.

The searing heat blasted over his skin and he screamed. The Arab drove the flaming brand as if he were sawing wood. The fire bobbed about his face as he scrambled to stay back. The Arabs had come to watch and laugh. It only made Bjorn roar all the harder.

Eventually he realized he had to surrender his weapon or the torment would not end. Worse, he might be burned. He was to die the next day. What care would the Arabs have if they burned his face?

He tossed the broken spear out of the cage. The torment did not stop. He pressed against the rough bars opposite the torch. His hands hid his face as the heat brushed his skin. The Arabs laughed and jeered. But soon his tormentors' threats grew dispirited until he pulled out the brand from the cage. He smashed out the flames against the bars, spraying flames and sparks over Bjorn. His legs and arms burned in a dozen places, but none seriously.

The Arabs drifted away, their merriment finished. He heard what might have been an alarm in the distance. It seemed to have drawn away the Arabs from the central camp. Yet by late night, they returned. Bjorn fell asleep, uncaring for whatever had happened to upset the Arabs.

The next morning he awakened to his cage being loaded on a cart. The Arabs were ready for war. Despite his hatred of them, Bjorn had to admire their discipline. They formed marching columns and obeyed their leaders. They exited the valley where they had been camped, following a vanguard formed of warriors in long chain coats and bright helms that gleamed in the sun.

Bjorn suffered the clouds of dust that rolled into his sweat-slick face and formed mud. At least the Arabs with him suffered the same. Flies buzzed around him. The cart rattled and shook over the uneven ground. It stuck at least three times on rocks or ruts and had to be levered forward by near-naked slaves.

At last they arrived at the battle lines. Bjorn guessed he was part of a reserve set to spring a flanking trap on the Byzantines. What seemed hundreds of Arabs huddled behind a steep crest. Horns, shouts, and clanging iron echoed into the bright blue sky from the opposite side. He was no better than a war beast to the Arabs. So he knew none of their plans.

A Norse-style ax rested in the cart with him as he waited to be released. His cart had been laboriously hauled as close to the top of the crest as the Arabs dared. During this time, the ax had fallen and slid to the foot of his cage. He studied it now. The double-bearded head was sharp and oiled. The shaft was dark and smooth from long use. Scores and nicks marred the length, forming a familiar pattern.

This was his ax. Prince Kalim's men had seized it when he and the others were first captured. Now it was restored to him.

"These Arabs ain't so bad," he said. He reached through the bars to touch the haft. His skin tingled over his neck and down his back. His beloved weapon restored. Only Gyna loved her weapons more.

Gyna. She was still alive. Gone north, or so Jamil had said. Bjorn did not believe the lies about her taking up with another man. Gyna hated all people, but especially strange men. She had love only for him, and even then Bjorn wondered at it. If he died today, he would never see her again. Perhaps she would be allowed into Valhalla where they would be reunited one day. But it did not seem a place where women would be allowed no matter how fierce they were in life. They went to Freya's hall.

He shrugged. He loved her. He wanted to see her once more in this world. But he might meet her again in the next. Or not. Fate decided these things. His mind was too weak to struggle with Fate's plans.

During his imaginings, the Arabs had crawled up the crest. Bjorn gave them a thin smile. Sneaky bastards. The poor Byzantines were about to take a hard blow from above. He was going to join this charge, too. They had no hope.

He felt the Arabs' tension expecting battle and death. Their eyes were wide and white. Their faces taut and brows furrowed. Their cheeks flushed. No one made a sound but for the clink of chain and sword.

Then a shout went up. The Arabs stood, raising their curved swords and screaming for death.

Someone popped open the door to Bjorn's cage.

"Ain't nothing else to do," Bjorn said. None of the rage or battle lust took him. This was not his fight. This was to be his murder.

He stepped out as Arabs rushed around him. He wondered at Jamil's prediction that he would be given a wide berth. His old ax was warm and familiar in his grip. A glance around revealed no archer tracking his movements. Had that been a lie as well? Perhaps he should not test Jamil. No matter where he ran, he would be lost and caught again. Better to die in battle.

He bounced his ax shaft on his palm as he hiked to the top of the crest then looked down. The Arab horde was streaming toward the rear of the Byzantines, who seemed unaware of the screaming mob rushing at them.

Bjorn gripped the ax in both hands, turning his head side to side to sweep the battlefield with his one eye. There would be an Arab leader here somewhere.

He would take that bastard's head with him to Valhalla.

It would be a gift to Gyna if they met again in death. If not, then he would drink mead from the Arab's skull and wait for Ragnarok.

With a roar to echo through Valhalla itself, Bjorn joined the charge.

10

Gyna had been imagining Bjorn while standing over Broken Balls. The red light of the dying campfire lit the left side of his face, emphasizing his deep eye sockets and the furrow of his brow. He blinked awake, shooting up and reaching for Gyna's sword stacked next to him.

The rest of the camp was like sacks of grain carelessly strewn around the beach. Their snores defeated the growl of waves from the beach down the slope. None of them reacted to Broken Balls's sudden awakening.

He grabbed the sword to his side.

"What are you doing, bitch?"

His shout pealed like thunder, at least to Gyna's ears. His slab-like hand wrapped around the grip of her sword.

But he had left her dagger untouched. Too bad for him.

Gyna snatched it away like a cat swatting at a dangling thread. Her sword had peace straps set, which Fargrim had insisted upon while she carried the weapon. Broken Balls, being a stupid pile of maggot bait, had not thought of this.

The dagger, however, had no such constraints. Further, Gyna always kept the blade loose in the sheath.

She flicked away the leather sheath with practiced ease. Broken

Balls had only an instant to realize he could not draw the sword he had grabbed.

The iron blade plunged under his chin and into the soft flesh of the neck. He clamped onto her wrist with one hand, dropping the sword. His small eyes went wide and blood gurgled up from the corners of his mouth.

But he held her tight and groaned against the iron that had invaded his mouth from beneath his chin. Gyna pulled back, but Broken Balls not only held firm but now struggled to his feet.

She twisted the blade. It made hollow, scraping sounds as it ground along his jawbone. Still the giant staggered to his feet with her locked in his grip.

"Why don't you die?" Gyna shouted as she wrenched back on the blade.

Broken Balls grabbed her throat in a giant hand and crushed. Even as his life blood flowed out his mouth and ran hot over Gyna's fingers, his strength did not diminish.

Unable to breathe, Gyna's chest tightened and she thrashed against the grip crushing her. She wrestled with the blade that had lodged in Broken Ball's jawbone. He stood stone still, eyes wide and unfocused. One hand wrapped around her throat and squeezing it shut. The other hand holding her dagger arm in place.

Her vision was darkening as Broken Balls's relentless grip closed her windpipe. She could not free herself even if she released the dagger. Broken Balls should have died, but could she have missed the thick veins of his throat and merely nailed his tongue to the roof of his mouth? That thought exploded in her mind along with flashes of white.

He would kill her after all.

She kicked him in the crotch, remembering to fight rather than struggle. This elicited a grunt and seemed to focus his eyes. They screwed down on her as he poured more strength into his hand. A small gasp escaped her lips as a bubble of air pressed out.

No good. She kicked again, but he did not release.

Panicked beyond reason, she released the dagger and grabbed

Broken Balls's one hand with both of hers. She thrashed and tore at him. Her eyelids fluttered as she felt ready to faint.

Then Broken Balls's hand opened and he collapsed.

He thudded like a falling tree, landing in the low fire. Sparks and embers flew up into the darkness.

Gyna collapsed to her knees, coughing and gasping. Cold air filled her lungs. Her eyes throbbed and her neck pulsed. She sucked her breath while her wits returned.

When the fog lifted from her eyes and her mind refocused, she realized someone shouted in the distance.

She leapt to her feet. Broken Balls lay atop the campfire embers with arms and legs thrown wide, gray smoke rolling out from beneath him. Her dagger hung from his throat and his eyes stared at the starless sky.

Her sword lay in the grass by her feet. She snatched it up and slung it across her shoulder. Its weight was like an old friend hanging a protective arm over her.

"You're not keeping my dagger," she said as she stepped forward to the corpse. The shouting was close, but she was not leaving another dagger behind.

Putting her foot on Broken Balls's chest, she hauled out the dagger with a thick, sucking squelch.

The sentry was running toward her, awakening others as he did. Fortunately, he was across camp. Nearer to her, sleeping men had only just roused from their dreams. They sat up, staring hard at the dark shape in the campfire.

Their confusion gave Gyna the moment she needed to make her escape. She ran the dagger across Broken Balls's shirt to clean the worst of the gore, then sped off for the deeper darkness that marked where pine trees served as gateways to the forest.

This was her land. She was raised here. She played along these shores as a girl. She ran through these forests with her friends. She knew where to go and where to avoid. She laughed as she fled.

Then fell on her face.

She had done all of that by daylight. Now she was fleeing in darkness, and one black shadow was much like another. The pain in her toes said she had struck a rock or root. The tree line remained ahead of her, but she had already put distance between her and the camp.

Would they follow her? What kind of bounty could there really be on her head? Yngvar had a bounty and as far as Gyna knew was Erik Bloodaxe's true enemy. She was nothing. Her price might be set at the level of a well-cared-for slave. But for a king to pay for her?

The answer came from the horn that sounded behind.

Fargrim was going to pursue.

She clambered to her feet again, adjusted the sword that had swung around her torso when she fell, then ran. The darkness of the pines seemed welcoming from a distance. Now that she drew nearer, she feared the nighttime forest. Besides the perils of deadfalls and uncertain footing, she feared the spirits that haunted such places.

But then so would Fargrim and his crew. She had to reach her father's old fortress. Even if the Danes still held it, being their captives would be preferable to remaining with Fargrim. After killing his brute, she did not expect any mercy from him.

She picked her way carefully. Fear demanded she run. But caution controlled her step. Her hands held against rough tree bark. Brush and branch pulled at her shirt, tugged at her boots and pant legs. Her hair tangled with twigs and pine needles. Yet the fragrance of the forest was a welcome change from salty air.

She followed the land up, always choosing inclines over slopes. Most times her own feet were barely visible in the dark. Yet the gods granted her a hole in the clouds to shed some light across her path.

Or perhaps they had granted Fargrim a light to follow her?

Shaking her head against the thought, she pushed ahead. The gods loved her more, didn't they? Why wouldn't they? In fact, she had given the gods little to care enough for her. She never sacrificed to them, never offered glory to their names. Nor had she ever called upon them. Perhaps that had been a mistake.

After what felt like half the night of striding through the forest darkness, she knew it had been a mistake.

She was lost.

The realization halted her. Alasdair and the others made running through a forest at night seem like child's play. But now her exposed skin grew cold and the pleasant fragrance of the pine forest held a trace of rot. The deep forest grew less welcoming of intruders like her.

Fargrim, if he had followed, must also be lost. That brought a smile to her. But how was she to kill him and the crew, get Yngvar's ship back, and return to Sicily while stranded in a forest in Denmark?

"Bjorn, you were right to call me mad." She sat against a tree, sliding down until she felt the cool earth beneath her. "This had all seemed a fine plan in the moment. What a fucking mess."

Bowing her head, she took stock of her pains. Her wrists burned from where she had struggled free from the ropes. Her knees and face hurt from when she had fallen on them. Every pulse of her heart sent pain through her neck. In the light, if she lived to morning, she expected to find bruises in the shape of Broken Balls's hand.

"At least I killed him." She sighed and rubbed her face.

The trickle of water.

She stopped rubbing. Listened harder. Then her eyes widened.

"Freya, Odin, and Thor! The stream!"

It was behind her. She wove between tree trunks, stumbling over rocks and rough ground, but found the small creek trickling behind her. A faint sparkle of the moon above shined on the flowing water.

"Not the stream, but you can lead me to it," she said. She knelt beside it to dip her hands into the cold water. She splashed it over her face, scrubbed the gore from her hands in it, then cupped it to her lips. Nothing tasted so sharp and fresh as this water.

The creek would lead to the stream that flowed from the higher lands to the west. This was the stream that fed both the fortress and the village where her father had been forced to live when the Danes first captured his fortress from him.

She had to only follow it either up or down stream to find either the fortress or the village.

"The gods even grant me a choice," she said, again splashing cold water onto her face. She laughed. "They do love me more than you, Fargrim."

Choices meant decisions, and Gyna disliked making too many of those. Throughout her young life she had bemoaned having no choices and no command over her own life. Yet once she earned the freedom to decide, she discovered it carried too much responsibility. She would rather follow Yngvar and blame him whenever a choice led to disaster.

She looked for a sign from the gods. A bird. Too late at night. A falling branch. Could not see it in the dark. The call of an owl. Silence.

The gods were not helping. Following the flow would take her to the fortress and possibly enemies. Going against it would lead to what she hoped would be a long-abandoned village. Not much help there.

Then she remembered the signal fires.

Her father had an agreement with Waldhar. When he needed aid he would light the bonfire and the Saxons would come with warriors. He had lit it the night Yngvar had come to collect taxes owed to the jarl at the time.

If she could set a bonfire of her own and Waldhar was in the fortress, then he would come to her aid. If Danes arrived instead, they might still aid her. But she would not have to risk confinement behind their walls to learn their minds, and she could spy on them before revealing herself.

She struck out against the flow of the creek, which led to the stream she knew so well. From there she travelled along the banks of the rushing stream, watching the moon follow her in the reflection of the water.

After two clearings passed, she arrived at the old village. It was not what she remembered. Rain and wind had turned homes to piles of rotting thatch and timbers. Some homes had been leveled to the foundations, leaving only ovals of rocks that formed the hearth. Once the fortress had been restored to Lopt, the people had carried away anything of value to return to their old homes.

Only to become captives of the Danes once more, thanks to Yngvar's treachery. The feeling of loss surfaced as she walked through the ruins. She believed she had settled her feelings for her father's fate. He had chosen to meet his death rather than surrender his fortress a second time. Yngvar had warned her father and had saved her life. Alasdair had shown her a gap in the stockade walls through which she had fled to safety. But her father would not have died had Yngvar not betrayed him and his Saxon allies.

She shook her head. Yngvar and Bjorn were too far away now. What was she doing here? What could a lone woman do to save a crew of men who were likely dead or scattered into slavery by now? If she did not light the bonfire, no one would come. If no one came, by daylight she could surrender to the owners of the fort, Dane or Saxon. She would be rid of Fargrim and fate would weave a new strand into the skein of her life.

But Fargrim had to die. The death of Broken Balls was not enough. That whole crew had to die. They had raped her. They must be made to pay for their crimes.

If she were to turn her back on Bjorn and the rest, she would have to surrender her sword. She would spend her life at the loom while gossiping with old women with warts on their faces that sprouted hairs to rival a seal's whiskers. Better to lose her head on the battlefield and fall among the corpses of her enemies than to die by idle chatter.

So she found the mound of burned wood from the last bonfire. It was nothing but sludgy ash, but it might have been the same fire that had summoned Waldhar to fight Yngvar. It had changed her life.

It would change her life once more.

Dry kindling was easy to find at the edges of the forest. Bigger branches and timbers to create a bonfire were far harder to come to hand. She repeated the names of every god she knew. She even begged the Christian god, though from what she had learned from Alasdair, that one was not much for revenge. Still, she needed every blessing she could beg.

What should have been a night's labor might have been merely an hour of work. She had accumulated enough debris and kindling to start her fire. This was far harder to do. Touchwood and a striking steel had been her accustomed tools. Yet after so many nights at sea where she camped on hostile shores, she had learned to start a fire with dry sticks and a stone. It was primitive and frustrating, but it was all she had.

Where the gods had been bountiful with timber, they were miserly with flame. Nothing she did could spark a fire. She tried using her dagger and a rock to generate a spark. It took nearly the same amount of time to get her fire started as it had to collect the wood for it.

But she did start her fire. The sky was beginning to brighten. Fargrim's men likely had become as lost as she had been. Their finding the stream would have meant nothing to them. Yet once her bonfire caught, it would be visible for miles around. They would head for it. So would whoever lived in the fortress.

When at last her pitiful flames had taken to the wood she had gathered and climbed up the stacked logs, she stepped back and sat in the grass. Despite the cool night air her hair clung to her face with sweat. Her back ached from carrying the wood and hunching so long over a flame that would not catch.

Now she had only to wait.

She leaned back on her hands and crossed her feet. Who would come?

For a long time she feared no one had seen the bonfire. After all, she had not built hers to the height that her father used to signal the Saxons. Perhaps no one could see it. The horizon was stained white with the approach of the sun. The moon had long traveled across the sky to vanish from sight. A new day approached and Gyna might be as lost as she was during the night.

Then she heard the voices. Men had located her.

She stood up from the grass, patted off the dirt from her pants, then flipped the peace straps from her sword hilt and loosened it in the scabbard.

Across the clearing, Fargrim and what seemed most of his crew stumbled into view. The yellow light of the bonfire washed across their astonished faces.

Fargrim pointed his sword at her from across the field.

"A fine chase, you bitch. I don't know what you mean by setting such a fire, but you're alone here. And I'm going to quench it with your blood."

The men of the fortress had either not seen the fire or chose not to answer its summons. Gyna gave a bitter smile.

That was a lot of work for a bad end, she thought.

Fargrim marched ahead and his men followed with their swords drawn and spears lowered.

11

The bonfire behind Gyna snapped and popped, sending sparks to smolder in the grass at her feet. The heat rippled across her back, but her face was cool against the predawn air. Fargrim and his crew were like yellow phantoms stalking across the field. The dark pines behind framed them clearly. Despite Fargrim's boast to extinguish the fire with Gyna's blood, they approached carefully. Their heads were tucked down as if they expected a line of archers to spring out of the glare of the fire and strafe them with arrows.

She wished she had anything behind her except miles of forest and streams. Even a wolf pack would be welcomed now. She stood alone against her enemies with only a sword in hand. Not even a shield.

Fate was cruel. The gods had enjoyed a tremendous jest at her expense. She had honestly believed she had outsmarted her enemies and would be dancing over their corpses by now. Yet all the dancing would be done by Fargrim and his men.

At least they would not rape her this time. She had a sword in hand and a dagger close to her other. They would have to kill her before touching her again. She set both hands on her sword and raised it toward Fargrim.

"Take a good look at the sword that will kill you."

Fargrim laughed, though he did not drop his guard.

"I don't know what you have planned, but you'll not succeed. Did you think to draw us into a trap? Who can help you here? You are outnumbered thirty to one. No matter what tricks you have laid, you can't fight your way out of this."

She had to agree, though merely scowled at Fargrim. His men began to fan out and would soon surround her. Her gamble on the fortress had failed and now she had to escape. As thrilling as it would be to leap at Fargrim and gut him while his men watched, she valued her life more.

"I swear it," Gyna said, brandishing her sword. "I will take your head with this."

Then she fled into the glare of the fire. Before the crew surrounded her, she cut close to the bonfire and used its orange haze to blind them to her direction. The flames brushed past her left arm but did not set fire to her clothes. It felt like jumping through a curtain of heat into a pool of cold water. She knew the village and knew the paths through it.

Fargrim called the chase. Fear lengthened Gyna's stride as she sped into the ruins. She sheathed her blade, knowing she could not fight. That slowed her, but she had already lost her pursuers.

Back to the trees, she thought. Find the stream and it would lead most of the way to the beach. With all of Fargrim's crew behind her, perhaps she could steal his ship. That plan was as mad as any other she had made. She knew nothing of sailing or ships beyond the minor tasks she had been given over the years. Rowing was simple. But steering, well, perhaps she could catch a current that would take her somewhere safer. More likely she would run aground a hundred yards from the beach and be no better off.

Gods give me a plan, she thought as she entered the forest again. I've used up all my wits on the last one.

She darted between the trees like a fleeing doe. In the morning twilight she must have been visible to her pursuers. Shouts followed her and she dared a glance back to catch shapes moving toward her.

"Woman, hold!"

The shout came from her left and was heavily accented. She whirled to see a man standing close to a pine tree. He held close to it, and draped in a green cloak with the hood drawn, he might have passed for a bush. Golden locks and a golden beard showed within the hood. She was not going to stop for him.

Turning to run, she slammed into the man's companion.

Her face flattened against his chest, and his arms wrapped around her in a bear hug. He smelled of pine.

"Whoa, girl," said her captor. "Did you set the signal fire?"

Rather than fight, she went limp. She recognized the accent and the skin of her face tingled with joy. She looked up into another hooded face. A flowing brown beard hung beneath a severe mouth. The rest was in shadow.

She spoke Saxon to him.

"I am Gyna, Daughter of Lopt Stone-Eye. Sister to—Gisela, wife of Waldhar. I set the fire. Danes have come. They are behind me now. Sound your horns."

It felt strange to speak Saxon again. She had learned Frankish enough to make good threats, but the language felt muddy to her. Speaking to a Saxon again was refreshing. The Saxon holding her did not release her, but his mouth fell open.

"Did you not hear me? Unless you have an army at your back, thirty blood-mad Danes are coming to kill us."

The blonde Saxon joined them. He pulled Gyna out of his companion's hold to look at her. He shoved back his hood as he studied her.

"You are my aunt?"

Gyna did not recognize the man. He could not be twenty years old. He had a long forehead and thin lips. He seemed incapable of smiling and his eyes were as cold as—Gisela's.

"Ewald? Gisela's oldest? But you were just a boy."

"I've not seen you in ten years, Aunt Gyna. Then you disappeared."

"Disappeared? I was sent away by your father!"

"Lord," said the man who had been holding her. "She is not mistaken about the Danes. They approach us now."

"Tell me you have an army following." Gyna glanced back and spotted the white shapes of Fargrim's men flickering between tree trunks. Dawn had come and weak light now filtered down through the canopy.

"I led the watch tonight," Ewald said. "Just me and dear Bernward come to see why a fire that should never be lit had sprung to life. Everyone else thought it was the ghosts of my grandfather's people and wouldn't come."

"Lord, we must flee and warn the others." Bernward revealed an iron horn tied to his hip.

"That will only draw their attention to us," Ewald said. "They do not see us yet. Come, Auntie, shelter under my cloak. These fools will pass us."

Ewald swept Gyna aside into bushes and threw his cloak over her. She did not see Bernward, but assumed he had done the same. Beneath the darkness of the heavy wool, she smelled Ewald's sweat and listened to his measured breathing.

She tried to think of when she had last seen this boy. Anything to keep her mind off the shouting and footfalls she heard passing nearby. Gisela had married at thirteen and had her son two years later. Gyna remembered a red-faced, screaming brat that had grown into an arrogant youth too similar to his father Waldhar for Gyna to want much to do with him. Yet now his strong arm sheltered her from enemies.

Time had moved on. Was she an old auntie now? Maybe it would be better to jump out at Fargrim and die in glorious battle.

It seemed as if they had remained covered for a whole morning. But when Ewald slipped off his cloak from their heads, the morning light was still low. Fresh air flowed over her face, cool and clean.

Bernward was not with them. Ewald helped her stand and took a better look at her. He did not say anything, but his serious face and the lines around his nose made him seem his father's son. Waldhar must be proud.

"Waldhar lets his oldest heir run free at night to be killed by passing Danes?" Gyna brushed her hair out of her face and adjusted her sword. "I thought he'd keep you close."

Ewald smiled, but yet it seemed full of sadness. He shook his head and looked to Gyna again.

"You wear pants and carry a sword. You are as wild as Mother said you are."

"Wilder than she knows. Now, where is your servant?"

"Bernward, show yourself."

The man rose out of the bushes like a spirit from a grave. Gyna nearly shrieked, for he stood close enough to touch yet she had never spotted him.

Ewald laughed, this time with genuine mirth. "He is my teacher. We learn to be canny scouts in this land. The Danes are always a threat. Now, we must warn everyone that a war band is roaming the forest."

The two Saxons escorted her through the forest as easily as if they strode paved streets. The rough passing of Fargrim and his crew was evident all around. They had trampled bushes, snapped branches, and left prints to follow. They were truly fools.

"It's over so easily," she said, shaking her head.

"What did you say, Auntie?"

"Nothing. When you capture these Danes, you must bring me the leader. He is mine. And they have a ship. That is mine, too. I will not be denied this, and once I explain things to your father he will understand."

Ewald nodded.

"And don't call me Auntie. It sounds old and we are not so close. I am Gyna."

"You are very good at giving orders," Ewald said. "Auntie. But you might consider that things are not as they were when you left us."

She paused. The forest suddenly felt darker, as if the past had crept around her and now squeezed out her future. Ewald stopped as well, facing her with a wry smile.

"What do you mean? What has changed?"

"We've no time to tarry with a crew of mad Danes running through our forest. You don't want them to return to your ship," Ewald twisted the words in mockery. "And flee before we can catch them."

"Listen, boy. Respect me or I'll teach you to. And my lesson will leave scars on your pretty face. Now, lead on."

Ewald's arrogant smile did not fade, but he turned to catch up to Bernward who had not slowed his pace.

"I meant no offense, Auntie," Ewald said, not looking back. "But things are different from when you were here last. You shall see soon enough."

Gyna's stomach tightened at the fear of what she might find behind the walls of the fortress. Every branch that grabbed her sleeve as she slipped through the forest felt like a ghostly hand teasing her. As Ewald and Bernward led, she had an urge to run after Fargrim's trail. At least she knew what dangers lay that way.

The fortress walls rose from between the trees as they approached from the forest. Black crows lined the palisades leaning together in groups as if gossiping. Even when men appeared over the walls, framed black against an ever-brightening sky, the birds merely sidled down the wall. They were anticipating a feast they did not want to lose sight of.

Bernward drew his iron horn and blew three metallic notes on it. The sound was grating and loud. The crows at last took to the air, unhurried and calm. They flew toward the shore, where Fargrim's crew was likely gathering after a fruitless night of running through the forest.

Gyna expected to sprint for an open gate, but neither Saxon increased their pace. In fact, Bernward no longer seemed as anxious to get to the walls. Ewald offered Gyna a thin smile.

"He was just eager to blow the horn. He never gets to have any fun being my teacher and protector. That was more to announce our return than to warn the others. By now I expect the Danes have realized they are surrounded by enemies."

"We go to join the battle, then?"

Ewald's smile faded. "No, there will be no battle. Ships like the Dane's are common enough at that landing. We saw their campfires at night. That landing is actually a trap and we would have attacked just before dawn. It's a good source of slaves and ships. Though by now most sailors know to avoid camping there."

"That plan could be turned against you," Gyna said, proud to find the hole in her nephew's thinking. "An enemy could offer you a decoy ship and attack the fortress while the warriors are outside the walls."

"The Danes have tried that before," Ewald said. "We've learned some hard lessons. But that was not the situation this time. Though I'm certain our warriors were shocked to find the Danes had all vanished into the forest."

The gates remained open, though a dozen bowmen guarded it either from the walls or the entrance itself. Though the men stared after her as she passed inside the gates, Gyna only glanced at them. She instead stared at the homes and buildings within.

Dawn still left deep shadows beneath the eastern walls to obscure everything there. Yet the main hall stood above all else on a small rise. White smoke was already rolling off the golden thatch roof. Tears hung in her eyes as she walked along rutted paths with the ghosts of old friends long forgotten.

"None of these buildings are the same," she said as she passed newly constructed homes.

"Fire," Ewald said. "We had to burn out the Danes when we took this fortress back from them. It was a bloody day."

"Were you there?" Gyna asked.

Ewald shook his head. "But Bernward was. He's not only a great scout but a great warrior as well. Killed a score of Danes that day, didn't you?"

"Yes, lord, a bloody day indeed."

"So new homes built on the ashes of the old," Gyna said. "Still, this place feels like home."

Ewald's smile returned, sly and knowing. "I wonder if you will still feel that way once you return to Grandfather's hall?"

Gyna's attention snapped back from the new buildings to Ewald as he led them down the track toward the hall. She still carried her weapons and her hand fell to her hilt instinctively. Bernward, who had lagged behind, frowned at this.

"Enough hinting," she said. "What is it that you're not telling me?"

"And what have you not said? I'm escorting you under good faith.

Leaving you weapons in hand and treating you like family. But how do I know you are really my aunt?"

"What?" Gyna stopped on the track. Somewhere from the grid of thatch-roofed buildings a rooster crowed and a dog barked in answer. "Of course I'm your aunt."

"You could be a trick of the Danes."

"I'm speaking in your mother tongue, you fool boy."

"Plenty of Danes speak our language, as we do theirs. How do I know you are my aunt? You just walked out of the forest like a spirit. Why are you here? Why are the Danes chasing you?"

"I'm not going to prove myself to you. How I got here is a long story. Take me to Waldhar and you can listen to the tale. I'm in no mood to tell it twice."

Ewald rubbed the back of his neck. "No, I suppose you must be my aunt. Now we are nearly to the hall. But you cannot see my father, Waldhar."

"He will want to know I've returned," Gyna said, letting her hand drop from the hilt of her sword. She gave Bernward a blithe smile as she did.

Ewald shook his head again. "You cannot see him. He is dead."

Gyna blinked. Ewald's smile no longer seemed smug and assured. It seemed false.

"And my sister?"

"Dead."

She stared between Ewald and Bernward. Neither man seemed as friendly as they had before they entered the fortress.

"Then you are chief?" Gyna asked, her eyes widening. "But you're a boy. And Waldhar had many brothers. It can't be."

"Nothing ever stays the same," Ewald said. "Auntie."

12

Battle lust and death spiraled around Bjorn as he waded into the back of the Byzantine formation. His heart exulted in the chaotic music of war. Screams of pain and terror. Desperate orders shouted over helmeted heads. Shields thudding together in the press of warriors. The clang of iron on iron. Or the wet thump of iron into flesh. Weeping. Groaning. Cursing.

This was the music for Bjorn's spinning dance. His ax, heavy and beautiful in both hands, swirled around him to carve a red path through the battle. White and blue robes of the Arabs, the dark mail and red plumed helms of the Byzantines, all were swept aside as he battered his way into the midst of the locked combatants.

He did not want to know anything else. Nothing else could fit into his mind. Not now, not with the rage of the bear god upon him. Weapons might have pricked his flesh. Something hot and coppery flowed into his mouth from the top of his head. Perhaps he had been wounded. In such a state, he could have both his legs hewed off but he would not know.

A plan had been in his head once. Something about a leader. But now just he wanted to hack and destroy. He longed to stand atop a mountain of corpses and glare down at the battlefield like a god of death. Bodies slipped beneath his feet as he plowed deeper into the fighting.

He sensed light in the dark of the battle. Enemies fell away to his left and right. His path ahead became clearer.

The battle was breaking up. Men were fleeing and others pursued.

He renewed his war cry. Blood flew off his mighty arms as he raised his ax overhead. Pursued and pursuer were the same to him. Bjorn had at last found the perfect battlefield. There were no allies here, only enemies in every direction. An endless field of enemies to reap.

This was what Valhalla must be like. Though he was the mightiest of all the warriors on this field, he did not doubt he would step into the feasting hall before the day ended.

He remembered his vow. The pause in the frenetic combat created an opening for this forgotten goal to fall back into his thoughts.

The Arab leader remained far out of sight. These men did not carry banners like the Norse. They had no honor. So they could not be as easily marked in battle. Yet Bjorn had fought so many battles that he guessed where the Arab leader would be.

In the center, where a Byzantine leader with some guts fought beneath his own bronze standard, Arabs clustered. They did not pursue the lesser men who fled all around them. They sought the prize of the Byzantine commander. Without doubt the Arab leader would desire to claim the Byzantine's head. Bjorn would have wanted it were he in the Arab leader's position.

A Byzantine streaked across his path, bloodied sword loose in his hand. Bjorn hacked him in the back to send him crashing to the ground. His mail coat had spared his life and blunted Bjorn's ax. But the staggering blow left him stunned as Bjorn sped away.

Despite his size, he moved with great agility whenever the bear god touched him. Pockets of Arabs and Byzantines continued to fight even as the main battle fell apart. Bjorn ignored these personal struggles and ran to where the bronze standard of some sort of creature, maybe a bird, wavered over the heads of Arab warriors.

He skirted aside two Arabs tormenting a Byzantine with their spears. His face was brilliant with blood as he danced between the sharp blades arrayed against him. He would die, but not before the Arabs had their fun.

A dozen long strides later Bjorn avoided another group, this time three Byzantines hacking wildly at an Arab who had fallen to his knees. He screamed and shielded his head with his arms, his small shield forgotten in the grass. Blood and flesh flew from his arms as his Byzantine tormentors chopped at him. Their swords were meant for stabbing and not chopping, making their strikes awkward and prolonging the Arab's death.

The detritus of battle littered his path forward. Bodies lay in piles like tide marks where the enemies had met. Blood flowed into glistening, dark pools beneath them. The corpses of an Arab and Byzantine lay on the grass, heads touching together like two lovers looking for shapes in the clouds floating past their lifeless eyes. Broken spears, bent swords, shattered shields lay scattered everywhere. The pale gray of dismembered hands and arms were stark against the green grass. He stepped on a perfectly severed ear and slipped. His arms flailed and the weight of his ax tugged him to one side. But he recovered and pushed on.

The scent of blood mingled with urine and vomit. Nearby someone had their guts emptied, for the reek of bowels carried on the hot breeze. The sickening stench stoked Bjorn's killing lust. He tightened his grip on his ax and the blood of his foes squeezed between his fingers.

He was at the back of the Arabs now. They were celebrating, hopping and shouting with swords raised overhead. A thin man with a long nose held the bronze standard and waved it as if it were a flag. One of their slain companions even seemed to join the celebration. His forearm stretched out even in death, as if asking to be hoisted up into their crazed dance.

Bjorn stopped short. None of them looked like a leader. They were all in blood-splattered mail coats each like the other. They had captured the standard, which from their giddy celebration must be a great prize. That much was shared in common with Norsemen. But having achieved this, they seemed to have excused themselves from more fighting.

The thin man passed the standard to his companion as they danced and laughed. Other Arabs spotted them from the distance, and raised their own swords and shouts above the wails of defeat from the Byzantines.

All of this transpired on a small rise. Bjorn had scarcely noticed the incline. But as fast as the killing lust rose in him, it ebbed away. As it did, more of the world around him came into his limited view. While the Arabs were drunk on victory and the Byzantines fled for their lives, he could learn all he had missed in his battle madness

The ocean was nearby. He had scented it earlier during transport to the battlefield. Now he was overwhelmed with other unsavory odors, but he was certain the sea was nearby. He watched the Byzantines flee. Their armor sparkled under the blue sky. The red and black plumes of their helmets made them seem like colorful ponies riding off in small packs.

A body of men in plain robes and no visible weapon sped along with them. Slaves, he supposed. Bjorn wondered what they were doing so close to battle. Perhaps the Byzantines needed servants during their fight. It seemed like something they might do.

His vision shrank back to its limited scope. The bear god had removed his mighty paw from Bjorn's shoulder. His battle was done. Now he had to escape, and the bear god had no interest in fleeing from a fight.

Jamil's promise had not come to fruition. Bjorn had killed more Arabs than Byzantines, at least from what he could recall. Yet no arrow had found him.

What a puffed-up pile of shit, he thought. Of course he ain't got the power to command warriors. He was a slave not long ago. Fucking Moor. I'll trim his beard right along with his head. Clean off his skinny shoulders.

Such thoughts called the bear god back to him. But it was only a glance at a favored son. Bjorn's hands tightened on his ax again, but the rage did not fill him. Jamil was not here. Neither was Saleet, who was the real power behind Jamil. He was the one that needed killing first. He had some sort of connection in Prince Kalim's court. He set the trap that had snared him and all his sword brothers. And he was the one who sent Bjorn out here to die.

Bjorn spit.

Then something caught his eye.

Those fleeing slaves. All but two were running after the main body of Byzantine warriors. It was those two fleeing opposite the rest that caused Bjorn to cock his head. His single eye throbbed with the effort to focus on figures so distant.

He would swear one moved like Yngvar did. The other slave at his side was small enough to be Alasdair. He did not know Alasdair's gait as well as Yngvar's. He grew up with Yngvar and could tell him apart from a hundred similar men. They were cousins, but lived in the same hall as real brothers. They had spent every day together since Bjorn could remember.

So as he stared hard after that peculiar gait, he could not help but feel he was watching his dearest cousin running from the battlefield.

"Can't be," he said, startled at his own rough voice.

Something heavy landed over his head.

The bear god rushed back to his favored son.

Bjorn roared and thrashed out at heavy ropes that pressed down over his face. He tried to raise his ax, but more ropes pulled him down.

A weighted net had been cast over him.

He spun, burning with rage. He did not see who or how many were behind him. At least one man held the net, and from the dark, naked skin he glimpsed between the tight weave, he knew the enemy to be one of his hulking Arab captors.

Screaming, he hacked with his ax. Not only did the blow fail, but now the ax head caught in the net. He lashed out with his fist, but the net simply expanded with him to drain the strength from his punch.

The more he struggled the more he became tangled.

Then he collapsed to his side, landing painfully atop his blood-slicked ax.

In battle, a man on the ground was as good as dead if he could not rise in the next heartbeat. Bjorn relied on size and strength to prevent himself from falling. He never trained to leap back up like Yngvar, Thorfast, and so many other of his other sword brothers did. Never fall until killed. That was his belief and it had served him in scores of fights.

Now he struggled to rise. The net tangled him the more he raged. Soon he could not even find his feet. Lead weights tied into the net rolled over his face as he bellowed curses and fought against the netting.

The huge figure of his handler now loomed over him. Where had this giant been hiding? Awareness had never been Bjorn's strongest talent. In fact, he had survived all those scores of battles because Yngvar and Thorfast, and later Gyna, had preserved him. Now alone with no one to keep him safe, the critical failure of battle madness was plain to him. Even a giant Arab with legs like tree trunks could sneak up on him.

It would cost him his life.

The Arab took no chances with Bjorn. He raised a massive spear in two hands as if he intended drive a tent stake into soft earth. Bjorn thrashed but the net clung tighter around him. His right arm was pinned.

At least he was atop his ax and his hand brushed against the smooth wood of its haft. He would go to Valhalla. He would hear that beautiful voice again as it called him to the hall of heroes.

The spear head flashed over him.

He cocked his head so that his one eye could see the killing strike.

He leaned toward it. Welcoming death. Screaming all his hatred and rage.

It struck down.

And fell wide.

The Arab growled, dropping his spear. He lumbered around. Bjorn felt hot blood dripping over his leg as the giant Arab reached out at some unseen foe.

Then the giant collapsed with a groan.

Bjorn fell silent. Above him the blue sky filled with the dark specks of crows come to their carrion feast. Shouting, both in victory and defeat, trilled in the distance. A faint breeze ran along his body, cooling the fresh blood of his enemy that had drizzled over his legs.

Then a figure crept up to him, crawling on his hands and knees as if trying to keep his profile below the horizon.

"The gods have given me a purpose." The figure spoke in a warm, fatherly Norse. He reached Bjorn's side then began tugging at the net. "And it is to endure until I have saved all of you foolish Wolves."

The man twisted his final words to make it seem a slur. But he chuckled as he worked at the net.

Bjorn raised his head against the weight of the net. He could not see the man clearly yet.

"Who the fuck are you?"

"You can't see me? My voice is unrecognized, though I called out to you over storm and swell as we sailed the wide sea? I who steered our ship to torment the Danes or sped us away from sea kings we dared not face, still you do not know me? I knew you had the head of an ox, but I never believed you to forget a friend."

Bjorn fought upright against the heavy net to look at the man kneeling beside him.

"Hamar? By Freya's tits! Is it you?"

"It is. And you are Bjorn Arensson, Bjorn the Blind, Bjorn Skull-Splitter, Bjorn the Mad, and Bjorn the ass that got himself caught in a net. If we survive this day I'm going to call you Bjorn the Fish from here on."

"I never knew I had so many names. Call me whatever you want. Better than being dead."

He strained to see Hamar through the tight weave of the net. His bold square face was undiminished by the trials he had endured. Though the rest of his body was as thin and wasted as week-old rushes. It made his head seem unusually large. His pale and dirty hair sat lank against his temples. His gnarled hands struggled with the net.

"What happened to your leg?" Bjorn asked the moment he saw the thick, white wrappings over his thigh. Rust-colored stains still seeped through them.

"Arabs set their dog on me. I almost bled to death. But the gods are not done with us. So they sent an Arab woman to heal me."

Bjorn lay back, surrendering to the weight of the net. Hamar growled in frustration.

"I will have to cut you out."

"Ain't no shortage of blades here. I promise I won't go nowhere while you fetch one."

Hamar laughed, then crawled closer to lean by his ear.

"Listen, Thorfast also survived the wreck."

Bjorn shouted with joy, though when he tried to rise up Hamar pressed his head back.

"Arabs are coming this way. Just play dead. You're covered in enough blood to be convincing."

"What happened to the Arabs that were just here?"

"The ones with the standard? They ran off to present it to their chief, I suppose. I'd been following the fat Arab, since I guessed he was going to kill you. Not that I needed him to find you in battle."

"How did you know about me?"

"I'm a slave warrior like you. I've been watching you practice alone with those Arab giants. They kept us separated, maybe because they fear what we can do together. But the Arabs value us for our sword skill. Anyway, I've no more time for stories. Three Arabs approach. Lie still. I will be back to cut you out of this net. Then we can flee by night."

"Thorfast is alive?"

Hamar patted his chest. "Aye. Now play dead."

Bjorn closed his eye as if settling in for a nap. Even wrapped in the netting as he was, he relaxed knowing he had help.

The gods were on his side. It was not his time to die. Let these Arabs pass and then he will go to meet Thorfast. His heart pounded with joy.

He heard their approach, mumbling among themselves. They stopped around his head. One's feet brushed against his ear. One prodded him with a toe, then after a short discussion they began to tug at the netting.

Bjorn felt the net peeling away. The three chatted in genial conversation, unaware he was alive beneath their noses. They concentrated at freeing his head and shoulders. Once they freed his arms, he would open his eyes and attack. He anticipated their shock as he burst up at them. Hamar would join the fight and make short work of them.

The gods truly loved him.

Then the Arabs stopped after working the net off his head. They debated in choppy, harsh exchanges over Bjorn's still body. One clicked his tongue as if disagreeing. He spent all his willpower to keep his eyes closed and hold his breath.

A blade scraped from its sheath.

He felt the cold, keen iron set against his neck.

They were not here to free him.

They were here to take his head.

13

Gyna stood in the hall that had once been her father's. In truth, it was only the layout and foundation of her father's hall. The original had been burned down in the last attack and this hall constructed over the ruins. Though by now the rafters were black with soot and the central hearth stones were caked with ash. The hall was dark and smelled like the stale breath of a drunkard. Saxons stood along the walls, seven on each side. They were unarmed but their cold eyes studied her. Though this precaution satisfied her, she still could not smile.

Ewald flanked her. The quivering shadows made him appear even more like her sister. He was handsome and fierce. Confidence—no, arrogance—radiated from his face like the heat from the hearth. Whether he had earned it or not, Ewald was in command of everything before him, just like his mother and Gyna's sister, Gisela.

She could bring herself to think the name now that she had died. Her death saddened Gyna, and she could no longer place what had caused her to hate her sister so much. Gisela had been their father's favorite and Gyna was their father's mistake. That had been enough for Gyna to want to erase her sister from her thoughts. Enmity built from that foundation.

Ewald gave a wan smile. He had refused to tell her more about what she would find in the hall. Waldhar was also dead, and that she did not regret. The fool had sent her away and probably at Gisela's request. Never mind that her banishment turned into the best event of her life, he had no cause to send her away. Other than when she had slapped his wife. Why had she hit her sister? She could not remember, but she undoubtedly deserved it.

"Do you like the new hall?" Ewald whispered as they stood facing the high seat.

"Just like a Norse hall," she said.

"Of course," Ewald said. "The Danes and all those Norse bastards stole everything from us. Even our old gods. Filthy thieves every one."

She had no desire to debate history with Ewald. She did not care for old things. Today and perhaps tomorrow were all she could hold in her mind at once. She shifted her weight to her left leg and waited for the return of whoever had taken leadership after Waldhar. That it was not Ewald was unsettling.

At last the commotion outside of the hall revealed that the war party had returned. She prayed Fargrim and his crew had been taken alive so that she could slit his neck personally. Thoughts of revenge blocked out any fear of who might have replaced Waldhar. Thirty crewmen had raped her. Even if in truth it had only been a dozen, they were all complicit.

The two doors at the front of the hall opened and a large figure blocked out the morning sun. He wore heavy mail and a thick wolf pelt across his shoulders. He kept his helmet under arm, it's horsetail plume waving against his bare leg. In the reflected light of the hearth, she saw the blood splatter on his feet and the hem of his mail. His face remained in shadow, but a long, braided beard flowed down to his chest.

She smiled. Some of Fargrim's crew at least had gone to their deserved fates.

The man strode inside, accompanied by his bodyguards. None of these men set their swords aside, for this was the chief and huscarls. His booted feet scraped against the dirt floor as he approached Gyna. Once out of the glare of morning light, she recognized the smiling face.

"Adalhard?"

"Fate is a strange thing, is it not? We meet again over the ruin of your father's hall. Almost as if it were ten years ago."

"You are chief now?"

She saw Adalhard's eyes flick to Ewald behind her, though it seemed unintended. He did not hesitate in his answer.

"I am, and so you should call me by my title." He pushed past her and approached Ewald. He inclined his head.

"Bernward told me you ran out to the fire alone. That was a foolish choice."

Gyna cringed for Ewald. Nothing hurt a man's pride more than to be called a fool in front of veteran warriors. But Ewald merely inclined his head.

"Bernward is a great teacher. And had I not gone to the fire, who would have rescued my aunt?"

She thought to correct Ewald, but he had indeed rescued her. She was inclined to think of it as her cunning plan having borne the desired result. But some unspoken tension hung between Adalhard and Ewald, so she remained silent.

Adalhard proceeded to his high chair and his huscarls took up positions at his sides. The men along the walls stood straighter and faced their lord.

"Come closer," he said to Gyna. "We are not strangers. I want to hear of your story. There is a long ship on my shore and a score of Danes being tied up in a barn. Then there is your walking out of the past from the ruins of Lopt Stone-Eye's village. This must be a tale worthy of a dozen songs."

She blushed, feeling the warmth on her cheeks. Adalhard waved her forward and she approached. Beneath the splendor of his war gear she became keenly aware that her sea-stained and blood-splattered clothing was little better than rags. The tear in her pant leg at the knee had lengthened, and she noticed the huscarls staring after her exposed skin.

Adalhard was still a handsome man even with the first touches of gray in his brown beard. A hard life had scratched lines around his eyes and across his forehead. Yet he had the open, carefree expression of a young man. Gyna knew him to be Waldhar's most devious brother and she trusted him no more than she would trust a wolf. Yet Adalhard counted Yngvar as a friend.

She bowed before him, though it rankled her to do so. Men needed their assurances of power, even when it was clear to everyone.

"It is a long story, but I will tell how I've come to your hall once more."

Speaking so politely angered her even more. Yet she had favors to ask and so had to remember her place. Bjorn had always told her to mind her place and she laughed at him for it. Among Yngvar's crew, as one of the Wolves, she was equal to everyone else. She had no place to mind.

But now she was a woman in pants who carried sword and shield to battle. In other words, she was little more than a crazed woman who did not understand her place in life. She had to appease not only Adalhard, but his huscarls and any other man who might sway his opinion.

"Tell me all of it," Adalhard said. "For the day is young and my men have earned their rounds of ale this morning. We will hear a good story."

The men of the hall called out in glad agreement and the mood shifted from tension to celebration. Even Ewald turned a raised brow to her.

"I am eager for the story as well, Auntie."

Finding all the attention on her, she straightened her back and ran her fingers through her hair. She wished she had combed it first, for three pine needles came out in between her fingers. She flicked them away and began her tale.

She spoke broadly of her adventures with Yngvar and his Wolves. But she spoke in great detail of their journey to Sicily and how they had been hired by Prince Kalim to attack the Byzantines and burn their ships. This story drew applause from the men and a round of drinks were dedicated to the heroism of the tale.

Then she took the story to the darker turns. The treachery of Jamil and his rat-lord, Saleet. Of how she alone escaped their trap and how she had come to be aboard Fargrim's ship. Of her rape and the promise of her death at the hands of King Gorm the Old of Denmark. Finally, she described how she had escaped to her father's village to light the signal fire.

"It was a foolish hope," she said. "But you did see the fire and Ewald did come to my rescue. So I owe you thanks, Chief Adalhard."

Adalhard's expression had shifted with every dramatic turn Gyna had described. True to his old self, Adalhard cared not if men knew his mood. It was never related to his plans, which were always carefully hidden as Gyna remembered from long ago. He once had designs on her as a lover and perhaps as a wife. But he abandoned that plan after he was captured by the Danes. He now stood from his chair and walked down to put his hands on both her shoulders.

His strong grip surprised her and she quelled her instinct to bat him aside. He was chief, and despite everything she felt about him was her savior as well. He could either condemn her to a life of boredom at the loom or send her back with warriors to Sicily. She had to endure the pretense of meekness.

"You poor girl," he said, his voice soft with sympathy. "You can be sure this man Fargrim and his crew are now tied up in the yard outside these doors. You will be avenged."

"Thank you, Chief Adalhard." She lowered her head. As she did, she glimpsed Ewald folding his arms and turning aside. "But I have a greater vengeance to take."

Adalhard set her back, both hands still firmly on her shoulders. His lined eyes twinkled with the golden hearth firelight.

"You mean this Jamil and Saleet? They are far from here."

"Not so far," Gyna said. "Yngvar's ship, my ship, carried us here in only a few weeks with fair weather. Nor did we hurry. With haste and Thor's blessing, I could return in less time. And with good fighting men at my back, I could negotiate the others' freedom."

She looked up now, hoping her eyes appeared vulnerable and enticing. Yet Adalhard's brows stretched to the crown of his head and his mouth formed an open circle with words caught within it.

"Chief Adalhard, I know I've only been here a single night. But time is my enemy now. I must return to Bjorn, to Yngvar and the others. They are unjustly accused and someone must release them."

Adalhard blinked. "So Yngvar has found his way into a cell once more. I first met him in a cell and it was a hard thing to escape it once. To do so twice, well, even the luckiest man cannot expect it."

"It is not escape," Gyna said. "He will be released."

"He shamed their holy place, whether he knew it or not. Such a crime cannot be easily forgiven. You are foolish to believe he will be freed."

Gyna shook her head. She had no place in her heart to believe in anything more than success. She counted herself as one of Yngvar's Wolves. Bjorn was her lover. Until she knew they were all dead she could not turn away from them. And if they were dead, she could not live without avenging them.

"Freed either in life or death, I must return to them. It would be helpful if brave warriors accompanied me. But I am fine to claim all the gold and glory all for myself."

Adalhard laughed, and so did his huscarls and the men gathered along the walls.

She had enough. She sloughed off Adalhard's hands and glared at him.

"You laugh but look carefully at me, Chief Adalhard. My sword is equal to any man's. Even yours, mighty Chief. Count the scars on my hands and arms. Feel the strength of my limbs. I did not earn these at the loom and hearth. I earned them standing over the bodies of dead enemies. It is true, I cannot hold the front rank of the shield wall. But when the time comes, every man on the battlefield knows my fury and few live to tell of it. If any wish to test me, then I grant them the humiliation of defeat. Do not laugh at me."

"You misunderstand," Adalhard said, his smile faded. "I do not doubt your strength. But would you fight all the men of this Prince Kalim and his servants? Even a full ship of Saxons would not prevail against an army. And we know these people, these Arabs. We have met their traders and heard the stories of their ancient lands. They rule kingdoms that dwarf all of the northlands. And you would challenge them?"

"I saw no kingdom bigger than what I have seen in the north. I don't go to conquer, merely to punish and take what I can along the way. If you will not raise a crew to aid me, I understand. But allow me to raise my own and seek my own death in my own way."

Adalhard returned to his high seat. He flopped down into it and set his palms on both knees. He blew out a long breath from beneath his heavy mustache.

"I will think upon what you have said. For now, we have the matter of your revenge against your captors. This we can agree to settle this very morning. In this way, we may feast victory this evening."

Gyna inclined her head. At least he would consider her request.

"But a ship is a valuable thing. No matter what you believe, this ship came to my shore and was captured by my men. You were a passenger at best, and more truthfully a prisoner. But you were never the ship's owner."

"I am one of Yngvar's Wolves," she said. "And I claim it for him. I will return it to him when he is freed. And if he and the other Wolves are dead, someone will burn my corpse on its deck."

Adalhard smiled and held up his palm.

"You may choose to return to Sicily. You may find such men as will aid you in that madness. But that ship is mine by right. You will not have it. I have ruled on this. Do not protest, Gyna."

He lowered his eyes at her as if daring her to defy him.

Gyna's face felt as if it were afire. But she lowered her head and turned aside.

"As you say, Chief Adalhard."

14

Picking out Fargrim from the cluster of captives arrayed in the yard outside the hall was harder than Gyna guessed. They huddled together, wrists bound together at their backs. She was certain the Saxons had tied stronger knots than they had on her. She realized she was rubbing her wrists as she searched for the captain among the huddle of once haughty Danes. Their clothes were torn and dirty from running through the pine forest all night. Their faces were covered in sweat and blood from battle. Their heads hung low, hiding their faces under matted, golden hair.

"Show me Fargrim," Adalhard said. "And he will be yours to punish as you will."

She inclined her head to Adalhard. In fact, she imagined gouging out his eyes and biting off his nose. The arrogant fool had claimed Yngvar's ship for his own. He was the second fool who thought he had rightfully acquired it. But like the first fool, he would never own it. Gyna swore it, though only in her heart.

"Fargrim," she called out to the group of men. "If you have any balls, stand forward."

None of the men answered. Had he died in battle? That would be too good for him.

Ewald and his teacher—or minder, as it increasingly seemed to her—Bernward watched Gyna as she approached the prisoners. Her nephew's scowl was so much like his mother's that Gyna could have mistaken him for her. But her sister was dead and she still had not reconciled to that, no matter how often she had wished her so.

"So you won't face me?" For the moment, she could abandon all her cares to the joy of revenge. For even if Fargrim had died, she would extract bloody vengeance on one of his men. She knew the faces of those who had assaulted her. They would do.

Yet she found Fargrim, head down and huddled with his men. She stopped in front of him. The bold sea king, or so he had styled himself, had now fallen. No more a shark, but now a sardine. She pointed and two Saxon warriors dragged him out.

She smirked. The battle had gone hard for him. What she had taken for huddling was his husbanding of a stab wound to his side. He had not worn mail when he followed Gyna into the forest. He had been unprepared for battle when he returned to what he thought was his ship. The stab wound was deep and leaked dark stains onto his torn shirt.

"Does it hurt?" She put her hands on her hips and looked him over. "I will show you what hurt is."

Fargrim raised his head and made to spit. Gyna was faster and slapped him hard across his face. The crack echoed over the yard. His crew growled and shuffled closer as if to protect him.

A score of Saxons in mail and carrying leveled spears warned them off.

Gyna glanced around. The edges of the yard were lined with the common people. They had come to see prisoners. But now with the offering of violence they had progressed from curious murmurs to open calls to violence. After Fargrim's slap, they cheered and called out for more.

"I don't have the strength to punish all your crew as they deserve," Gyna said. "So I will put it all into you. My chief has awarded you to me."

"You bitch." Fargrim glared at her, gritting teeth stained red with blood.

"Had you listened to me from the start, you would not be dying like a tied pig. No sword in hand for you, Fargrim. You will wander in Nifleheim where the Great Worm will chew your rotting flesh until Ragnarok comes."

Adalhard joined her. "Make your judgement now. Does he die or go to the slave block?"

"Of course he dies," Gyna said, eyes never shifting from Fargrim. "I will kill him. Give me my dagger. I will have his head."

Fargrim's eyes widened in horror. He understood Gyna's intent. Taking a man's head was challenging enough with an ax. Taking it with a dagger was prolonged torture. Gyna's heart fluttered at his terror. She gloried in it, never looking away. Her cold dagger was pressed into her hand. Ewald had handed it to her.

"You look strange, Auntie."

"Have him held down before his men. I will need fresh clothes when I am done."

The grim spectacle drew the onlookers closer. Gyna remembered the press of men atop her, their stench, their punches and rough hands, their invasion of her body. Fargrim had to pay for all of it. The onlookers would have much to see.

In the end, he screamed after enduring Gyna's initial torments. She marred his face, sliced off his ears and nose, and only then did he scream. Cutting his head away with a dagger, no matter how sharp or sturdy, was tiring work. Fargrim died in a spray of blood long before his head lolled back on a tether of skin. Gore rained off Gyna's face as she worked. Though Fargrim had died, his crew endured the bloody spectacle until at last she tore free his head and held it up to fill her mouth with his draining blood. This she spit over his crew, causing them to flinch and cower.

The crowd cheered her. The warriors looked on impassively. Ewald stared wide-eyed while Adalhard remained with his strong arms folded over his chest.

She plopped the severed head to the dirt before the captives.

"Let ravens and vultures poke out his eyes and eat his flesh. All of you remember why you suffer. You challenged me and lost."

She never learned the fate of Fargrim's crew. They were rounded up and led away, presumably to a captive pit to be held for a slave market or ransom. After drenching herself in the blood of her foe, she was sent to the stream to bathe and given new clothes.

So her own imprisonment began.

Adalhard welcomed her. He had taken a wife Gyna did not know, a dour woman with a long face and eyes pale as water. She spoke with a strange accent and called herself Nenna. Adalhard seemed to only notice Nenna when the prettier maids attended her. Gyna did not hate meek women like Nenna, but she had nothing in common with them. She limited her contact with Nenna, though she had been invited to pray with her. She was a Christian and apparently had her own priest.

Gyna had earned a blood-thirsty reputation after Fargrim's grizzly decapitation. Everyone kept distance from her for the first days of her stay with Adalhard. She had been granted a corner of the main hall where she could sleep, just as she had done in Yngvar's hall. Only she found the corner cold and empty without Bjorn to push up against. She had awakened one night believing Bjorn had rejoined her only to discover Adalhard's hounds had curled up with her. They were good dogs. Bjorn would have loved them.

She stalked the hall and the yard, not assigned any task or asked to repay any kindness. Nothing could be asked of her for she owned only weapons and the fresh clothes she had been awarded. The deerskin pants were to have been for a young man who died in a fall from the stockade wall. His heartbroken wife donated these to her.

By the fourth day of wandering within sight of the hall, she realized she was Adalhard's esteemed prisoner. For what end, she could not guess. Her acceptance of him imparted legitimacy for his rule among the oldest of his followers. She was the daughter of Lopt Stone-Eye and the sister of the old chief's dead wife. She had some claims to this fort, however tenuous.

Then she understood.

She sought out Ewald that night. After the feast when Nenna dragged her attractive maids away from Adalhard's drunken attentions and the warriors slumped between their emptied mugs, she caught Ewald's eye. He spent every day with his uncle Adalhard or Bernward. It seemed he was as much a prisoner as she was.

They slipped outside into the cool air. Though it was dark, torches lit the surroundings of the hall. A guard leaned against the wall, spear set to the side and his arms folded. He offered a curt nod and did not take any interest as she and Ewald slipped to the edge of the light.

"Adalhard's afraid I'll help you make a claim on his leadership," Gyna said without preamble. "He's watching to see what I'll do. Then maybe there'll be an accident that kills one or both of us. Maybe you'll fall off the wall like the poor bastard who was supposed to be wearing these pants."

Ewald stared at her and her sister looked through his eyes. He was a perfect blend of mother and father. Though his golden beard was full and neatly trimmed, Ewald was still a young man. He offered no expression or any acknowledgement of Gyna's accusation. Yet he did not turn aside.

"That's the truth of it. If he sees us speaking together, or that guard tells Adalhard we went into the courtyard together, well ..."

Ewald at last nodded, understanding the unspoken threat Gyna placed before them. He sighed and glanced back at the hall.

"Many of the men, the youngest ones, think I should have been chief after my father."

"And why aren't you?"

"I was not at the battle when he died. I had taken ill. Not just sick. I was upon my bed and soon to die. God preserved me and I lived. But I was not there to aid my father in his need. Uncle Adalhard was and the older folk love him. He is some sort of hero for having survived King Gorm's slave pits."

"That's because he met Yngvar there," Gyna said. "And he would not have escaped otherwise, no matter what anyone says. Now what of your other uncles? They don't dispute?"

"They have their own halls to rule," Ewald said. His bright face had darkened as he considered his family. "They don't want this land the way my father did. They say the Danes will take it back from us again and that the earth is too wet with blood to ever yield good crops."

"Waldhar died a battle hero," Gyna said, nodding with approval.

"He might have sent me away. But I can't deny he was brave. How did my sister die?"

"She was sick with me. Mother lived on for a while after Father died. Uncle Adalhard comforted her during this time. But she never got better and joined my father in heaven. Uncle Adalhard proclaimed his rule the day my mother was buried."

'You want to challenge your uncle but you don't have enough men. And for such a small clan to battle amongst itself would bring destruction. And the Danes would eat up what was left. You can't prevail here, even if you win. Adalhard does not trust us but knows well what I just told you. He cannot risk violence."

"I am not so weak, Auntie." Now the arrogance flickered back to life. It had subsided in the days since meeting in the forest. "I have allies beyond these walls."

"And you are allies with Bernward watching you for your uncle?"

"Bernward is my man, though my uncle believes he is sworn to him." Ewald smiled and looked back to the hall.

"Look, we cannot idle out here for long," Gyna said. "Here's what I propose. Get me back to my ship. Bring your loyal men and go to meet your allies. Here's what I will offer you, and the gods will punish me for this. If you deliver me back to Sicily, you may keep the ship as your own."

Ewald's brows raised and he seemed about to earnestly thank her. Then his brows furrowed and he paused. "Auntie, if I capture and crew that ship, then it is mine. You cannot gift me what I own already."

Gyna chuckled. "It might seem that way, boy."

"Don't call me boy."

"Don't call me Auntie."

They stared at each other, both stones that would not dislodge without the hand of a giant to pull them free.

"It might seem that way, boy," Gyna said, drawing closer to Ewald. "But the old gods have put a curse on any man who sets his hand to that ship. Go see Fargrim's head, or whatever the ravens have left of it. It's hanging over the gate. He claimed that ship."

Ewald snorted. "Well, Auntie, my uncle owns that ship now and his head is firmly on his shoulders."

"For now," Gyna said. "The gods walk with me, Ewald. I did not believe it myself at first, but now I know they do. If I ask them to punish Adalhard they will. If I ask them to knock down the walls around this fort, they will. I don't know how, but it will be so. The gods will grant me that ship, and I will destroy any fool who sets himself between me and it."

Ewald shrank back, the arrogance slipping from his face. He narrowed his eyes and his voice was thick with skepticism. "The old gods have no power over this place. The one true God protects us."

"Only as long as you walk on your god's land. Step upon my ship, and you sail with Thor and Odin. And without me aboard, that ship will go to the bottom. Now, we speak as if we already plan to take the ship together. So do we have this agreement?"

"We do," he said. "I admit I have been thinking of a way to take that ship since you brought it here."

"Silly boy, your uncle is leaving it for you to take. He wants you to go, even if it is to your allies that would oppose him. At least then he would know enemy from ally. And he would be free to kill you next time you meet."

Ewald reflected on the consideration, stroking his beard as his eyes seemed focused elsewhere.

"Auntie, wouldn't that leave him weakened against the Danes? He would not want us to go so easily."

"Boy." She twisted the words. "It won't be so easy. He's leaving you the ship, and probably will find a way to tell the Danes the son of Waldhar is vulnerable on the water. We will have to fight free. And we'll kill Danes for him while the Danes kill us, his foes. All the while, he can bring reinforcements from across the strait. Must your Auntie think of all these things for you? What kind of chief will you make? Your first real enemy will bury a dagger in your guts while drinking to your long life. Open your mind, boy!"

Ewald ignored the jab. His eyes were wide, staring at the scene Gyna had created for him. She hoped he imagined the Danes streaming across the decks with red swords held overhead.

"But if you stay, with me here," Gyan said while Ewald was still trapped in his imagination. "Adalhard will eventually find a way to condemn both of us. And he will have your followers to fight and it will be messier for him. But he must remove us. No man rests easy with a viper in his hall, even if the viper is in a cage. For someone may open that cage while all others are asleep. So take advantage now, while he still leaves hopes you will flee. Gather your men. We can provision on the journey away. Take me to Sicily. Swear this on your god, and I will keep my gods on your side."

Ewald looked into her eyes. The heavy lines around his mouth were Waldhar's. The fire in his gaze was Gisela's.

"I swear it, by God."

Gyna smiled.

Hours later, while Adalhard's loyal warriors snored, Gyna departed with twenty-odd young men along with Ewald and Bernward by the front gate. The guards there seemed to have all fallen asleep as if by magic. But Gyna knew they hid their eyes from the traitors they had long wished to leave their midst.

Then she was aboard Yngvar's ship again. A new crew of Saxons were at the oars, but they knew their business well enough.

They sailed away into the dark sea where gentle waves rolled as if in welcome.

Though Gyna did not know where they sailed or whether Ewald would keep his oath.

And she begged forgiveness of the gods for her arrogance in invoking their names. Then she prayed they would not punish her for it.

But she knew, unlike the Christian god, the old gods placed no value on mercy.

15

The iron edge against Bjorn's neck pressed into his skin, cold and sharp. Its blade drew a line of burning pain. His eyelid fluttered even as he forced himself to continue to play dead. He saw nothing but a vague red of the sun above him shining through his single lid. Yet he imagined the three Arabs kneeling around him. One had steadied Bjorn's head between his hands and the other placed the dagger against his throat. The last one must have stood aside, probably holding the container for his severed head once the grizzly work was finished.

The net still entangled him. They had only worked him free down to his shoulders. They were not after his body, after all. The Arab holding his head chattered as if in idle gossip while his two companions listened, humming and grunting as their friend spoke.

The Arab removed his dagger with a dissatisfied curse. The one holding Bjorn's head groaned with impatience. Then Bjorn felt one straddle his chest then sit down on his torso.

He would feel the heart pounding in terror beneath him, Bjorn thought. Even tied up, he had to fight. He was going to die but at least he lay atop his beloved ax. He would go to Valhalla and wait for his companions there. For now he knew Thorfast lived and Gyna had as well. Of course, the Fates might have sent Yngvar and Alasdair to their deaths. But had he not just seen them fleeing in the distance? He would soon find out.

The Arab's weight pressed down on Bjorn's midsection. But perhaps the thick netting prevented the Arab from detecting his thudding heart. The Arab adjusted his seat and placed his warm, rough hand against Bjorn's jaw to adjust the angle.

"Eh?" The Arab snatched his hand back as if he had touched hot iron.

He must have felt a pulse.

Bjorn roared and snapped up. The sun dazzled his eye, but the dark shadow of an Arab hovered over him.

He drove the crown of his head into the Arab's chin. He yelped and fell to his side. Bjorn thrashed against the net, but even with his desperate strength he might as well have been wrapped in iron chains.

Hamar charged from wherever he had hidden himself. Bjorn could not see, but he heard his friend's footfalls and shouts for death and Odin.

The Arab holding Bjorn's head now looked down upon him. Upside down in Bjorn's vision, the Arab's eyes were wide like a dead fish. Bjorn could do nothing more than roar his fury. But the Arab scrabbled back and squealed.

Hamar's sword clanged against iron, but the voice that screamed out was not his. Bjorn thrashed harder, hoping that the Arabs had loosened the net somehow. Yet it seemed they had made it even harder to move. He cursed.

"Get me out of this," he shouted to Hamar.

But he received no answer. The Arab whom he had knocked aside now rose up.

His eyes rolled as he struggled to focus, but he did not panic like his companion. He patted the ground for the dagger he had lost when Bjorn had head-butted him.

Now Hamar and his foe stepped into view. They circled each other. Hamar limped on his injured leg. The Arab crouched over a gash in his waist that leaked crimson down his dirty gray robes.

The Arab backed into his companion, causing him to fall across

Bjorn as if they were embracing as friends. Their noses touched. The Arab's breath smelled hot and sour as it washed over Bjorn.

Using his head, he shoved the Arab's face aside then bit into his throat. With no other weapon than his teeth, he had become an animal. He crushed down and the Arab screamed. It rang in Bjorn's ear, deafening him to anything else.

Yet he bit down harder, his mouth full of soft skin. The Arab's beard broke away into Bjorn's mouth, piling on his tongue along with sweat and the first squirt of blood.

He imagined himself as a great wolf, with fangs to pierce flesh and a long snout to drag across his foe's throat. Though he had neither, he still tasted hot and salty blood welling into his mouth. The Arab screamed and punched against Bjorn's chest. But he dared not pull back lest he tear his own flesh.

Then the Arab fell away.

Hamar stood over him now, blood from his sword running into the ground in a stream. His face shined with sweat and was flecked with blood.

Bjorn turned and spit the gore and whiskers from his mouth.

"There's one more," he said. "Above my head. I can't see him."

"The coward has fled," Hamar said. He dropped his sword into the grass then knelt. "I'm going to cut you out. You're worse than a fish in this net. Hold still else I slice your flesh."

Bjorn scraped his tongue along his teeth to dislodge the remnants of beard in his mouth. The bitten Arab now lay on his stomach in the grass, his fear-frozen eyes fixed on Bjorn. Tears still leaked from them.

"Glad it hurt," Bjorn mumbled to the corpse. "I'd have made it worse if I had both my hands."

After a struggle to cut the first cords of the net, Hamar carved through the webs until he had sawed down to Bjorn's waist. He kept looking up, his square face searching every direction for enemies.

"Almost done," Hamar said. "Arabs are still running after their enemies."

"I think I saw Yngvar and Alasdair among the Byzantines."

Hamar paused, but did not look up. "Now that would be a strange thing."

"I know Yngvar. Curse this one eye. I cannot see the distance. But I would swear it was them."

"The gods have played with us before," Hamar said. "I see they have not tired of it. Thorfast survived, though I wonder if he still lives. Why not Yngvar and Alasdair? By now it seems as likely as not."

Hamar gave a shout of satisfaction. "You're free. Now get up and we must flee. These men came to collect your head and it won't be long before someone comes to see what they're about."

Bjorn stood, fetching his ax into his hand. He stretched, feeling cold relief work into his limbs. A cold tingle worked along his skin.

"You're as tall as a tree out here," Hamar said. "Can't you duck down? Anyway, the other side of this rise is free of Arabs. We can flee from there. There was a cave by the shore where I think we could hide. We must find it."

"Sea's that way," Bjorn pointed with his ax across the battlefield. He searched for Yngvar and Alasdair, but the figures scurrying around the wide, green field were smears to him. He saw rugged, stout hills covered with lush green brush. The strange trees with leaves like sword blades formed a small forest around their feet. The bright sun licked his face with humid heat.

"We can't head that way while our enemies have the field," Hamar said. "We hide for a time, then travel by night."

Hamar plucked Bjorn by the elbow to lead him away. Bjorn scanned once more, but knew he would find nothing. The gods had granted him a glimpse of what might be, but they granted him no time to learn more. The figures on the battlefield were gathering into clumps. He knew their leaders would soon bring order to the madness. Flight would become much harder.

He ducked low, but found his waist too sore to hold the position long. They ran across the top of the small ridge where the Arabs had captured the Byzantine standard. Corpses in banded metal cuirasses and red cloaks littered the ground. Arabs in their mail shirts lay among them. But Bjorn and Hamar did not stop to loot.

They dipped to the other side of the ridge.

Even with a single eye Bjorn recognized the giant Arabs surrounding their smaller masters.

"Jamil and Saleet," Bjorn said as he and Hamar drew up short.

"And a bowman," Hamar shouted, shoving Bjorn aside.

The arrow sped past him, a trail of wind whipping across his cheek.

He needed no more provocation. The bear god returned to him. The world became wide and red and Bjorn raised his ax to charge.

Saleet shrieked and shifted behind the three giant Arabs and their long spears. Jamil touched his chest but froze in place.

The archer simply notched another shaft, calmly lifted his bow, and released.

Pain flashed hot and white in Bjorn's left arm. The arrow had been shot true at his broad chest, but as he charged across the grass with ax raised, he stepped into a rut and twisted. The stumble had saved his life. The arrow instead pierced the meat at the bottom of his left arm. It snagged in his skin, snapping from the explosive force so that the arrowhead fell away.

The pain also batted aside the rage filling Bjorn's head.

The shock of it halted his charge. Time felt as if it slowed, as if the bear god guided him in a survey of the field.

The three giant Arabs set their spears and lumbered forward. They were naked to the waist, brown skin glistening in the heat, and wearing only leather vests and ballooning pants. The archer must have been the one Jamil promised would slay him. He was stood to the side with a short bow and a narrow quiver of gray-fletched arrows at his hip. The archer worked with deliberation, his fingers flicking through arrows to find the one marked for Bjorn's heart.

They were all distant enough that flight was still a viable choice.

Hamar had escaped over the shallow ridge. Bjorn glimpsed his head vanishing beneath the line of grass.

He would throw his life away here. Even though his direst enemies were near, his fury alone could not carry him. It would kill him instead.

All these years he believed he carried the battles he fought with Yngvar. Yet now he realized his friends protected him and shielded him from the recklessness of his own rage. He had broken shield walls and had trampled frightened swordsmen to cut a path to enemy leaders. But he could never have survived the battles without his companions.

Now he stood as the sole target on the field. His rage would throw him upon the blades of his enemies and bring him ruin.

Before he realized his decision, his feet had pivoted. He was already thumping up the shallow slope following Hamar. Feeling a tingle at his back, he expected an arrow through his spine. He cut hard to the right. It was instinct informed by experience. The first shot had leaned to his left and so the archer might bias his shots in that direction. The thought flew threw his mind with the same speed as the arrow that hissed past him.

He had guessed correctly. That would be the archer's last shot before he roared over the ridge.

The Arabs down on the battlefield were regrouping. A disordered mass of them headed toward the high ground where he stood.

Hamar was running parallel to this group toward the open fields where no enemy moved.

The pain under his arm was fierce. As his arms pumped with his running, the broken arrow rubbed against his body. The wound burned and slicked his side with blood. He had endured far worse than this. Nothing compared to the loss of his eye. But he needed every advantage to escape this trap, and bleeding soon tired even the stoutest warrior.

Saleet's high-pitched, hysterical screaming followed. Bjorn dared not look back, for other Arabs had spotted him running and were now moving to cut him off. Their lusty cries echoed across the grass, causing Bjorn to redouble his efforts.

Hamar, despite his injured leg, was already well in the lead and headed for a clump of palm trees. It seemed an unlikely place to hide, for the trees were thin and the brush rose only to waist height. Worse still, it was circling back toward Saleet and Jamil. Bjorn had no better ideas and poured all his strength into lengthening his strides.

An arrow snapped into the grass by his foot. But he flew past it and continued after Hamar, who was already stumbling into the trees.

The other Arabs waved their swords in the distance. Bjorn saw the sun flash on their honed edges.

Yet he had outpaced everyone, even to his own surprise. His side pulled tight with pain and he could barely gasp his breath. He leaned against the rough bark of a palm tree.

Then his eyes went wide.

Hamar was untethering a horse from a tree. He nodded to another tied to a different tree.

"Jamil's horses," Hamar said as he gulped his breath. "Saw them earlier. Hurry."

Bjorn patted the neck of the small horse as it snorted and shied away from him. He knew the scent of blood frightened the animal. But Bjorn loved horses. He was not above eating horseflesh, of course, yet only as a desperate choice. He had endured all sorts of teasing over the years for his love of animals.

Now his love of horses rewarded him.

He not only calmed his own horse, but Hamar's as well. He understood them, respected their intelligence, and knew he was asking a favor of them. Other men called them beasts. But he knew they were smarter than some men.

So they both mounted the small horses and the animals did not need any encouragement to flee from the angry mobs rushing at them.

Bjorn laughed, holding his hands tight into the horse's mane. Behind him Saleet's shrill curses chased after them. The Arabs that had sought to cut them off lost heart seeing them mounted.

The animals galloped away and Bjorn roared in laughter. He dared not risk turning back to see Jamil and Saleet cursing him as he stole their mounts. He might fall. Yet imaging their anger filled him with joy and banished the pain in his arm.

Yet once they were away, neither he nor Hamar could command the horses. Neither of them were riders except in the most basic sense. The horses carried them where they chose.

Soon he realized they were being delivered to wherever the horses thought of as their home.

"By the gods, Hamar, we have to get off these horses before they take us back to the enemy."

"How?"

Hamar had draped himself across the horse's neck and held on like a frightened child. His fear must have contributed to the horses' as well. The animals had not slowed much.

"Just jump off. Don't land on your head."

Bjorn leapt to the dirt, crashing hard on his side and feeling a rock drive into his hip. Hamar did as well, falling onto his back and rolling.

The horses circled and neighed but eventually ran off to wherever they were headed.

Bjorn raised his head. They were closer to the palm trees and mountains. Smoke from some unseen hearth lifted into the air back across a rolling field. Nothing seemed familiar to him. He called to Hamar.

"Do you know where we are?"

Hamar lifted his head and looked about, then dropped back into the grass.

"Somewhere near the Arabs."

They were lost among their enemy. Bjorn set his head back and stared at the deep blue overhead.

He believed he heard distant laugher.

The gods were mocking him again.

16

Gyna smiled as she sat on the rails of her ship. The sun scattered across the gray water. The cool, salt wind rushed through her hair and whipped the thin cloak over her shoulder. Her shirt filled with air and ballooned at her back. But she was grateful for the fresh clothes. They brought her as much comfort as the weight of the sword on her hip and the rub of her sheathed dagger in her right boot.

The young Saxon men were all as brothers. Golden hair and mustaches flying as they rowed. They sang as they rowed, and laughed and bragged otherwise. Not every one had taken a sea chest when fleeing, so not every oar was manned. Their strong backs gleamed with sweat and the muscles of their thin bodies rippled from their effort. Others sat resting on the deck, awaiting their turns at the oars.

Ewald did not steer, but stood with Bernward who assumed the duty. He squinted into the distance, leaning on the tiller as the longship turned on the water with the ease of a floating leaf. She had heard Hamar remark on how well the ship steered. The danger was always the wind, particularly a storm. A light ship was blown easily, and had to travel with the wind or else risk being capsized. Too often they had ended up far from their intended destination because Thor let his storms rage overlong.

But not so on this journey.

The gods had not taken their ire out on her. Perhaps she had suffered enough for their pleasure. She had surmised correctly that Adalhard wanted Ewald to leave and was glad to see him take the traitors along. Had she been in his place, she would have alerted the Danes and sent them to kill Ewald. That would be far neater and less risky than doing it himself. She wondered at Adalhard. Was he more merciful than she thought? What good was mercy? Ewald was a hungry, arrogant whelp with a real claim to leadership and fighting men to back him up. Why grant him a ship and free passage to his allies?

She laughed aloud at Adalhard's stupidity.

Ewald caught her laughter and nodded. They had been at sea for a day. Gyna wondered where these allies of Ewald's might be, and how he had contacted someone so distant. To her the coastlines all appeared the same until much farther south where the Moors built their strange square houses. She had always been content to let others tell her where she was going. But just reckoning the days, they had to be far south of any Saxon land.

Today they were finally striking into a wide river mouth. Many ships from sleek longships to the fat-bellied Knarrs favored by merchants headed into the river where dark pine trees guarded the banks.

She slipped off the rail and went to the prow. A young Saxon stood there, his blue eyes narrowed against the glare.

"I know this place," she said to him. "This is the Seine River. We're going to Frankia."

The Saxon nodded. "So Ewald has said. A great count has called for aid and friendship with our people."

Gyna held the rails as the ship rocked into the waves before the Seine. While she had learned enough Frankish from Bjorn and the others, she had no special love for this place. Nor did she like what she had heard. The Franks were forever trapped in wars against each other or Norsemen or Bretons or Burgundians. It seemed the world chose Frankia as its battlefield.

If Ewald answered some random call for mercenary aid, he would not only risk this ship but also likely remain trapped in Frankia. Bjorn's grandfather, Ulfrik Ormsson, had come here on an adventure and never left. Frankia did not release its heroes. It buried them.

She stalked across the deck to where Ewald chatted with Bernward. He looked up with a smile.

"We are close now, Auntie. We have come to Frankia, a place you must know well."

"What are we doing in Frankia? This is nowhere near Adalhard's territory."

He shrugged and looked across the deck at the backs of his rowers.

"Who says I want his little dung heap? My father and uncle were fascinated with that pile of sticks on a hill. I guess they never learned to think of more, seeing how they fought for it their whole lives. I dream of more. I could be a king if I could claim the land. I cannot do it alone. But if I were to ally with the Franks I would have the aid I need to make my own claim."

"So your ally," Gyna spit out the word like an over-chewed hunk of gristle, "is really some petty Frankish noble who wants to use foreigners to fight his battles. And if you live through it, he'll aid you in—in whatever this foolishness is you're about. Gods, boy, you don't even have a plan, do you?"

Ewald's smile fell and his brash arrogance returned. He curled his lip.

"Auntie, I have a plan. I have a ship and I have a crew. I am known to Lord Humbert through his messengers. He has asked for me to attend him so we might discuss how we can aid one another."

"Lord Humbert? Sounds like a true master of war. And you think he'll build you a kingdom without any claim to it of his own?"

"We would be allies. Bernward agrees with me and he served my father. As long as I act in good faith with Lord Humbert I will have all the strength I need."

Gyna stared at Ewald, who seemed pleased with his reasoning. She looked up at Bernward. He stared gravely at her as he guided the ship into the brown waters of the Seine. He seemed to challenge her to say more.

She realized the truth behind this odd journey.

"I see," she said. "I'm sorry I did not understand how deep your plan runs. You're a shrewd man."

"Ah, not a boy, Auntie?" Ewald's face lit with satisfaction.

Her smile flickered. "No, not anymore."

She did not look at Bernward but returned to the rails to stare at the dark trees and gray rocks speeding past. She inhaled the last of the salt air and sighed.

Frankia, she thought, a land for deceit and trickery.

Poor Ewald was Bernward's fool in all of this. The old warrior had designs of his own, though Gyna was uncertain what they might be. Yet Ewald was young and had friends as idealistic and foolish as himself. His status as son of a great chief gave this whole adventure legitimacy. But in the end they were being led away from home to join a foreign war that would benefit only a single man, Bernward.

Whatever happened to men who worried for their farms and families? She shook her head. All these hotheads were willing to jump on a ship and sail away with a plan as frail as hoarfrost. Of course, she had done the same with Bjorn on their journey to the Midgard Sea. At least she believed a reasonable reward awaited her at the end of that journey.

Ewald would have to sort out his own problems with Bernward. Perhaps these other young men were also Bernward's? That thought made her shudder. It felt like a repeat of her woes as Fargrim's captive. Now she understood why Adalhard had let them go without informing the Danes. He was really letting Bernward go and would not conscience aiding in the death of his nephew.

"Gyna, why do you realize these things too late?"

She asked herself this question as the riverbanks sped past, then glanced at Bernward who concentrated on navigating the narrow waterway against oncoming traffic out of the Seine. This entrance was carefully controlled by the Franks, who had learned this river was an open door to the heart of their country. For now, Bernward would have to deal with patrol ships and fee collectors and eventually stop at Rouen. She knew that much from the stories told around the mead hall. The rivers were the main paths of travel, especially for Norse longships.

Rouen.

She blinked. That was the city Bjorn's father lived in. Aren Ulfriksson was his name. She could secure aid from him. He was a powerful man and his son was in great need.

Though Aren and Bjorn hated each other, as far as she understood. Aren had let his brother raise Bjorn and had nothing to do with either him or his mother. He spent all his time with Vilhjalmer Longsword, who ruled from Rouen.

But surely he would help his only son? She had to find out.

For without a doubt Bernward had read her realization of the truth. She was unskilled at hiding her thoughts. So Bernward would likely push her overboard one night. He probably never wanted her aboard this ship except maybe to lay some tentative claim to it. Now that she and Ewald were so far from home, both of them would probably meet a foul end.

She sighed again and leaned on the rail.

"Do I have to save everyone? It's hard enough to protect myself."

They arrived at Rouen after having been stopped by patrol ships to pay tolls. Ewald had not thought to accommodate for expenses and so had to turn to Bernward for help. Unsurprisingly the veteran had the silver coins to pay and secured their passage to a berth in Rouen. They would anchor there and spend the night on the deck, unwelcome in the city. The great stone walls of Rouen were shabby and stained black. The bridge across the Seine sat low enough to block all but rowboats. Ewald seemed stymied by this problem, but Bernward informed him they would portage the ship around the tower and continue onto another river that would lead them north again to Lord Humbert.

Gyna watched Bernward carefully. He gave no sign of betrayal. In fact, he was a model servant and mentor to Ewald. The two were in constant communication, and even now, as the ship bobbed at dock and the sky blazed orange, they spoke together with three of the other men. The rest of the crew were stretching out to find a spot on the deck for the night.

"We're not going to provision here?" Gyna asked as she approached Ewald. "Seems like we should make an arrangement to have fresh food and ale ready in the morning. You've got coin for that, don't you, boy? All I have is my charm."

Ewald's face flattened as he turned to her. "Auntie, we are only a few days to Lord Humbert's hold. We have plenty."

Gyna leaned over the rail and spit into the dark water below. Conversations from sailors in other ships nearby floated over to her. She wished she could join them instead of deal with her nephew.

"Plenty," she repeated. "Boy, have you ever sailed anywhere before? I don't mean drifting on a log across a pond. I mean a long journey like this. There's no such thing as plenty for the future. One good wind and this ship spills everything into the water."

"That's on the open sea," Ewald said. "We'd just pull up to a bank and wait out any storm."

"You mean wait for the locals to rob us of what we have," Gyna said. "And this being a Norse ship, even if you haven't put the beast head on the prow, well, we won't have much help from the local lord. Probably he would be the one robbing us. That's just one of a hundred ways the Fates could weave a black thread into your plans. So, King Ewald, you'd be serving the interest of your people if you at least had more than we need. The future is never certain."

Ewald's shoulders dropped and he looked to Bernward. "Do we have coin enough for extra supplies?"

"No, lord," he said. Bernward looked across the docks to the city. "We have enough to reach Lord Humbert. We are guests here. I do not think our journey will be as fraught with danger as your aunt believes."

Gyna smiled. "Well, your auntie is going ashore to see what she can find with her charm alone. You should come and learn from me. Unless you think there's nothing you can learn from this old lady. But I'd say if you're going to be a king one day, you better learn how get what you want for nothing. All kings can do that. Want to see how it's done?"

"I believe that's called theft, Auntie."

"Not when it's freely given to you." She took Ewald's arm. "Come with me while there's still light. I'll teach you how it's done."

Ewald laughed. "Well, I've never seen such a grand city as Rouen. I suppose it can't hurt to see it before the sun sets."

"That's right," she said, drawing Ewald to her side. "And take your sword. Can't look weak when bargaining."

"Lord, I don't think this is wise." Bernward now stepped forward. Gyna noted how he had to hold his hand back from reaching out.

"Oh Bernward," Gyna said. "Don't be worried. I'm his aunt. I just want to show him how to make a deal. It's in his blood, but I doubt my sister ever let him have the chance to make deals that matter. Isn't it true, Ewald?"

"Well, that is true. I learned how to fight and spy and survive off the land. But not to make deals."

"Well, a king who has to hide in bushes is no king at all," Gyna said. "You need other skills. And you should start learning now."

"Still, lord, there will be time for that." Bernard now put his hand on Ewald's shoulder and guided him back to his side. "We are simply passing through this city. Tomorrow we will be gone with first light. We cannot delay, for Lord Humbert is expecting us."

Ewald's bright smile faded and he seemed about to accept his master's command.

Gyna had one chance to push this before she had to use more direct means to get Ewald out of this trap.

"Boy," she said. "A king does not take orders from his servants. That's one lesson you don't need to go anywhere to learn."

The crew went silent and the men nearby stepped back from her. Bernward's cheeks reddened and his eyes narrowed. Ewald's eyes were wide and mouth agape.

Gyna pressed closer.

"Make your own choice. I'm going into the city. You should come with me. But that decision is yours to make. Not mine. Not Bernward's. Will you let your servant pull you by the shoulder and make your choices? Then you are not a king, are you?"

She stopped short of proclaiming Bernward king in Ewald's place.

That was his likely ploy, she figured. Bernward exerted control over a young man with royal blood. He maneuvered him into this alliance with the Franks so they could build a small estate away from Ewald's family, who otherwise would lay claim to it for themselves. But away from Adalhard and the rest of his family, he could rule with Bernward directing him. Then after all was settled Ewald would die in an accident. Bernward would claim the land. He probably would be working with this Lord Humbert throughout.

"Well? Don't stare with your mouth open. A king has to be decisive."

Ewald blinked, then pulled out of Bernward's grip.

Now his mentor was the target of his brash arrogance. He tilted his chin up as he spoke.

"I will go with my aunt. We won't be long. Keep the ship safe for us."

Their stare was a clash of swords. But Bernward had to lower his head or else raise suspicion.

"Be careful, lord. I believe this is an unnecessary risk. Perhaps I should come with you."

"A great idea," Gyna said with as much enthusiasm as she could fake. "Bernward is older than me. Imagine what he could teach you. Do come with us, Bernward, and continue to guide Ewald at every turn."

"It's a simple trip into the city. My aunt is fine, and I will bring my sword." Ewald held up his hand with imperiousness matched only by Prince Kalim. At least he was a true prince of a mighty land. Ewald was barely master of his own thoughts. At least he was easily led, probably why Bernward chose him for this plan.

Bernward made to protest, but Ewald had already turned his back. He instead gestured that Gyna lead.

They both stepped over the rails onto the docks.

Now she hoped finding Aren Ulfriksson was as simple as knocking on the gates of the castle where she assumed he lived.

She had to find him.

This was her last chance to regain control of Yngvar's ship and return to Sicily. She had to rescue them. Every day she wasted led Bjorn and the others closer to death.

If they had not died already.

The delays gouged at her heart. Why did the gods burden her with this responsibility? And now the safety of her nephew as well—an arrogant fool more likely to run to his doom than accept her aid.

The walls of Rouen loomed high above her. Ewald gasped with delight.

Gyna drew a deep breath and prayed.

Let Aren be here and let him love Bjorn enough to send him aid.

Neither request had much hope. But she would never know until she entered the city.

17

"Auntie, this makes no sense."

Ewald pushed against her iron grip. She loved the surprise in a man's eyes when they realized she was their equal in strength. She did not appear as strong. But bulk did not make for power. Rowing and swordplay tested in battle built strength, which Ewald never had to taste for himself.

"Don't squirm or yell," Gyna said.

Her voice bounced off stone walls. They stood in a wide audience chamber in the main fortress of Rouen. Their weapons had been collected at the main gate, and Gyna felt their absence as keenly as if she were naked. The bare wood floor was well worn from countless petitioners. An empty chair stood across from her on a short dais. It too was worn from the man who had ruled atop that august seat. That would not be Aren, but the Jarl of Rouen.

The Jarl of Rouen, Vilhjalmer Longsword, had just recently been murdered by enemies set in ambush.

Another sword through the heart of my hopes, Gyna had thought at the news.

Yet Aren Ulfriksson was here and he would meet with Gyna, who claimed to carry urgent news of Aren's son.

She had not truly intended to teach Ewald any lesson about

making deals. Yet to have come this far, she had charmed guards and convinced servants of her and Ewald's urgent task. Their perceived threat was low being one woman with a single warrior—who looked so in awe of the city that no one could consider him a serious threat.

"You have no proof of Bernward's treachery." Ewald lowered his voice but glared at her.

"I know what I'm talking about," Gyna said, hoping her exasperation did not taint her voice. She watched the two doors behind her, which hung open with four spearmen flanking them. A dull orange glow showed beyond where torches lit the stonework halls.

"Bernward served my father, and was faithful to me since I can remember. You dishonor him with your accusations."

"Well, somewhere along the way, Bernward got ideas of his own. He's the one taking you to this Lord Humbert, if he's even a real lord. More likely you're running in a circle to join with other Saxons on the Frankish border. But I don't know. I don't care. He means you no good. You're his tool. And like a tool you'll be set aside when there's no use for you anymore."

"But you can't know this is true." Ewald's voice rose again to echo off the stone walls. Gyna whirled back on him and raised her finger for silence. She stood closer to him.

"You said it yourself, he makes all the choices for you including this journey. Even after you swore your oath to me, you still had to get his approval." Gyna snorted then spit on the floor. "He's a shrewd one. I'm not sure about the others. You say they're your friends. I say at least half are Bernward's dogs. Your dear old auntie will be swimming in the Seine with a rock tied to her legs once we get back to them. Mark my words. We're both safer away from all of them, especially Bernward."

"I cannot betray him," Ewald said. His voice quavered and his cheeks reddened.

The back of Gyna's hand itched to slam across his face. Was this baby the son of the great Saxon Chief Waldhar? No wonder Adalhard had claimed leadership.

"You're under my protection," Gyna said. "This is the last favor I do for my sister. And I bet Adalhard knew I'd take care of you when he let you go. I'm a fool to do this, of course. Gods, are you going to cry?"

"No!"

"If you cry I will geld you right here."

"I'm not crying. By God, I am a man!" His voice cracked.

They stared at each other.

"If you even sniffle I will break your nose."

Ewald folded his arms and faced the empty chair. He accepted her accusations far better than she had expected. He must have suspected the truth but needed someone to plant his face in it. Still, he might feel differently when he again meets Bernward himself. For such a reckoning would come.

Gyna had to get the ship before first light.

Another door, smaller but no less heavy than the main doors, rattled in the wall to her left. Then the door opened and the man she assumed was Aren Ulfriksson entered.

Gyna stood straight and slapped Ewald's shoulder to remind him to present himself properly. Then she stared at the man tottering toward her.

If this was what Bjorn was going to look like as an old man then maybe she should let him die now.

A man of about sixty years old limped across the wooden floor. He was bald now but for a thin fringe of white hair that hung in strands to his sloping shoulders. His wrinkled flesh was thick with age spots. One like a brown turd stuck to his left temple was especially revolting. He was so fat that his voluminous and fine clothing could not diminish his girth.

"You are the ones that come with news of my son?" Though he was a Norseman, he spoke Frankish.

His voice was old but refined. Three other warriors had followed behind. Compared to Aren they were like children, though they were strong and clear-eyed men who watched her with interest.

"I am Gyna Loptsdottir," she said in Norse, bowing low. "And this is my nephew, Ewald."

"Speak Frankish to me. And I will remind you I am a jarl, though of what anymore I cannot say."

"Yes, lord," Gyna said, bowing. She rapped Ewald's shoulder again, for he had not bowed with her. Aren's watery eyes flicked over him but held no interest.

"I have not seen my son in several years. I can assume he is in some sort of trouble, seeing that he is absent. Though I wonder why he would send a woman and this young man?"

"He has not sent us, lord. It is a long story in the telling, but Bjorn is held captive along with Yngvar Hakonsson. They are prisoners of Arabs in faraway Sicily."

Aren's old eyes widened, though his lids were so droopy with age he still seemed hardly awake.

"I am flattered you think I can be of any help to him from so far away. But I have my own affairs. My lord and dearest friend has been murdered. This very city might fall into enemy hands at any day. I am afraid I cannot do much for him."

"Rouen will fall?" Gyna could hardly believe what she had heard. But she waved away the question. "No matter, Bjorn and Yngvar are your only blood kin in this world. They both need my help, but I am a single woman. I can kill men ten at a time with my sword, but the Arabs have numbers enough that my blade will dull before I ever reach him."

Aren laughed, putting his blue veined hands over his belly.

"That is a boast better spoken from a man twice your size. Who are you to my son? You were not with Bjorn when he was last here."

"I am his lover and companion in the shield wall. We live and fight together, shoulder to shoulder. We are sworn to protect each other. So I have come this far seeking your aid."

That sounded better than the truth, she thought. Fortunately, Ewald did not understand Frankish but just studied Aren's ancient body with a dubious gaze.

"Tell me the story of how that came to be, and what has befallen my son and nephew. I am an old man now. I need something to excite me."

Gyna expected them to be invited to a mead hall and given food and drink to recount their stories. But Aren stood as if he had to leave in the next moment, and the three men behind him folded their arms as if they would not move. Her expectant smile faded.

"Well, it is a long tale. But I shall tell all of it. Perhaps you should sit, lord?"

"Only the true Jarl of Rouen may sit on that chair," Aren said without turning from her. "I will never disgrace it with my old body. I was merely Jarl Vilhjalmer's oldest friend, but it does not make me lord here."

"Of course," Gyna said, bowing again. But Aren did seem to act as if he were jarl. He just needed to have enough authority to take the ship and give her a real crew. She began recounting her tale with Bjorn.

By the end of the long story, Aren had barely shifted his expression. His followers, however, had become engrossed in the telling. They helped her find words when her Frankish failed. They now stood close and seemed admiring of her tales of heroism. She had not even deviated much from her fears of Bernward.

"So now you have heard all." Her voice cracked, as her mouth was filled with wool and her throat dry from so much speech. Yet no offer of drink was made. "Every day I tarry I risk Bjorn's and Yngvar's lives. I need a crew to take back my ship and sail with me to Sicily. There will be great rewards for all of us. But these must be taken by the sword."

Aren scratched his cheek making a dry, rough sound with his yellow nails.

"A tale worthy of my father," he said. "His blood flows in my son's veins."

The men behind them nodded in agreement. Ewald, who stood tapping his foot, finally broke into the pause.

"Auntie, are you done retelling the history of the world? You were pointing to me and toward the ship. What has Jarl Aren decided?"

She waved him off as if he were a fly. Aren smiled thinly at the gesture.

"Our Saxon brothers are as hot-headed as ever. You say the man aboard Yngvar's ship is an enemy. Yet what proof do you have?"

"None," she said flatly. "I need that ship. It belongs to Yngvar and

Bjorn, not to a Saxon or his Frankish lord. Tell me, is there a Humbert who rules north of here?"

"None that I know."

"Then that is my proof. The story is false and Bernward has other ideas, maybe ideas that will hurt your interests. Bjorn needs your help to claim that ship and its crew. They follow my nephew here. I promise we will sail directly to Sicily and trouble you no more."

"You think if Bernward is removed, the rest will do as this young man says?" Aren asked.

"They will, or at least we will know who will and who won't. If we need more crew, then there must be men ready to plunder rich lands. There is never a shortage of them."

"And you know the way to Sicily?" Aren smiled brighter, revealing black teeth.

"I will need someone to show me the way." She felt heat on her cheeks. "It is a shame the only one among the crew who knows the way is Bernward himself."

Aren nodded. "Well, my son and nephew beg for aid once more. I do not know how many more times I can rescue these boys. They must one day become men."

In any other setting, she would have knocked out that old man's black teeth and spit in his face. Her knuckles crawled with the urge to strike bone.

Yet she lowered her head and marshaled her voice. "Their need is great, lord. Only your generosity may help them now."

Aren chuckled. "It is your sword arm and wits alone that will free them. I offer no more aid than I can from the safety of these walls. And such safety will soon be lost to me. Jarl Vilhjalmer is dead without heir, except for a bastard son who might even now bleed under the daggers of his enemies. My killers must be soon arrived. Perhaps I should go with you. Let not the last son of the great Ulfrik Ormsson die hiding behind walls of stone. Let him die away on the open sea, testing his sword against great warriors. As his brothers died!"

He leaned back and roared with laughter. His men smiled alongside him. Gyna shared a confused look with Ewald.

"But I am not a warrior. Never have been. I have lived my life and have no regrets. I was no father to Bjorn, no uncle to Yngvar. But if I may do one thing before I pass from this world, let it be a final act of aid to my kin. Show me to Bernward this night. I will take fifty warriors and force him from the tiller. The ship will be yours. The Fates will weave the rest of your tale thereafter."

Gyna's heart lifted and she could not contain her smile. She bowed lower. "I will raise a runestone to your fame, Jarl Aren. You will be remembered for your generosity."

Again Aren thundered laughter that bounced about the stone chamber.

"You do not know the life I have led behind these walls. I am even less known for my generosity than I am for my sword skills."

"Auntie, what is happening?" Ewald's voice was filled with trepidation. His worried brow reminded Gyna of her sister, and that thought softened her response.

"We are taking the ship back," she said. "And you are going to lead the crew to Sicily. It is better than the trap waiting you in the north, whatever it might be. I promise, you will return to Adalhard with a king's fortune. If you must become a king, then build your kingdom as the heroes of old did. Raise a band of warriors and take the land you want by force. There is no quick path to kingship, especially where Bernward leads. It is for his benefit alone, I am sure."

"He has served me since I was a child."

His eyes were wet. Gyna had no heart to chide him. Bernward was the worst kind of traitor. She shook her head and guided him by the arm.

"Let us follow Jarl Aren."

So Aren collected his men. While he did not raise fifty men, he brought more spearmen in battered mail than Bernward had aboard the ship. They marched through the city, where at day's end traffic had ebbed. Still, men and women fled from their approach.

"Remember, Jarl Aren, we need the ship ready to sail with all speed. I hope it will not be damaged in this action."

"I am old, not daft," Aren said. He waddled at the rear of the column. He carried a sword, but wore it awkwardly.

At last they came to the dock.

The ship was gone.

"Auntie, they left us."

Gyna's fists tightened so that her nails dug into her flesh.

"I guess Bernward didn't need you after all. I don't know where he has gone, but when I find him he's going to the grave."

18

The broken arrow shaft lodged in Bjorn's underarm was more of an irritant than an injury. He wrapped a strip of cloth around it after washing it out in the clear stream running beneath him. The cloth had come from a local home that he and Hamar had visited. The frail, sun-baked farmer and his family had tried to bar their doors against them. Rather than need to fix a destroyed door, he eventually allowed them in. They took food, skins of water, and cloth for bandages.

He and Hamar both needed bandages. While the arm wound stung but otherwise did not hinder him, it could easily go bad. Bjorn had seen strong men brought down by simple cuts. He could not afford the same fate when he knew Thorfast and Gyna at least still lived. Perhaps Yngvar and Alasdair as well. Hamar's leg wound was still not healed and even now stained the fresh wrap around his thigh.

He scooped warm brook water over his face and scrubbed the dirt. Flies and gnats fled from him as he washed, but the moment he stood up they swarmed him again.

Hamar crouched on a rock, chewing on the stringy goat meat they had taken from the farmers. At least it was meat and enough to last a few days if they ate sparingly.

"I am glad for my freedom," Bjorn said, joining Hamar by his rock. He held out his hand and Hamar broke off a piece of the cured meat for him. "But I don't know what to do with it. You can't find that cave again? Where Thorfast was to meet that woman?"

"It was along the shore," Hamar said. "But everything was confusion at that time. The Arabs brought their hounds and I was nearly killed. I cannot remember the exact location. But it must be nearby and must be part of these hills."

"Fucking hills," Bjorn said. "Fucking hills then rolling plains, then more fucking hills. I hate this land. Flies and hills. That's everything besides Arabs and their slaves."

Hamar laughed. "Freedom is worth more than gold. Even if it is simple freedom to swat at flies."

Bjorn chewed on the stringy meat. It was so salty he would have to drink the brook dry once he finished. His jaw was soon sore and he forced the rough clump of meat down his gullet.

"Well, it's not like we can go asking anyone if Thorfast passed this way. I don't know what to do. Yngvar always told me what to do. He'd point and I'd run, just like a hound. He must have thought I was a fool."

"No," Hamar said. "Why would you say that? No one ever thought you a fool. We all followed Yngvar. We all had a voice in the plans, but we were content to let him decide. We followed because Yngvar was a great leader."

"Is a great leader," Bjorn corrected. "Feel it in my guts. He's still alive."

Hamar grunted. "Nothing can surprise me anymore. I am shocked to have survived this long among so many enemies. We could try to find Thorfast, but he could have gone anywhere. Perhaps he fell afoul of the Arabs again. That happened to me."

Bjorn shook his head. "He's smarter than us. He wouldn't get caught. Known him all my life. He probably found men to follow him. If Yngvar was not around, then he'd be our leader. You know that."

"Well, how would he do that? He was being chased by a dozen

Arabs into these hills. He might still be hiding somewhere among them."

"Then we should look for signs of his passing there. He was with a woman?"

"He should have been," Hamar said. "We were on the way to meet her when we were overcome. I could not defeat the dog chewing on my leg, so I played dead hoping the beast would release me. It succeeded but I was carried away and did not mark Thorfast's fate."

"If he's with a woman, she'll slow him down. Unless she is like Gyna."

The name caught in his throat. What had been her fate? If she had been taken to Prince Kalim, would she have been forced into slavery? Would she serve him on his bed? The thought sent tingles of rage over the back of his neck. How would he enter the palace to rescue her as a lone man? Was she even there?

Hamar coughed into the silence. Bjorn's chewing on the cured goat meat matched the sounds of the brook running past them.

"We can't chase after him," Bjorn said. "Ain't going to work. We'll be dead of hunger before we even catch his trail."

"Aye." Hamar's voice was dry and hopeless. He rubbed his injured leg and said no more.

"Well I ain't saying we do nothing. You slouch like I just stole your woman. Sit up and listen, man. I'm trying to think crafty like Yngvar and Thorfast. I need your help to do it. I'm just a one-eyed berserk. Not much for crafty thinking."

"I know the stars and the seas. I know swords and shields. I know little else that's not about ships." Hamar's nails scratched across the bandages on his leg. "But I'll do what I can."

"So let's do what we know," Bjorn said. "You know ships and swords. I know swords. So we know two things between us. We ain't the brightest stars in the sky. But we're not fools. We're never going to find Thorfast if he's still alive. We'll never get to Gyna wherever she is now. Even a fucking island of hills and flies is still too big for us to search. But it ain't so big the we couldn't find someone if they were making noise."

Hamar looked at Bjorn, who twisted around so that he could fit his friend into his vision. Hamar stared back, not understanding his meaning.

"Listen, Gyna and Thorfast will be trying to stay hidden. Same for Yngvar and Alasdair, if they're who I saw running for the shore. We're doing the same. We're all fucking hiding from each other because we don't know better. My guess is we're the only ones who know all the others are still alive."

Hamar nodded. "That must be so."

"Right. We need to make noise and have them come to us. We need to set a signal fire that tells them we live and we are waiting for them. Ain't no other way we're rejoining otherwise."

"That is a good idea," Hamar said. "But a fire will draw our enemies as well. And how do we create a fire that says it was set by us?"

"Well, you are dumber than me." He thumped Hamar's shoulder with his fist, smiling. "I mean we need to do something that makes news spread like fire. So even if Thorfast is hiding in a fox den he will still hear of it. And we must do something that only we would do, so that they will know we are near. Then we wait for them to show themselves as well."

Hamar shrugged. "It could work. But maybe all they will find is our heads hanging from the city gates."

"We risk the same just sitting on this rock and hoping the gods send us one more boon. But the gods have already spared our lives, and they won't do more. So I said we're good at swords and ships. Think on that. Help me, man. My head hurts having thought this far."

They both sat back in silence. Bjorn smiled contentedly, for he had never created such a plan in his entire life. Charge and kill had been his answer to every challenge set before him. Now he actually had a thought that might equal Yngvar's.

Perhaps the gods had granted him a final boon after all.

"Well I'm good with ships," Hamar said, carefully unpacking his thoughts. "We're both fighters. So maybe we need to steal a ship. One of the prince's ships."

"Not to piss on your idea, but we're two men. We can't steal a warship then sail it by ourselves."

Hamar continued to itch at his wounded leg. "We can steal a small ship, one of his little patrol ships."

"Not big enough to get attention," Bjorn said. He waved a fly off his face. "Everyone for miles around needs to talk about this. And that doesn't say we did it."

Hamar's head lowered as he thought. Bjorn let more flies dance across his shoulders before chasing them off. Perhaps his plans were too ideal. What could two men do that would become the talk of the coast and represent them? He shook his head at his foolishness. Of course there was nothing.

Then an idea flashed into shape. He snapped forward on the rock and clapped his hands together.

"You're right," he shouted, his voice echoing through the palm trees covering them in blue shade.

Hamar leaned forward, his square face catching the dappled light. "We steal a small ship?"

"Small but not too small." Bjorn's one eye now focused on what he imagined he could do with such a ship. "No one would call it a threat. But then we fill it with oil. They burn lamps here. Palace is full of them. So stuff it with oil and set it aflame. Let's do it with two ships. Yes! Two ships full of burning oil. Send them into the docks. Right into the prince's ships. Then we proclaim ourselves. Let everyone know what we did. But we will be away before they can catch us. We will need another ship for that."

"That's a lot of ships," Hamar said.

"It is. Didn't say this was easy. But it does say we did it. Thorfast, Alasdair, and Yngvar would know we did it. Gyna would hear of it in the palace. And they'd know it was us."

"Because we burned Byzantine ships like this before," Hamar said, slapping his knee.

"And if we show ourselves, then we might even lure Saleet and Jamil out. They'll want to catch us before the prince learns they let us slip free."

Bjorn imagined holding Jamil's and Saleet's heads up to show

Prince Kalim what his fate would be once all of the Wolves reunited. The glory of his fantasy nearly caused him to fall from the rock.

He and Hamar laughed and celebrated with another hunk of cured goat meat. He chewed heartily, now imagining all of his friends gathering to him, cheering him for his wits and bravery. Most importantly, he imagined them all at sea together again. In his mind, they still sailed upon their old ship—though this could not be, for it was surely lost by now. Still, he imagined the sea spray on his face, the cold wind tearing at his cloak, and the fog-shrouded fjords rising gray in the distance. Under his foot was a sack of gold coins. On the mast was the bloodless head of Prince Kalim. Gyna stood by his side and under his arm. His other arm rested on the haft of his ax.

Such a vision! He had to make it real.

The sting under his arm reminded him that his plan was fraught with danger. Had that arrow flown closer to his body, it would be his rotting head on Prince Kalim's city gates. He rubbed the bandage.

"We need to keep our weapons sharp and free of rust," Bjorn said, pulling his ax up from where it leaned on the rock behind him. "And we must keep ourselves fed. Otherwise, we will have no success."

Hamar grunted. "We should have taken a whetstone from the farmers."

"And striking irons," Bjorn added. "There's much we need before we carry out this plan. Do you think we could return to the farm and get more of what we need?"

"Of course we could," Hamar said.

After they had refilled their skins and drank once more from the brook, they retraced their path to the distant farmhouse. Flies followed them across the grassland but Bjorn no longer cared for their harassment. As the sun drew down, he saw the farmhouse as it had been before. A rectangular orange light shined in the shadow of the flat-roofed building. Someone flicked back and forth through it.

"Looks like they're settling in for the night," Bjorn said. He sniffed at the air, smelling the sweet notes of a cooking fire. "Let's see what they've prepared for the evening meal."

They strolled across the field toward the open door. Bjorn had his ax slung across his shoulder. Hamar, whose leg still troubled him after exerting it during their flight, managed to keep pace.

They came within sight of the house.

And walked into a trap.

The first arrow hit the thin grass at Bjorn's feet and bounced up to thump against his leg.

19

Gyna blinked, unbelieving at what she saw from the bank of the Seine River.

Ewald was less astounded and rushed ahead of her and Aren's warriors toward the muddy banks.

"The ship!" he shouted as he ran. "They've got our ship!"

Gyna looked to the Frankish warrior at her side. He was a lean man with a thin head with ears that protruded like two handles of a clay pot. He kept his brown beard trimmed and so pointed he could use it as a quill. He had been introduced by the name of Norbert and ordered to lead Aren's men in search of the missing ship.

They had only gone down river a short distance to board a waiting patrol ship when they spotted their target being towed back to them.

"A Northman longship draws much attention," he said. "I was confident the patrols between here and Paris would catch it. We've suffered enough predation from Northmen through the years to take a dim view of even a single ship."

"Couldn't you have told me that earlier rather than let me worry?" Gyna folded her arms and watched Ewald waving at the ships passing.

The ship was caught between two others of equivalent size. They were much like the longship, though these had higher sides and fuller hulls. Ropes and boarding hooks had entangled her ship. Only three men were on deck to help steer as the other ships dragged her toward Rouen. The crew of the patrol boats waved cheerfully back to Aren as they passed.

"Now what?" Gyna asked. "Where did the others go?"

"We will have to hear their report," Norbert said, twisting the point of his beard between his fingers.

They returned to the docks where Aren waited with his three loyal bodyguards. Gyna noticed that his back had a slight curve that was not obvious before. He must be extremely old by now, perhaps sixty or more. Few people survived to such an age. Only nobles could afford a life that did not kill them by age forty.

Once Gyna's ship had been gathered to the docks with aid from Norbert's men, the leader of the patrol ships disembarked and presented himself to Aren. He was a strong man though a head shorter than Gyna. He did not notice her as he bowed low.

"Lord, we caught this ship full of Norsemen speeding toward Paris."

Aren nodded and swept his watery eyes across the empty deck.

"And what of the Norsemen?"

"Once they knew we had trapped them, they pulled ashore and abandoned their ship."

"So they left you a prize to claim in trade for their lives," Aren said. "You let them flee into the countryside?"

"We were slow in getting ashore, lord." The stocky man bowed again, lower this time. "We did follow but they had fled into the woods and it was twilight. I sent runners to warn the locals and alert the militia. But we could not abandon our own ships. What if that was a ruse to lead us away from our own vessels?"

Aren waved his gnarled hand as if dismissing everything. "They are not Norsemen, but Saxons. They are far from home, and I believe they will head north. There is trouble everywhere in this land, now that Jarl Vilhjalmer is gone. I can send riders ahead to warn of trouble but can do little else."

He turned to Gyna. "Do you know anything more of their plans?"

"I knew only the lies Bernward told me, and I was wrong about his plan to use my nephew's status. So I might not be as clever as I thought."

"Or his usefulness was done," Aren said, smiling at Ewald who was pretending to understand everything he heard. "You might have saved this young fool's life."

"I'm certain I have," Gyna said. "I think he was an unwitting hostage to letting Bernward and his men leave with my ship. I don't think I'll ever know, and it doesn't matter. Because now I need to find men for this ship and take Ewald toward greater danger."

Aren nodded again. They fell silent. The shouts of dock workers ending their day echoed through the night air.

"I have given much thought to my son," Aren said. "Not just since you arrived, but even before. I have regretted much in the way I treated with both him and my nephew when they were here last. Now that Jarl Vilhjalmer is dead, I have no family left. I have loyal men. But it is not the same. I had a son, and a true Norse hero if the tales you tell are true."

He stared at the ship and reached a trembling hand toward it.

"I might have lived a different life," he said. "Look at that ship. It's like the one my father sailed. There are no shields on the racks, no hard-bitten men working the rigging, but I can see him standing there now. Young, strong hands on his hips and head back in laughter. His mail gleams and his helmet is rimmed with gold. He is a sea king of old and none may defeat him. He will sail with you to meet his grandson. To restore him to this deck so that he may live the life that I—his very son—did not live."

Gyna looked to the empty deck. The back of her neck crawled with a chill. She saw nothing but gray planks. Yet Aren's eyes beheld a ghost. Was the spirit of Bjorn's grandfather, Ulfrik Ormsson, standing there invisible to all but his son? She shivered.

"Jarl Aren," she said quietly. "Bjorn is a mighty hero. Yngvar is a great leader. All this time I have wondered if they have survived capture at the hands of the Arabs. In the quiet of the night, I sometimes believe they must all be dead. That I am chasing nothing but my own foolishness. Yet now you say the spirit of their greatest ancestor waits on this deck. Then surely they live still."

She felt heat rising in her eyes. Aren did not look aside from the ship. For without doubt he must behold his father in all his glory come down from Valhalla to aid his kin in their hour of need.

"Auntie, what in God's name is everyone doing?"

"Shut up," she hissed, then slapped at him. "There is great magic here."

Ewald's eyes widened and he looked around. The other Franks stared at the deck with the same expressions of amazement. One man behind Norbert made the sign of the cross.

"I will provision this ship," Aren said. "And I will grant you what men are willing to go to my son's aid. You must find him. When you do, you must not tell him that I am sorry or that I am weak. You must tell him I demand greatness from him. That he carries his ax to his enemies and wins glory. That he slays the king who took his eye. And that when he is called to Valhalla he will be carried from a battlefield piled with dead enemies. I demand he not die in a pit or upon a bed."

The tears flowed down Gyna's cheeks. She knelt before Aren, head lowered, and outstretched her hands. "Lord, draw your sword that I may swear to you all will be done as you have asked."

She waited with head lowered. After a pause, the blade scraped free and dipped forward to her. Setting her hands on the cold iron, she looked up and blinked through her tears.

"I swear before all the gods and upon my very life, I will serve you in this or die in the attempt."

Aren smiled. He did not weep, but his eyes glittered as he withdrew his sword. He sighed as he struggled to guide it back into its sheath. At last, Norbert aided him and he nodded his thanks.

So they had concluded the recapture of the ship.

After two days of resting and preparing as Aren's guest, Gyna had provisions and a crew. Norbert would be their leader and personally represent Aren on this journey.

As they stood ready to cast off back toward the sea, the sun appeared from behind dark clouds. Everyone took it as a sign of favor from whatever gods they held dear. Aren had come to the docks to see them off.

"You could join us," Gyna offered, hoping the old man would not accept. He did not.

"I owe much to Jarl Vilhjalmer," he said. "And his bastard will need protection. I am old but I am not without power. I have lived my life behind these walls. I will die here as well. I pray to the old gods that we shall meet once more. But I do not hold it likely. Send me news of my son. And give him strong sons of his own."

Gyan's face heated and she glanced at Ewald, who was pouting in the stern. Everyone else spoke at least rudimentary Norse and understood enough to laugh.

The ship that had carried a Saxon crew into these waters now left under the power of a mixed Frankish and Norse crew. The morning was fair, and by the time they dumped back into the sea from the mouth of the Seine, the sun was high and bright over them.

Norbert ordered the crew but deferred always to the man at the tiller when it came to the ship. On the open sea, he was as much a passenger as Gyna or Ewald.

The young Saxon kept his own grim company in the stern and away from anyone else. He could not speak their languages, and even if he could seemed surly enough that none would approach him. By the late afternoon of the first day at sea, Gyna approached him.

"You were never going to be a king," she said. "And Bernward was probably glad to see you leave him."

"They were my friends," he said, staring out at the distant stripe of coast they followed south. "And Bernward has been my teacher since I can remember. I cannot believe he would betray me."

"Well, if you're going to be king, then be ready for treachery at every turn. Even your best friend. Even your kin, including me. Kings have no friends."

Ewald squirmed at the thought. "Well what now, Auntie? I am stuck aboard this ship with you. I need to know what I'm going to face."

"Lots of danger," she said. "You carry a sword. Are you good with it?"

"I have bested some of the strongest warriors in my practice."

"But have you stuck that blade through a man's heart and watched his eyes go dull as he dies at your feet? Bit of a difference." She watched the muscles of Ewald's jaw tighten under his full beard. For one so young, he had a good amount of hair. That came from Waldhar, she decided. She let the slashing waves fill the silence before continuing.

"You'll get that sword blooded before this is done. We travel to Sicily. My guess is you've never heard of it. It's a strange place with strange people. All of them want to kill us, doesn't matter which ones you're facing. But there are thirty good warriors here, a full crew. We bring our friends to the battle."

"From all you've said, it seems you plan to take thirty men against a nation of enemies. It seems you intend to kill me."

Gyna laughed. "Stick with me and I will keep you safe. One day you'll keep your dear auntie safe. But for now follow me. And we're only going down to secure Bjorn and the others. I figure we will need to capture something the prince would be willing to trade for their lives. A ship of jewels or a favored woman. Something he'd see as a fair exchange for the lives of a gang of Norsemen that'd make poor slaves."

"But you said they ruined a holy place. Won't they be put to death for it?"

"Possibly," Gyna said. "But the gods would tell me if they were dead."

"You talk to the gods?"

"The gods talk to all of us. Not many listen or watch for what they say. If it turns out they are dead, then we have a different task. We've got to burn the whole city and make sure everyone is dead, especially the prince. We'll need more help for that, but I won't rest until that is done."

"You are as mad as my mother said." Ewald set both hands on the rail and stared ahead. "But I have shamed myself at home. Uncle Adalhard will never take me back. I have put faith in false friends. The worst that can happen to me is that I die on this adventure."

"There are worse things than death," Gyna said, slapping his shoulder. "But your auntie will keep you from them. For now. Keep your sword loose in the sheath. Danger is soon coming."

The days sailing south reminded her of months before when they first made this journey. It was deep summer and the weather hotter. The shift in the climate and the coast astounded men who had never gone so far south. Once they gained the Midgard Sea, what Jamil the Moor had called the Mediterranean, they all felt as if they had crossed into a different world.

A week with Norbert convinced Gyna he was a solid man she could depend upon in battle. Ewald had stopped sulking enough that he could exchange smiles with others. They had laid a basic plan to enter Licata. They would pose as Norse mercenaries, which was not far from the truth. It was how they entered the port the first time. It should succeed a second time. From there, they could learn the fate of Bjorn and the others.

As they sailed toward the blue clump that was Sicily, her stomach tightened. She had truly returned to Sicily as she had sworn to do. The air was humid and hot. The sea was calm and had been so the entire week they followed the coast. The gods were shepherding her to her fate. Did they intend to mock her arrogance or reward her recklessness? After so much struggle, she now had to make good on her vows.

It was a pressure of a kind she had never felt before. Everyone relied on her. But did her skill meet the demands of this burden? Beneath all her bluster and confidence was the small daughter of Lopt Stone-Eye who played with cloth dolls in a quiet corner of her father's hall. How had that girl come to lead a crew of thirty men into a strange land seeking plunder and revenge?

They had passed numerous ships along the Midgard Sea. Most were uninterested in a lone, low-sided ship. The giant ships that wandered these waters had no heart to chase them. They kept a distance and offered no threat. The smaller ships that might have dared to keep pace with them saw the swooping angles of a Norse ship and thought better of violence.

But now that Sicily grew wider and higher on the horizon, the triple-masted ships with their triangular sails became more curious.

They passed closer and some followed a short distance before turning away.

Now, as she stood in the prow and reached toward Sicily, she saw three triangular sails full with the wind. Behind her, men groaned as they rowed against the wind.

The sails lined up on each other as the ship faced them.

"Sails," she shouted over her shoulder. "I think they're heading for us."

"They are," Norbert confirmed, joining her. "And they've got the wind. I don't think we can escape."

Gyna watched the ship speeding directly at them. The distance was a deception, for those sails would soon be upon them.

Ewald joined as well, staring resolutely at the approaching ship.

"Welcome to Sicily," Gyna said to him. "Get that sword ready."

20

The late afternoon sun skimmed across the water, flashing along the choppy waves. The three sails rose higher as Gyna watched from the prow. The crew had been rowing in shifts. Half of the thirty men were rested and the others were slick with sweat. They grumbled about the humidity and the sweat that clung to their brows. Yet all their complaints ceased when Norbert called out the sails driving for them.

The entire deck was silent but for the grinding of oars in their tholes. They could not out-pace the enemy ship with its three full sails.

"We could reverse our rudder," Gyna said. "Catch the wind and flee."

Norbert, who stood with her, shook his head. "We can try, but the time we spend will be to their advantage. This is not our ship. While I have known many different decks in my day, this is still an unfamiliar ship. If we drop that rudder, it goes to the sea bottom and we are finished."

"Maybe they mean us no harm," Gyna said. "We are close to shore. Perhaps they come to inspect us?"

"At that speed, they will ram us," Norbert said.

He then turned from her and shouted at the oarsmen to redouble their efforts. His navigator at the tiller was already pulling the ship around and out of the path of the approaching enemy.

Gyna loosened her sword. She pulled Ewald closer. "Get a shield from the rack. They'll strafe us with arrows first. Then they will close and board us. That will be their mistake, but they will never catch us otherwise. This ship's too slippery up close."

"Why can't we outrun them?" Ewald asked.

"Because we're not the rightful owners of this ship. When Hamar was at the tiller, this ship could fairly fly like a seagull. But it's just us today. We'll fight instead."

"I thought the gods sailed with you on this ship?" Ewald's face had lost its color as he stared at the ship. Now the white foam breaking across it was clear along with the gleam of armed men waiting on its decks.

"The gods are unreliable," Gyna said. "But if your sword is sharp, you can always count upon it."

The chase never fully launched. Despite Norbert's shouting, the men could not get the speed they needed. The ship did not turn in time, though Gyna had often seen Hamar spin the ship like a child's toy. The enemy ship was faithful to them.

"Bowmen," she shouted. "Shields!"

The rowers pulled in their oars and snatched plain wooden shields off the rack. Men dove to the deck seeking cover.

"Get down here," Gyna shouted to Ewald, who crouched under a shield. He stood in the center of the deck, where he could be shot easily if an archer took aim at him.

She pulled him against the gunwales facing the enemy. Her back pressed hard into the wood. She drew her shield across her head and body, tucking her feet into her body. She nudged Ewald's shield into a better position so it overlapped with hers. An arrow only needed the smallest gap to rain death upon them both.

The first shots thumped into the decks. A heavy thud shuddered through the wood at her back where an arrow had struck the hull.

A man shouted a painful curse. Ewald moved to look but Gyna elbowed him back.

"Hold on," she said to Ewald. "They're keeping us down so they can grapple. I wish we had arrows of our own."

True to her prediction, the ship rocked hard as the enemy wake crashed against the hull. Harsh, foreign voices cried out for blood. The first hook slammed onto the rail.

"Up now! Keep your shield facing them!"

She sprang out of her hiding place. One man lay on the sack writhing in a pool of brilliant red. She spun about, keeping her shield forward.

An arrow struck its rim then snapped. Splinters struck her eyes, blinding her for an instant.

Ewald shouted beside her.

Gyna shook the splinters out of her face. Directly before her was the enemy ship at an angle to her own. Down the rail she saw the enemy ship had landed a single hook that had held. Three men were hauling their own vessel closer. They were Arabs. They wore either thin vests or went bare-chested. Three of them hauled on the rope that had caught their ship and were pulling it across the short distance.

"Cut that line!" Gyna shouted at men who still huddled under their shields.

This was the only moment they had to escape. A single line held them. If they could break free now, this ship could win any race from a dead stop. But if more lines caught them, then blades would have to decide.

Yet the young crew was not experienced in sea battles. They were slow to recognize their peril.

More arrows shot directly across the rails. Two more of her crew fell back screaming.

"We have no bows?" She knew the answer, but could not believe they had not carried any. Yet bows require special care along with their arrows. They were hard to keep dry at sea on a ship like hers. So no one had carried them except perhaps as a personal item that would avail nothing in this clash.

Two more hooks with ropes sprang toward them like striking

snakes. One splashed into the sea. The second one landed on the rails and caught wood.

The boarding was inevitable now. Gyna drew her sword and picked her spot along the rails where she would defend.

"We're not getting out of this," she said. "Stay on board and let them come to you. We kill them one at time as they file across."

Ewald stared across the shortening gap between the ships. His face was ashen but a strange countenance overtook him. He seemed to pull back like a cat ready to spring.

She smiled. Her nephew was ready to show these Franks and their half-Norse brothers what fury a real Saxon could bring to battle.

While her crew had no arrows to keep the boarders away, they did have spears. Norbert howled at men to bring these to bear. At last one of the Franks began to hack at the first rope that had snared them.

But it was too late.

The first enemy leapt across toward Gyna. She was the weakest point without spears to back her up. So the enemy focused on her.

She caught the Arab on her shield. He was light but bearing down on her with his full weight she still struggled to slough him to the deck.

The enemy ship slammed against hers and rocked her backward. She stumbled but remained standing. The next man leapt across.

Two enemies had crossed to her. Fortunately, Norbert sent his spearmen as reinforcements. The first enemy boarder on the deck died from a quick strike through his kidney. The second boarder had fallen back on the man who had been following him.

Then Ewald sprang.

Onto the rails.

Then across the narrow gap into the enemy throng.

"You stupid boy!" Gyna's heart nearly shuddered to a halt as she watched her nephew throw himself into waiting enemies. She expected him to die before she could even reach the rails.

His sword slashed down and rose again, trailing red. He screamed and hacked. His shield battered the foes to his left. His sword swept back the blades arrayed against him on his right.

Gyna sprinted, sliding as the ship tilted with the waves.

Norbert screamed at her to stay back.

The first rope snapped away.

But Gyna had to rescue her stupid nephew. She set her foot on the rail and pushed up.

Ewald had already killed two men and was flush with battle fury. The Arabs flowed away from him as he danced forward into a trap he likely did not recognize.

She recognized it, though, and had already launched herself into the air before it closed.

Her feet slammed down onto clear deck. The Arabs were still enfolding Ewald in their snare. But her sudden crash broke it open again.

She stabbed in short, quick strikes. The tight quarters were impractical for anything else. One Arab dropped. Another plowed her aside with his shield.

But she crashed into Ewald.

"Get off this ship, you fool!"

"I am a god!" His face was flecked with red and his cheeks flushed. She saw the wild in his eyes. Both Waldhar and her sister, she thought. Too bad he was going to die.

"Then fly like a god!"

She slammed back with her shield, knocking open a path back to the rail. To save Ewald, she needed a free hand. She flung her shield edgewise at the next Arab, then grabbed Ewald's collar.

"Back!"

He was lurching forward. The ship rocked violently and threw him off balance.

Gyna used the momentum to hurl him to the rail. Another Frank was there, either to board the enemy ship or plug the gap she had left.

"Take him!" Gyna pushed a stunned Ewald at the Frank. He grabbed Ewald's arms and hauled him across the rails like a caught fish.

Then the enemy ship parted from hers.

"Shit!"

She looked along the rails. Both lines had been cut. Norbert had men using long oars to shove away from the ship. The Arabs had climbed onto their own rails to shoot at them. But the rocking ship sent their arrows astray.

Something heavy slammed against her head. She crumpled and landed on the deck. Shadowed faces hovered over her. A spear point gleamed as it hovered over her heart.

She tried to turn, but feet crowded her. The point rose in preparation for a strike.

Then the spearman howled and fell away. Hot blood dripped over her face, splattering into her eye and dripping into her mouth.

Spitting, she tried to scramble to her feet, but found two men willing to haul her up.

Norbert stood by the rails watching as his ship sped away. His face was bloody and grim and he held no weapon.

Three more sails were converging on them. Another Arab ship approached out of the glare of the sun. They had been stalked and trapped. She never knew it.

"Auntie!"

Ewald's scream echoed across the widening gap. He struggled against two men holding him between them, much like herself and her captors. Yet she did not struggle. The battle fury had left her weak and winded. Ewald stretched a hand toward her, but his ship turned aside and caught the wind.

The newly arrived Arab ship turned to give chase. But the ship Gyna had boarded had given up pursuit. Their part in the trap was done.

"Thor fill your sails," she whispered to the ship as it turned away. Oars dipped into the water and it shot ahead. "Do not forget your Jarl Aren's command. Find Bjorn."

The Arabs holding her tore her away from the scene, throwing her against one of their masts. The spearman who had been about to kill her had himself been impaled by a spear, one probably hurled from Norbert's hands. Now one of the Arabs wrestled this out of the corpse, then pointed it at her.

Dark blood oozed off the blade as her enemy snarled at her. She still had a weapon in hand. For the first time in her life, she had no will to use it.

I will see them in Valhalla, she thought. I die atop my enemies with a sword in hand. I cannot be defeated.

She had tried her best, as foolish as her attempt had been. One woman with a single sword could never achieve what she had set out to do. She knew it now, looking down the long spear pointing at her. She pressed against the mast to gird herself for the impaling blow.

The Arab gripped the spear in two hands and lowered it at her guts. His teeth flashed in his snarl. His crewmates surrounded her, laughing and hungry for her death.

Then the Arab captain shouted down the spearman.

He rushed forward, batting down the spear and cursing at his stunned crewman. The others backed off, grumbling but obedient.

Gyna stood, holding her sword in a loose grip. She stared at the captain, who after shouting for order turned to her. He had a smooth and cheerful face. His beard was wild and blood splatter marred his gentle demeanor, but he approached her with something like gentleness.

He nodded to her sword. He held no weapon of his own. His words made no sense but were soothing and calm.

She dropped the sword. Another crewman snatched it away.

The Arab captain smiled, he guided her away from the mast as if she were merely a bullied child who needed a strong hand to guide her to safety.

The ship rocked and creaked. Men drew in the sails against the wind. The ship drifted with the current. Gyna strained to see past the brooding shadows of the enemies surrounding her to the sparkling waves beyond.

Her longship had found both the wind and oars. The Arabs would never catch them now. They had escaped, and she smiled.

The Arab captain spoke gently to her as he led her away. His voice was as calming as the gentle rocking of the sea. She did not mind surrendering to him. His strong hand had her by the sword-arm as he led her through the throng of his crew.

Some could not part, for they lay dead on the deck in dark

puddles of blood. A lone Norseman also lay among the corpses. A broken spear shaft protruded from his back where it pinned him to the deck.

At last the captain halted and turned her to face him. His pleasant smile made him seem a genuine friend. How could such a kind man command so many bloodthirsty brutes?

Then something slammed into the back of her head and she collapsed into echoing darkness.

21

Bjorn jumped back at the arrow shaft that had bounced off his leg. Hamar walked beside him across the grassy field, oblivious to any danger.

All around was grass. No stone or dip in the land could offer him any cover. Every tree or covering terrain was far beyond easy reach. He and Hamar were strolling through the open toward a farmhouse they had previously raided for basic supplies.

The door hung open, welcoming them with orange light. The scent of a meal wove through the air, inviting them forward. A womanly shape flitted about the interior of the flat-roofed farmhouse.

And an unseen archer had just shot and missed.

"Archer," Bjorn shouted. "Run to the house!"

He grabbed Hamar's arm and dropped his ax into his other hand. They pulled left and the archer's shot skipped across the grass just before him.

Hamar now shouted in surprise. They had to get to the house where they could take cover.

But the archer was on the roof.

Bjorn spotted his dark shape huddled as he aimed his next shot.

They split up, running in a zigzag pattern toward the house. Bjorn cursed his overconfidence. No place in this land should be considered safe. Now he was marked by an archer on a rooftop too far to reach.

The archer made no effort to conceal himself. He continued to train his bow on Bjorn. An instinct caused him to skid to a halt just as the archer shot through the space he was about to step into. Then he resumed running, twisting left and right then left again. He tried to avoid predictability.

No more shots followed. Though he and Hamar were still close enough for a single shot at one of them, the archer pulled back over the roofline.

The farmhouse was now in reach. Hamar, limping along, slowed before reaching it.

"Get against the wall!" Bjorn shouted. But Hamar's injured leg had endured too much. He stumbled and crashed to the ground.

The archer did not reappear.

Bjorn rushed to Hamar's side. "Get up, you fool. You're dead out here."

"My leg can take no more," he said. "The wounds still hurt."

"An arrow through the neck hurts worse." Bjorn grunted as he wrestled Hamar off the ground. He had landed on his water skin, bursting it. Water soaked the white cloth around Hamar's leg.

Still the archer did not reappear on the roof.

He did not need to.

Three giant Arabs lumbered out from around the other side of the house.

Bjorn froze. These were his trainers and tormentors. Each man a match to him. Saleet had picked these men to contain him and bring him back to strength. They knew how he fought.

He let Hamar slip back into the grass.

"This is my fight, friend. Catch your breath. I'll return soon."

Bjorn straightened up and took his ax in both hands. He felt the bear god's paw upon his shoulder.

Yet for the first time in his life, he shooed away the touch.

"I must surprise them," he said. "They will kill me if I fight with madness. Forgive me, mighty bear."

He watched for the archer, who must be repositioning to land a killing shot if Bjorn were to prevail. Bjorn sneered at his unseen presence. Saleet and Jamil had picked a poor marksman for their task. He had fired in haste and without accuracy enough times that Bjorn now thought of him as an irritant rather than a threat. Yet the pain under his arm reminded him even a fool could kill with a lucky shot.

The three giants grinned as they fanned out before him. They carried heavy swords that needed two hands to wield. Their shoulders bulged with the effort of hefting them. Sweat glistened on their bodies as they stalked closer.

"All right," Bjorn shouted at them. "You think you know me. But I'll be pissing on your corpses soon enough. Come on! I've been dreaming of this fight for a long time."

The orange light cast from the farmhouse door blinked out. The wooden clack echoed across the grass that rustled with a gentle, hot wind.

The lead Arab charged with sword held high.

Bjorn slipped away from him, knowing he was a distraction for the giant flanking from his blind side.

They would always move toward his blind side and force him to readjust. They had teased him with this tactic in his drilling with them. Yet they were not smart enough to realize they had also been teaching Bjorn how to compensate.

He struck low, and not with a chop they expected. He used the bearded point of his ax like a spear. Driving this forward before seeing his target, he was rewarded with a strike into yielding flesh.

The Arab giant wheezed and fell back. The point had plunged into his gut then tore a deep cut from which bright blood sprang.

He whirled back toward the original feint. It would take no effort for that giant to finish his blow. Bjorn raised his ax in time to knock it aside.

Then he forced his ax into the face of his attacker, who had to stumble backward or else lose his eye to the attack.

The third attacker slashed down with force enough to cut a horse in two. But Bjorn expected this brute as well, and had stepped backward so all he felt was the air cracking before him.

He whirled his ax overhead and slammed it down onto the final attacker's head. His skull split and the giant collapsed. Bjorn cracked his ax free and leapt over the body. The corpse would block the Arab following behind. He needed every advantage against them.

Sure enough, as he turned, one of the giants was skipping awkwardly around his fallen companion. Behind him, another rose holding his guts in with his hand. He roared like a bear himself.

Fighting with his wits more than his strength satisfied Bjorn in ways he had never experienced. His foes relied on their strength and size alone, and Bjorn now turned it against them. The injured brute could not lift his sword with only a single hand. He had only one man to contend with.

Bjorn howled and used the reach of his long ax to hook the neck of the giant that fumbled around the corpse of his companion. He pulled forward and the Arab fell.

From that moment, Bjorn had won the battle. The Arab on the ground took an ax blow to the back and died without a sound. The last Arab held his stomach wound with a hand thick with glistening red. In his other hand, he struggled to raise his oversized sword.

Again using the reach of his ax, he hacked at the hand over the wound. The blade sunk into flesh and dragged it away. Bjorn continued through, shoving the giant to the ground. The Arab glared up and cursed him the moment Bjorn's ax whirled around and sank into his neck.

The Arab collapsed at Bjorn's feet. His massive body thumped into the grass and Bjorn let his ax follow.

He now stood with sweat dripping down into his single eye. Laughter overcame him. Three dead giants surrounded him and he had not even scratched himself.

"This is what it feels like?" he asked through his laughter. "Never had a sweeter victory."

"He's getting away," Hamar said. He had raised himself up on one arm and pointed toward the horizon. "The archer."

Bjorn saw the small form flitting away into the darkness. Perhaps he had run out of arrows or else realized he could not prevail even with the advantage of a bow. Bjorn spit at his retreating shadow.

"Gone to tell Jamil and Saleet they've failed to kill us yet again. They'll learn to not trust their work to fools."

He fetched Hamar to his feet, throwing his arm around his shoulder. They both stared at the closed farmhouse.

"Are you lame, or will you recover?" Bjorn asked.

"Rest is all I need. I have pushed my leg beyond what I can endure. But I do not trust this place."

"We'll take what we need, and get you a new water skin. Then we will go back to find that cave along the sea. It must be near."

Bjorn chopped the door down with his ax. Inside the farmer and his three young sons stood before him with short knives. Behind them two daughters and the mother huddled against the far wall.

Waving his ax to clear them away, the farmers shuffled back. Bjorn kicked over a table. From another he grabbed a plate of grapes and stuffed them into his mouth. He chewed then spit out the vines as he collected everything he wanted. None of the farmers spoke, though the youngest girl whimpered. When he had filled his arms, he left them.

"We've got what we can from them," Bjorn said, offering his armful of goods to Hamar. "Got a striking iron, more cloth, things we need. Take some, and use me for a crutch. We've got some walking ahead before the night falls."

"It's not so far that we can't reach shore before nightfall. But we will never find the cave in the dark."

"We'll find it in the morning," Bjorn said. "Now don't complain. We've got to be in high spirts to achieve what was planned. I want the docks at Licata to burn brighter than the moon at night."

The trek back toward the shore was longer now that Hamar's leg had failed him. They stopped along the way, letting him sit on the grass and rub his thigh. Each time he cursed the dog that had savaged him.

"I'd be happy to spend all my days killing that dog for what it did to me."

"Don't be mad at a dog. He was just protecting his people. It's what a dog should do, after all."

When they gained the shoreline again at the foot of the hills south of Licata, Bjorn set Hamar down in a copse of palm trees.

"Wait here and I will scout the shore for anything dangerous or of use. Last thing we need is someone creeping up on us while we sleep."

He set off toward the sea breeze that beckoned him. Flies had retreated with the onset of night. But now mosquitoes plagued him, bringing itches to his arms and legs. This land was unmerciful.

The shore was dark with stars that slipped between high clouds. Bjorn saw nothing upon the water. Yet his vision in the dark was even worse than in daylight. He realized belatedly that Hamar had smirked at his offer to scout. Of course, he would not see anything until it fell atop him. He smiled, gently chiding himself as he continued to follow the thin tree line along the shore.

"Hamar, you're too kind. You might've said something."

To be certain no dangers lay hidden along the trees, he continued ahead. If he did run headlong into an enemy, he was feeling confident after his battle with three giant brutes. His only regret was Jamil and Saleet were not there for him to finish off.

He realized they treated him as little more than a boar to be hunted. They counted on his rage and his violence to eventually undo him. So they had set their fools upon him, perhaps expecting he might slay one or more before they brought him down.

Now that he revealed he could fight with his wits, would they treat him with more respect? Would they lay a more careful trap? How had they guessed where he would go even when he had not planned to return to the farmhouse until the moment he set out for it? Was he so predictable?

Had they already guessed his next step?

The thought gave him pause as he picked through the thin brush between the trees.

This entire plan might be too obvious. Where Saleet and Jamil had underestimated him, had he not done the same to them?

As these thoughts consumed his imagination, he lost the thread of his wandering along the shore. Now he stumbled to the end of the tree line and realized a small fire burned where the beach and grass met. Men were clustered around it, their lean bodies quivering shadows against the yellow light.

They had beached their ship and men were strung out between the fire and its sweeping, low-sided hull.

It was a Norse ship.

Bjorn's foot crushed down on a branch and he froze like a hare before a hound. Nearly thirty men, a full crew, stood or sat around the fire. He strained to hear their speech.

Frankish.

He ground his finger into his ear, then listened once more. He could not catch full sentences, but heard the Frankish words.

"Now if this ain't the gods at work," he said. He set his ax down by his foot and watched a while longer. What were Franks doing here in a Norse longship?

He stared at the ship with his one eye.

Stared a long, unbelieving time.

That was his ship. The one he had sailed for so long with Gyna at his side and his companions at the oars. Hamar would know it. He loved that ship.

It was here and in the hands of other men.

Strangers.

The bear god touched him and he welcomed it. Rage flowed through him.

Thieves. Enemies.

He snatched up his ax and charged out at the closest group sitting in the grass.

All thirty men must die.

22

Gyna's blackout did not last. She awakened before she crumpled to the deck. But the blow to the back of her head had sent blood leaking around into her mouth. She realized she was face down on the deck. Wrong hands relieved her of her weapons. They dragged her upright and clapped chains around her.

Chains of black iron and rust. Impractical for a sea-roving vessel, she thought. But little was better than iron to keep a prisoner bound. She would not escape.

Once secured, the kind-faced captain stroked her bloodied hair and spoke soothing words she did not understand. His men carried her to the stern and threw her among piles of rags and a ruined sail. The chains chaffed her flesh and her head swam. She felt ready to vomit, both from the blow and the fear of what must come next.

Yet none of the Arabs paid her any mind. The dead Norseman was stripped of anything the Arabs wanted, including his boots, then dumped into the rolling sea. Their own dead were treated with more reverence and stacked in neat rows and covered with blankets. The crew then completed what must be a patrol circuit, ignoring Gyna as she lay bound among the old sail that smelled of salt.

Finally, by the late evening, they returned to Licata. Gyna recognized the distant domes of the prince's palace. They gleamed with dull golden light as the sun retreated for the day. She pushed deeper into the sails, hoping she would be forgotten there.

Yet after the ship thumped into its berth and shore hands called out to the crew in happy exchanges, the captain returned for her. He brought two unfamiliar men who wore heavy chain shirts over their robes. Sweat streaked their faces, and one man could not chase off a black fly that tormented him. They spoke with the captain and then fished Gyna out of the pile of sails and rags.

"Where are you taking me?" Making demands satisfied her desire for control, however false it was. Her two guards said nothing, but hauled her to the docks she had left more than a month ago. She was back where she began.

In worse trouble than when she had left.

The chagrin of her plight drew a weak smile to her as the guards hauled her onto the shore where a wagon awaited. Two other thin men naked but for loin cloths were already in chains and seated in the bed. One was dark like stained wood and the other was pale-skinned with a shaved head. Both of their faces were swollen and bloodied from the beating they must have suffered before capture.

The guards lifted her still in chains and threw her between these hopeless men who stared at her with eyes barely visible beneath puffy, bruised flesh. She landed on her side then struggled to upright herself as the cart tugged ahead. The driver and her guards sat up front and chatted politely with each other.

She leaned against the side of the wagon, letting the bumping and rocking throw her about. They entered Licata, passing the guard tower where Yngvar had sent her to check on their gold. That seemed an age ago.

He was probably dead by now. Same for Bjorn, Alasdair, and even Thorfast. She would join them soon.

What had been the point of all this struggle? She could not find an easy answer as the cart trundled past uncaring city dwellers who could not spare her a glance. The clean sea air gave way to the stench of the city. The sweetness that had once filled her nose had vanished.

The palace of Prince Kalim rose higher the deeper the cart penetrated the city. The driver and his two guards laughed all at once. Just another day at their work, she thought. But for her it was the worst day of her life. The day she would be condemned to die in chains in a dingy cell beneath her enemies' feet.

She should have done anything but return here. Fargrim might have been persuaded to keep her rather than ransom her off. She could have remained with Adalhard. She could have followed Ewald to whatever strange adventure awaited him in the north of Frankia. She could have stayed in Rouen and served Bjorn's father, Aren. She could have died alone in the wild while seeking freedom.

Anything would have meant more than selling her life for no gain at all.

Crushed by her failures, she did not struggle when the cart rolled to a halt in the courtyard of the prince's palace. Her companions had been beaten into submission and did not move the entire trip. In fact, two palace guards leapt into the wagon then levered both of them off the wagon bed. They fell to the ground as if they were dead. The light-skinned man might have actually died, for when he landed he made no sound or motion. The dark man shouted angry words that died away in a wheeze.

When the guards turned to her, the driver's guards removed the chains and let them clank to the wagon bed. Her new captors then took her down between their arms and led her away opposite of where the other two men were taken.

She could not remember much of this palace. The grandeur of it had confused and overwhelmed her. That was probably the intent of the builders, she guessed. Now she had no idea if she were being taken to where Bjorn and the others might still be held.

They led her down a long hall lit with oil lamps that stank of fat. A small guard room held four more men who looked as happy to see her as a cat does a bath. Their sour expressions lightened when they realized they had a woman in their prison.

Gyna tilted her head back in challenge. Here would come the rape and brutalization she expected. One of the men with a white scar cutting his dark, lined face grabbed her by the chin and examined her. His smelly, rough hands twisted her head side to side as he sneered at her.

She wanted to spit in his face. It would only invite harsher punishment. Why worsen the end of her days? Instead she looked to the rafters while the jailor examined her.

He released her with a disdainful snort. He snapped out a few commands to his subordinates and they dragged her down sagging wooden steps into foul darkness cut only by the light of a candle a third man carried behind them.

The scent of rot and feces assailed her. Her jailers seemed immune to it, but to her it was as good as a punch to the gut. The stairs creaked beneath her until they arrived at the bottom. The thin light showed a long corridor of heavy doors. Dirt floors were covered with dark stains and puddles that caught the light of the candle. The Arab behind them shouted down the row of doors. Muffled shouts of the prisoners returned.

At least a dozen men must be kept here. The jailers spun Gyna toward a heavy door that one man drew open. It scraped over the ground revealing total blackness.

They threw Gyna inside. She crashed onto hard, cold earth. Pain spiked in her knees and wrists as she landed. Her left hand was in something cold, wet, and sticky.

The door slammed behind her, and the bar clacked into place on the other side. Darkness rushed over her. She lay still, listening to the prisoners calling out.

She waited until the shouts subsided. She did not move, fearful of the endless black. Where were the walls? The ceiling? Was there another in here with her?

"Anyone home?" She stretched out her hand, finding nothing but air. "Anyone want to be my friend?"

As far as she could tell, no living thing was in the cell with her. She decided to search the darkness later. There would be time.

For now, she turned back to the door. The faintest of light showed around its edges. A small rectangular window was also in the door, filled with short iron bars so that not even a finger could be shoved through it. It was just a means to view the inside of the cell before opening the door. She pressed her face against the cold bars. She shouted between them.

"Bjorn? Yngvar? Alasdair? It's Gyna. Are any of you here still? Thorfast? Speak to me!"

The shouting from the prisoners renewed, but nothing made sense. She struck her fist against the hard wood of the door. "You'll have to shout louder if you're there. I can't hear you over the noise."

"I know those names."

A man spoke directly across from her, answering in Norse. Gyna's hands went cold from the shock.

"Are you one of the crew?" Gyna pressed her face harder against the bars, trying to see through the intense gloom. Yet the vague light revealed little more than the rough outline of the door across the hall.

"I was a friend to Thorfast. I traveled with him for a time. We fought together, but had to part ways. I expect I would have done better following him."

"Wait, friend. I don't understand what you mean. Thorfast and all of the others were captives of Prince Kalim. Who are you that knows Thorfast and the others I have named?"

More of the prisoners shouted through their doors, but soon their voiced died off. None spoke Norse and Gyna did not speak their language.

"I am Ragnar. I came here with a ship that I dreamed would leave filled with gold. But the ship sank and all of my friends died. I alone survived, and made a life wandering among this land with bandits allied to the Romans. That's how I met Thorfast. He had survived the shipwreck that had killed all his companions. We were sword brothers for a short time. He told me of Yngvar and Alasdair. And of Bjorn and Gyna. We did not have time for long stories. But I remember enough to learn the names of his friends."

"Shipwreck?" Gyna's voice fell to a near whisper. Then she pressed against the door with her whole body. "What do you mean shipwreck? I had their ship. They were prisoners and probably locked in these very cells."

"They were sold as slaves," Ragnar said. "According to Thorfast, they were being shipped to their owners across the Midgard Sea when Romans attacked and sank them. Thorfast came ashore with another man, Hamar or Harold. I cannot remember the name. But that man was killed when Arabs found them. Thorfast found another survivor, a Roman slave called Sophia. I guess she saved his life. He was repaying her by taking her home for revenge against those who had enslaved her."

Gyna shrunk back from the door. All the others were dead? Bjorn had drowned? Young Alasdair who was such a strong swimmer went to the sea floor? Yngvar whose keen mind could solve any problem died a slave? Only Thorfast lived.

"Are you still there?" Ragnar asked.

"Yes, I am just ..." She clamped her hand to her mouth as tears flowed over it.

"It is a hard thing to lose sword brothers, especially like that. Know Thorfast intended to return here to take revenge for his friends. Perhaps you will meet him again. By now he must have reached Sophia's home."

She cleared her throat and wiped tears from her eyes. "Where was that?"

"I am not certain," Ragnar said. "They were headed to Pozallo, where Sophia's cousin was a commander. But an Arab army blocked our way. Thorfast decided to thread through the army in disguise, but I followed my Roman allies north. My leg was hurt. It still is. That's how I got captured again. Couldn't keep up with them and the Arabs got me. But as for Thorfast, I have heard nothing more of him. Last I saw he was walking into about two hundred enemies. He was either a fool or a brave man."

"He was both," Gyna said, resting her head against the door. "He was my friend. They were all my friends. No, they were my family. And now they are all dead. Are you certain?"

"I have met no other Norsemen on my return here or in these cells," Ragnar said. "Though I am but newly arrived. I suppose they will get around to torturing me for information on the Romans."

"Who are the Romans?"

Ragnar laughed. "Ah, well, you might call them Byzantines. They have a fortress at Pozallo, though I wonder how long that will remain before the Arabs decide to tear it down. They call themselves Romans. They are barely clinging to the east coast of this island. The

Arabs have only to decide to be rid of them, and I think they will fall easily."

Gyna remembered the ships burning at Pozallo and how Yngvar and Alasdair had dared the walls of its fortress. She remembered Bjorn's expression of childlike glee as the flaming ships lit his face with golden light.

"Ragnar, we must escape this place and soon." Gyna pressed her face once more into the small bars. "We need to meet Thorfast and together we will have revenge on the men who did this to us."

"Revenge is fine," Ragnar said. "But I have a strong preference for life. If we escape, I mean to get away from this horrible island. It has been a curse to me since I came within its coasts."

"I have a ship," she said. "And a crew of thirty men."

And an idiot nephew whose stupidity led me to this fate, she thought but did not speak aloud.

"Yet you are in this lightless place with me. There must be a good story to tell. Forgive me if I cannot see the value in a ship while locked in a cell."

"Of course not, you fool. We will break out and you will stand on the decks of the fastest ship you've ever sailed. There will be your freedom and your passage back home. Like you, I want to be away from this place. But not before I drink the blood of my enemies."

"And this ship will somehow crash through these walls?" Ragnar's voice matched her own irritation. "If there was an easy way out of these cells, wouldn't every man here have escaped?"

"There is no easy way," she said. "But these doors open. And the men who guard us wear no armor. I am still strong and well fed. I have not been abused. They expect a woman to be weak and trembling. But I can kill them with my bare hands. And if you can join me and we can get weapons—"

"And if Loki himself joins our side and tricks a palace of guards to look aside, then we will have freedom. Listen to yourself, woman. You count overmuch on luck."

"I count on my wits," Gyna said, sniffing. "And we will need luck. We will need the gods. But the gods will not see us if we hide underground in defeat. If we call upon them and offer them the glory of our deeds, then we might gain their aid. For I know they are watching me. If you knew my story, you would believe it too."

Ragnar fell silent. Gyna waited for him to agree, then realized sounds were coming from up the stairs.

She shrank back from the door as footsteps creaked and clapped down the stairs. The candlelight now seemed like a blaze in the dark. The rectangular window glowed like the sun for an instant before a shadow blocked it. Guards mumbled on the other side. She sat on the ground as if to appear defeated and weakened.

Her cell door scraped over the ground and the door filled with men. She would not be able to fight this man, even with a weapon in hand. She counted five heads that she could see, all wearing white head covers.

The lead man stepped in and the light of candles flowed around him. He stepped up to her and nudged her with his foot.

"I heard a Norse woman had been captured. I knew it must be you."

Jamil the Moor stood over her, speaking Frankish. He wore a fine gray robe. Dancing shadow filled his wicked smile.

"I promised we'd meet again," Gyna said. She shrank back from him, hoping to appear hopeless and weak.

Jamil stepped closer.

"Now to teach you a lesson, you whore. If only your one-eyed dog were here to witness this."

23

Gyna still lay with her face in the cold dirt cell floor when she heard Ragnar call to her from across the cell. Jamil had been gone for hours. Her head still throbbed from the vicious beating he had delivered her.

"Speak, woman," Ragnar said. "Are you still alive?"

She wished she was not. Her side ached with intense pain. Jamil's kicks might have broken a rib. She squirmed in response to Ragnar's voice. He could not see her, of course, but she could muster no strength to answer.

Rather than rape her, Jamil had beaten her with a wooden club. Two men held her in place until he had pounded her into submission. In the end, she could only ball up and endure the beating.

He had not sought to kill her. He only struck her head once, and it was a glancing blow due to her own struggling.

"You are dead," Ragnar said. "If after so long, you cannot answer then you must not be alive."

She moaned as loudly as her ribs would allow. Slowly rotating onto her back, she faced up into the darkness. She could hold no position that did not bring her pain. Every beat of her heart sent throbs of agony through her limbs and body.

"At last," Ragnar whispered across the darkness. "It sounded as if you were being milled into dust. Can you move?"

The thought occurred to her that her legs might be broken. Her left knee throbbed. But she pulled both knees up to her chest, slowly and painfully, but she could move them. Whether she dared stand was another matter.

"I am hurt," she called back.

Ragnar's laugh echoed through the darkness. Someone far down the row of cells joined him, though that distant laugh was filled with madness.

"I don't know what that bastard was telling you, but he sounded angry enough to kill you. Be glad you still live."

"I have to get out of here," she said. Her voice was weak and low, and died in the darkness before reaching beyond her cell door.

But she had to escape now. For she remembered Jamil's cursing her.

"Your one-eyed lover thinks he can threaten me." Jamil had shouted at her between the blows of his club. "He thinks he can hide from me. Saleet has the power of the court behind him. Bjorn will not survive long."

All of Jamil's threats had vanished beneath the repeated hammering of his club. It had beaten all of the memory out of her. But now it returned after hours of long suffering in the dark.

"I have to escape," she said again.

"I cannot hear you," Ragnar whispered louder across the hall.

She sat up. Her waist screamed with pain. Her head still swam from the blow she had received on the Arab's ship. Pain flared along her hips and spine. Her side screamed with agony. She would lose a battle with a sparrow, never mind a real fight with an Arab warrior.

But pain could come later.

Now she had to stand and escape.

She recalled Jamil's last words before he left her in a pile on the cell floor. He had crouched beside her so that she could smell the oddly sweet scent of him by her face.

"Bjorn will come forward the moment he sees you hanging from a cage off the walls of Licata. He thinks he has won a great battle, killing Saleet's men. Thinks he is a clever man. But when he finds his woman on the edge of death, he will lose his mind. I am certain. Then he will hang from a cage beside you. I shall enjoy watching the birds peck out your eyes and tear your flesh."

She got to hands and knees, holding her breath against the pain in her side. Sweat beaded on her brow as she struggled against it.

Then she stood.

Her knee buckled but held. Her side ached and her mind flashed white with pain.

But she continued to stand.

She balled her fists and glared up at the ceiling lost in darkness.

"I am not bait for a trap," she said through gritted teeth. "It is you who must fear me."

"What are you saying?" Ragnar asked, his voice rising higher. The mad laughter from down the row of cells continued.

She shambled to the door then leaned against it. Rolling her neck and flexing her fingers, she realized that except for her ribs and left knee she had not been as badly injured as she thought. Hard muscle had protected her from the worst of it. That Jamil had avoided striking her head meant he had held back and thus robbed his blows of full force. The beating had been part terror-tactic and part venting of his frustrations.

Yet it had been enough to draw out Gyna's wrath. That would fuel her escape back to the coast.

From there, Ewald had better be returning for her or else have given his life in the attempt. She would not be a captive were it not for him. If she lived, she vowed her nephew would never forget this.

"Ragnar, do you speak the language of these people?"

"I have learned enough Greek to speak with anyone. Most of the Arabs know some of it. I know some Arabic as well, but not much."

"You are a smart man," she said, her voice still hoarse with pain. She wrapped her arm gently around her ribs. Speaking amplified the pain all along her sides.

"Thorfast said so too," Ragnar said brightly. "But he also said I was a fool."

"He thinks everyone is a fool," Gyna said. "When we meet him again, I will slap him for you. But today let's use your smart head to get us freed of this blackness."

Ragnar laughed again. It was an easy laugh. Though Gyna had not yet seen this man in person, she imagined him with a pleasing face and eyes thick with laugh-lines. She decided she liked him.

"These doors are only barred from the outside. So if one of us escapes, we can free all the others. It is a poor choice for a prison."

"I don't think many people escape this place," Ragnar said. 'There is a room of guards above and a whole palace filled with more after them. And then even should we get out of the palace we would be within the city where there are still more guards. Do you expect I have learned the secrets of flight, that I might lift us both into the skies and away?"

Gyna smiled. "That would be too easy, but still worthy of a song to see the two of us flying over Prince Kalim's palace."

"I would be sure to piss all over it before I flew away," Ragnar said.

Her laughter hurt her ribs. But she endured it, for she had not laughed in too long. She rolled her forehead against the hard wood of the door as she thought. Eyes opened or closed, she saw nothing but dark. So she turned her mind to how she could escape this trap.

Alasdair sprang to mind. She had spent many long days learning how to sneak about with him. He had a natural talent that could not be taught to other men. But Ewald had learned the same and hid so completely from her she never saw him until the last moment. So the skill could be learned and trained. And she had trained with Alasdair.

"We're not going to fly," she said. "And we're not going to fight our way out. Not hurt as I am."

"As am I," Ragnar said. "Do not forget I am only here because my leg caused me to lag behind my companions."

"No flight, no fighting," Gyna said. "But we can walk. So that is what we must do."

"Why did I not think of it?" Ragnar said in mock surprise. "I should've just walked out of here long ago."

"Do not make light of me," she said. "It is said that the shadow is darkest beneath the candle's flame. We only need to look as if we belong here and no one will see us. You say Thorfast walked into two hundred enemies in disguise. We both learned that trick from the same master. If he can do it, then so can we."

"I know he attempted it," Ragnar said. "But I do not know how successful he was. We did not delay after we parted company, but raced north to warn the Roman garrison. I've heard no more of him."

"Well, I've heard Bjorn still lives. And you know Thorfast lives. I am gambling my life that Yngvar and Alasdair have lived, and maybe many others as well. I did not see their ship go down. But it seems to have happened close enough to shore that many survived. This cannot be anything but the work of the gods. They are with me, Ragnar. So stay by my side and you will win freedom with me."

"Very well," he said, his voice a harsh whisper across the hall. "So how do we walk out of here without fighting?"

"No fighting," she said. "But a little killing is necessary to get started. They think I am beaten near to death. Jamil held his blows. He wants me alive and screaming to become bait in a trap. So I am stronger than they think. If they send a guard or two inside, I can easily kill them."

Ragnar's laugh boomed out. The crazed prisoner down the hall laughed harder with him. Gyna nodded impatiently until Ragnar's laughter died in a cough.

"Two armed men and you without a weapon. You are mad."

"They can carry nothing longer than daggers in this space. Any other weapon would be too long. I disarm one and kill the other with it."

"Such confidence," Ragnar said. "Then what?"

"Let's worry for it one step at a time. We have to get their clothing for our own, then find a way out of this palace disguised as them."

Ragnar moaned. "We'll be back in these cells before we reach the end of the hall. But it is better than waiting idly for torture and death."

"Good man," Gyna said. "Call them down. Tell them I've died. Is there anything in this cell I can use against them?"

"I have a bronze bot for shitting in. They put our food in it too. Maybe you can find the same?"

Gyna felt her stomach lurch at just the thought of it. But she kicked around her cell until she found something light but hard by the door. She picked it up in two hands.

"I've got it. Let's get this plan underway."

Ragnar began to shout in a strange language. Gyna curled up on the cold earth floor and grabbed the pot to her. The stench of it was enough to make her heave. It was empty and dry, thank all the gods. She could fit her hand into it like a glove but it was too loose to serve as a weapon.

She waited while Ragnar shouted until someone answered with a shout in return. The madman down the hall continued to roar and laugh, and he started to bang his door. Others joined.

Soon Gyna heard a cursing Arab descending the stairs. He stopped across the way at Ragnar's cell and shouted to him. Light spilled in from the small window, painting a yellow stripe across her leg. She decided to pull up her pants to expose her calf as added incentive for the Arabs to investigate.

Soon the Arab stopped arguing with Ragnar. He banged the opposite door and then cursed.

"He's leaving," Ragnar shouted back in Norse.

Gyna then started to moan as loudly as she could. She held her head as if she had been brained with a hammer.

The Arab held his candle to the window and filled her cell with light. She went still and silent. Her arms crushed the bronze pot to her body as she curled around it.

The bolt rattled in the door as the Arab lifted it off. The door creaked as it scraped over the ground to open into the hall. Light splashed across her, but she did not move. She could not leap up fast enough, not with her knee and side so pained. Patience had to win out.

The Arab grunted something at her, but she did not respond. He did not enter the cell. After a long moment, he closed it again and set the bar. But he did not leave. Instead, he went to the foot of the stairs and called up.

A brief exchange ensued across the stairs. A muffled voice above rained down curses. The Arab just outside Gyna's cell sounded impatient and worried. Eventually, she heard the jangle of another Arab clomping down the stairs and cursing with each step.

The madman howled and the other prisoners called out. Ragnar dared to shout a brief report to her.

"Two are coming. One has a short sword. Be ready."

She could do much with a short sword, she thought. She smiled as she listened to the two Arabs argue outside her door. She lay as still as she could, but slowly fit her fist into the bronze pot.

At last the door opened again. She kept her eyes closed and body curled tightly over the pot as if she had died atop it. In truth, the sharp pain in her ribs helped keep her breathing shallow.

Light bathed her and red light shone through her closed lids. The Arabs mumbled among themselves. Their feet shuffled inside and closer. One was on either side of her. She wished she knew which had the short sword.

A foot prodded her from the right. She moaned in response as if half-alive.

This drew an aggravated moan from one, who began cursing as he reached down to yank her over.

She spun easily, swinging her fist in the bronze pot like a hammer. It collided with the head of the man kneeling over her. The blow yielded a satisfying hollow, metallic clank and the Arab collapsed down.

The other man shouted in shock. Gyna lurched to her feet, the frenzy of the moment carrying away all pain and fear.

This one held the candle. He was short and fat, and his wide eyes gleamed with the flickering yellow light. Gyna grinned.

Then her knee collapsed and she stumbled.

The fat jailer recovered his wits and drew his dagger. Gyna still had the bronze pot over her fist. The other jailer lying beside her moaned and shook his head.

She saw the dagger hilt in his belt. It tilted toward her as if inviting her to draw it. She shouted with glee as she snatched at the handle.

But her hand was covered with the bronze pot, which clinked uselessly on it.

In the same instant, the fat jailer jumped atop her. Her ribs felt as if they had all exploded in her chest. The candle fell to the side and began to gutter.

Shouting from every prisoner filled the halls.

She saw the flash of iron rising to strike. She grabbed with her free hand, stopping the blow before the iron plunged into her heart.

The fat jailer's breath was hot on her face. He was strong and her left arm was her weaker limb. But she swung the pot around and slammed it against the jailer's head.

She repeated it a dozen times until the Arab finally collapsed, their hands both still locked around the struggle for his dagger.

But when he fell atop her, either dead or unconscious, his grip failed and Gyna claimed the dagger.

She shoved him off.

The bronze pot was dented and warped around her hand, now oddly conforming better to her wrist.

Behind her the first Arab groaned and scraped against the dirt as he rose to his feet.

She whirled to face him, certain her dagger could reach his throat before he could call for help.

They both stared at each other in surprise. He must have been shocked to see her in such hale condition. She was shocked to discover he was nearly two heads taller than her and thick muscle.

Then the candle guttered out and darkness swept over them.

24

Bjorn charged, screaming a wild curse. His old ship was beached by the gently gurgling waves that rolled onto the blue sand. The night sky was filled with stars to showcase the familiar sweep of its graceful hull. A gentle breeze flowed around it, swaying the rigging in a calming rhythm.

And strange men had made their camp around it.

The dim firelight spread a wide but faint yellow circle around them. Nearly thirty men dressed in cloaks and carrying spears or longswords made camp. Bjorn's single eye managed to capture the whole beach. The bear god was upon him, guiding his feet and filling his arms with strength. The god would not leave him until the sand turned to mud with the blood of his foes.

A man sat in the grass near to him. He wore a bandage wrapped around his forehead to cover his left brow. Red blood seeped through the cloth.

Bjorn's ax slammed through the man's skull down to his jaw. He had only just reacted to the attack, backing up for his longsword beside him. Now he slumped back. The contents of his broken head flowed out after Bjorn's ax lifted out of the cleft.

He twisted on the ball of his feet and hacked at the dead man's companion, who sat cross-legged opposite him. He had grabbed his sword, but it seemed he merely intended to inspect it.

That man's head spun away from his shoulders as Bjorn struck it off in a single blow. Even he was startled at the clean strike. It was the kind of hideous kill that could break a shield wall with fear alone.

The gory death had the same impact now.

The men scrambled away as the second body flopped to the ground, pumping a jet of blood three spear-lengths into the taller grass. The enemy screamed in terror.

Their Frankish cursing confused Bjorn. For an instant he thought himself home in the north once more. Even the ever-present heat vanished and he thought a chill passed over him.

"Face me, you cowards!"

He swung his ax at the retreating men. He was two bounds from the next enemy, but he had the wits to snatch up a spear and level it. His eyes were bright with fear, but he knew how to keep Bjorn defending. He set the spear low to the ground the way a horse might be warded off from a charge.

"Do you know whose ship you have stolen? Your heads will line the rails. I swear it!"

He charged ahead, skirting the set spear for a different clump of warriors who were just gathering their shields together.

"Bjorn Arensson!"

He heard his name. He continued to charge.

"Bjorn Arensson! We come from your father."

His ax slammed down just as the first man raised his shield. The round metal boss clanged against the ax blade. Sparks flew and the man slid back. His companions hid behind shields and bucked against him.

"Gyna is captured!"

He drew back. The words stopped him as firmly as set shields.

"Who are—"

The two men flanking him smashed their shields into him, driving him back. They pressed forward until Bjorn's foot slipped in a pool of blood. Off balance, he struggled to keep upright. But the shield warriors crashed against him again and he flopped onto his back.

"Get his ax." Someone shouted the order, and before Bjorn could regain his footing a third man swept his ax aside with his foot.

He rose, and a shield again bashed across his head. The pain blinded him and he roared in fury.

"What of Gyna?"

He held his arms across his head and fell flat. A shield struck him again, this time only glancing. Yet it hit his wounded underarm and he again cried out in pain.

"Don't kill him! We need him alive."

At last the men around him pulled back. Yet they glared hatefully over the rims of their shields. These round shields were painted half green and half white. The white paint had peeled and the rims were formed of old leather. These were well-used shields facing him, and the men bearing them knew their work.

For a moment only the rolling waves and the gentle rustling of grass gave any sound. Bjorn's eyes followed the two shield warriors as they backed away, still crouched behind their shields.

A golden-haired man appeared over him. He was young but had a full and well-shaped beard. His eyes were wide with fear and his cheeks flushed against pale skin. Yet he still seemed somehow royal in his bearing, and somehow familiar. He spoke with a thick accent.

"You are Bjorn? The one Aunt Gyna came to find. I cannot believe this. God is truly with us. She was right."

"Aunt Gyna?" Bjorn sat upright. A dozen men leapt back with sword and spear now ready. He felt hot wetness trickling down his face, and realized it was not all sweat.

He looked behind to the two corpses spread out in the grass.

"You are allies?"

"I am Ewald, Son of Waldhar. Gyna was my mother's sister. She has endured much to come to your aid. But look at you."

Another man with a narrow head and proud bearing joined Ewald's side. Unlike the young man, he held a drawn sword.

"I am Norbert, sent by Jarl Aren to bring you to safety. These men are my loyal crew."

His heart sank as he realized the men who would have saved him now glared at him with hateful frowns. He pawed at his face, wiping away blood and brains.

"Fuck," he said, slouching. "I took you for thieves who stole my ship."

"We have already endured much to find you," Norbert said, still not returning his weapon to its sheath. "Were it not for the generosity of your father, I ..."

Norbert looked past Bjorn to the two dead behind him. He then turned aside.

The man called Ewald, who claimed kinship to Gyna, now knelt beside him. He put a friendly hand to his shoulder.

"Aunt Gyna felt the same way about this ship. She guarded it with her life all the way from this place, to Denmark, and back to this place once more. Now she is either a prisoner of this so-called Prince Kalim or else floating dead in the Midgard Sea."

Bjorn grabbed Ewald by his shirt, yanking him forward. Norbert raised his sword as if to strike.

"What do you mean by this?" Bjorn let Ewald go and raised his hands for peace.

Norbert watched him as if he were a rabid dog that might strike at any moment. His sword remained readied.

"Just before we came to this place, Sicily or Licata or whatever this land is called. Just then we were chased by ships crewed by men called Arabs. We were boarded. Well, we were about to be. I jumped the rails to bring the fight to these Arabs. But I was alone. Aunt Gyna followed to save me from my own recklessness. But she was left behind when we cut free."

"Cut free? You fled?"

He looked accusingly to Norbert, who sneered in return. Then he softened his expression as he answered.

"We were beset by two great warships. Our only advantage was our speed. So we led them on a chase and evaded them after a time. To stand and fight would have meant all of us becoming captured. How then would we find you, lord?"

Norbert was clear he did not consider Bjorn a lord.

"Of course," Bjorn said. He lowered his head. "I'm sorry you were sent to find me. I am a fool, if you didn't notice already. I kill enemies. About all I can do. Ain't good at much else. This has been too much for me to do alone. Someone has to lead me. I don't want to think of all these fucking problems. I just want to do what I'm good at. And it ain't making grand plans."

He gestured at the sea as if it explained everything. Norbert and his crew remained silent. Ewald straightened his shirt and stood once more.

"Gyna needs you," he said. "I need you. You wish to be led? Then let me command you. Stand and clear your head. Out on that sea, Gyna has gone into the hands of enemies. As a woman, I imagine they would not kill her but keep her for ... other purposes."

"Don't say it," Bjorn said. "I know. If the Arabs worked for that weasel-shit Prince Kalim then she would go to the pits. If they were raiders, then she could be anywhere."

"They were soldiers," Norbert said. "They were organized, wore surcoats of like colors, and they flew a banner of their lord. I know nothing of these people, but I can tell a soldier from a desperate pirate."

Bjorn growled in frustration. "Then she is a captive. And it won't be long before Jamil and Saleet realize they've got her. Fucking beasts. I'll spread their guts over this cursed land. I swear it."

Ewald smiled. "Aunt Gyna said as much when she thought of you being captive. You two are much the same. But tell me, how are you free?"

Bjorn slowly struggled to his feet. Norbert stepped back and slid his sword into its sheath. It seemed the signal to his crew to stand down. A dozen of them rushed to their fallen companions. Others looked on in sadness. Others still sat down once more. Their wounds were fresh upon their bodies and their weariness was evident.

"It is a long story," Bjorn said. "And I must know how it is Gyna went to my father and brought me my ship and fighting men."

He turned to face the corpses. "I have nothing to offer these heroes. A fucking shame. I am shamed. Nothing I can do now will bring them back. But teach me their names. I'll be sure to remember them, and if I ever get from this place with the treasures I sough, I'll pay the blood prices to their kin. I swear this."

Norbert at last relaxed and sighed. He patted Bjorn's shoulder. "We are here at orders from our lord. But I would lie if I do not admit all of us were more interested in treasures than finding you. And times in Frankia are bad."

"They are never good," Bjorn said. "Maybe for the ten years of my youth, and then it has only ever been war."

"It is far worse now," Norbert said. "Our people are once again unwelcome. I fear the Northman will be pushed into the sea. But we have nowhere else to go but Frankia. Anyway, these are all young men. You might be pressed to find their parents alive when we return. But that you made this oath to repay them, I am satisfied."

"I have a friend nearby. His leg is hurt. Also he's the steersman for this ship. No matter how keen you think you are at the tiller, my friend can make this ship fly like a gull over the waves. None are better. Let us fetch him to this camp, then we can share our stories. Got a lot to tell you."

Bjorn led Ewald and a half-dozen men back through the light trees to where Hamar waited. His companions were silent and stood clear of him. But Bjorn did not sense hostility. They would be angered at him until the next enemy faced them. Then they would love him. Every sword brother loved him, no matter what they thought of him before battle. He killed enemies. That was his skill and his pride.

Hamar was shocked into silence as well. The crewmen made a stretcher of their cloaks and carried Hamar back to camp.

"My leg is not so hurt that I cannot walk."

Yet to Bjorn it seemed the protests were to preserve his pride rather than truth. Fear had driven Hamar long upon a leg that could not bear the punishment. Now he had found his limit and none too soon.

Once returned to camp, Bjorn discovered the corpses of his unfortunate victims had been cleared away. A sound scent of blood and death hung in the air to mark their passing. But Norbert seemed to have calmed his anger and that of his crew during his brief absence.

They huddled together, backs to the fire that burned lower with every hour that passed in conversation. The crew preferred to speak Frankish, but Ewald only knew Norse and not to any great degree. He had been raised a Saxon though his mother had been a Dane. So whenever anyone slipped back into Frankish they had to repeat themselves for Ewald's benefit.

Bjorn's eye teared at their accounting of her in battle. Ewald kept his head lowered to hide the flush on his cheeks.

"I had never experienced a battle like that," he explained. "When I scented the blood and saw the enemies before me, I became as another man. I thought myself as a god. But I was only a fool. Aunt Gyna threw me back to our ship before it slipped away. I cannot forget the look on her face as she realized she was being abandoned. I know she blames me."

"She blames everyone for anything she doesn't like," Bjorn said. "Can't remember a time she couldn't throw blame on another. Don't take it so hard. Your aunt might've done the same if she wasn't looking out for you. You've got her blood, after all."

"Ewald showed his brave spirit," Norbert said. "I agree it was madness to cross to the enemy ship. But I cannot deny it inspired many of us, myself included."

So Bjorn had learned Gyna's tale. He told his tale in turn. Revealing that Thorfast still lived did not impress anyone, for none knew the significance. Norbert simply nodded in polite acknowledgement. So he continued until he had recounted his slaying of Jamil and Saleet's underlings and their arrival at this coast.

"Your story tests belief," Norbert said. "That you are still alive is a sign that God favors you. Or at least the old gods have not yet gone from the world."

"I do not put my trust in the Christian god," Bjorn said. "Though I would if he could aid me. But I want to destroy my enemies, not love them. So, yes, Odin and Thor look down from their halls and laugh at me from time to time. But soon they will cheer my deeds and revel in the glory of my revenge."

"Now that we have found each other," Ewald said. "We must put every effort into finding Aunt Gyna once more. She has been gone two days now. I fear for what might happen in that time."

"I agree," Bjorn said. "But the hour is late. I ain't much of a thinker when I'm awake. Right now, I think we are better resting and laying our plans by daylight."

No one disagreed and camp was made. Bjorn and Hamar slept apart but near enough to the other crew. Bjorn did not find sleep easily. He stared at the familiar swoop of his longship. He could see his cousin, Yngvar, leaning against the prow while searching the horizon. Alasdair stood dutifully beside him. Along the rails, Thorfast and Gyna argued over one of their trifles. Thorfast's white hair blazed with hard sunlight and Gyna's flew with the wind.

Such a scene. His heart pounded with the excitement of it.

For once more the Wolves would unite. He would be the man to do it.

Yet sleep had found him and by morning he awakened to a thin rain that pattered across his face. The new sun fought the rain clouds, but they formed nothing better than a squall that would soon pass. Nothing to impede a day of sailing.

He joined with Norbert and Ewald. They shared a simple meal of dried fish and ale. But it was better than anything he and Hamar had tasted. The two of them shared elated glances as they finished their meal.

"So what plans have you dreamed of, Lord Bjorn," Norbert asked. He now spoke with more respect.

"Calling me lord sits strangely with me."

"But you are the son of my lord. What ought I call you?"

"The name your lord gave me," Bjorn said. "That is enough. Our plan before the gods sent you to us was to steal a ship for ourselves and burn the prince's ships at anchor. Wanted to draw them out to battle. But now that Gyna is their prisoner, I can think of nothing but a direct attack. Either we break into their palace and free her, or else we take a hostage to trade."

Norbert frowned. "We faced but two ships with full crews and were repelled. How much worse will we fare against a standing guard? Can we reach this palace easily?"

"Not at all," Bjorn said between drinking from a skin fat with foamy ale. "But the city itself is not heavily guarded. There are no walls to scale. A tower is the only worry we have. The palace is a different matter. But if we move with speed, we could be upon it before they can raise their defense."

"Could that work?" Ewald asked hopefully.

Norbert grunted. "We could gain the city, possibly. But we could not reach the palace before it was alerted. I've not seen it, but if a prince lives there then it will have walls and a garrison."

"It does," Bjorn confirmed. "But what else is there to do? Gyna ain't going to walk out on her own."

"I suggest a feint," Norbert said. "We attack to draw the guards while a small party of men approach the palace. There is no easy way to pry an enemy out from behind his walls. You might capture something of importance that could be traded for Gyna. At least you need to find a way inside first. This plan would benefit from initial scouting. Get to the palace and learn its weak points and the habits of its guards."

Bjorn shrugged. "I can't think of anything else except charging ahead and killing anyone in my way. I'm not good at sneaking about. That was Alasdair's task."

"I am a scout," Ewald said. "I could learn what you need to know."

Bjorn looked at the smiling young man. Daylight revealed a confident and proud face framed in golden hair. He was unmistakably Saxon and certainly the son of a Saxon chief.

"Well, that should be our plan," Bjorn said.

With plans settled they broke camp and returned to the sea. Hamar wept when he set his trembling hands on the tiller once more. He was given a sea chest to sit upon, and Norbert would relieve him as needed.

Bjorn smiled as his old ship raced across the waves toward Licata. He did not know the course, but Hamar only ever needed to sail a route once to remember it with prefect clarity.

Ewald stood with Bjorn in the prow, his brows furrowed and his eyes set on the hazy distance.

"We will succeed," he said. Though it was a statement, Bjorn knew the young man questioned their chance of success. He was right to doubt it.

Bjorn slapped his back but kept silent. He scanned the skies for a sign of the gods' favor. Though they had delivered him from death and returned him to his ship, Bjorn still needed to lean upon them.

Yet the sky remained gray and the gods shared no inkling of their favor.

25

The darkness that swept across Gyna was as thick as a wool blanket. The madman down the row of cells continued to laugh and scream through the utter black. She held her dagger out, ready to strike but at what she could not see. She had glimpsed the last of the two guards before the candle extinguished when dropped by the first guard. She expected he was dead, or at least unconscious. Now that last guard stood somewhere before her. He shifted and his sandals scraped over the wet earth floor.

She bounced light on the balls of her feet. She would not move first and reveal her exact position. Yet if she left the guard a chance, he would call for help and foil any hope for escape.

The guard made his choice.

He slashed out with his short sword, counting on its length to sweep the blackness and find her nonetheless. The choice was arrogant, foolish, and nearly successful.

The sword's pointed tip sliced through Gyna's shirt, opening a hole over her stomach. She twisted to avoid the reverse strike she expected. In the same moment, she lunged forward with her dagger out and it found the Arab.

His scream matched the howl of the madman's. Their voices joined together in an ear-ringing shriek.

She plunged her dagger toward where she guessed he stood. It struggled against hard muscle and she drove herself into the stab until she ran up against her foe. Hot blood flowed over her hand. The Arab's sword arm, finishing the arc of its swing, flopped about her shoulder as if he were welcoming her into an embrace.

With a grunt of effort, she tore the blade sideways to widen the puncture wound and spill her enemy's entrails. He screamed again. His sword clattered to the ground. The awful stench of punctured bowels filled her nose.

The Arab collapsed in the darkness.

She heard nothing more other than the madman cackling down the hall.

The cell's air was damp and cold and cooled the hot blood splashed over her legs. She heard labored breathing along the floor.

The first Arab she had pummeled with the bronze pot wrapped around her fist had not been killed.

Dagger still in hand, she dropped to her knees and patted the blood-slicked floor until she found him. She shook off the bronze pot and it clinked into a wall lost in blackness. Her fingers sought the soft flesh of the Arab's throat, and once she found it she carved it open. Her enemy choked and shuddered, then made no more motion or sound.

She rested in the darkness. Sweat rolled into her eyes. The pain in her ribs bloomed in red-hot agony once she realized the battle was finished. The frenzy of the fight had preserved her against pain. But now her knee and side rebelled. She doubled over with a groan.

"Are you alive?" Ragnar whispered from the darkness across the way.

She looked toward the voice, but could not find her own to give answer. Her cell door hung open. It created a rectangle of the faintest gray against the utter black of her cell. The already horrid stench of this pit redoubled as her two enemies leaked the contents of their bodies onto the cell floor.

"I am free," she said, her voice gasping and hoarse. "But my knee and ribs have been hurt. I will gut that dog, Jamil. I'll break each of his ribs one at time. I swear this."

"Get me out of here,' Ragnar said. His door rattled in the darkness. "Unless your limbs are hacked off you must endure. This is our only chance. Hurry!"

The door rattled once more. She stood slowly, cradling her side. She felt through the hot and bloody mess until she found the dropped short sword. It was a familiar weight in her palm. It brought a smile to her.

"Are you chained?"

"I can hardly walk," Ragnar said. "They've no need to chain me."

She slipped out of the cell. A torch or lamp shined light from halfway up the bare wood stairs to her right. The feeble light shined just far enough to reach her cell and Ragnar's. She saw the dim shine of eyes glaring out from the small rectangular window of the first door.

"Hardly walk?" Gyna stared back at those gleaming eyes. He would slow her down, perhaps even lead to their recapture. She owed nothing to this man.

But then something thicker than sweat trickled down her cheek. She was splattered with blood of her two enemies. The sight of that alone would reveal her to enemies.

"Open the door," Ragnar said. "We've no time."

She lifted the bar and pulled it open. It squealed as it swept into the hall.

"I'm only doing this because you were a friend to Thorfast."

Ragnar was lost in shadow, but he cut a strong shape in the wan light. His smile was a dull yellow.

"I'd kiss you if I didn't think you'd brain me like those two Arabs."

"If you're a handsome man, don't let the guts clinging to my shirt put you off. But if you're a dog's ass, then back in that cell."

Ragnar chuckled as he stepped outside. Gyna handed him the short sword. She preferred the dagger for close fighting. He accepted it with a gasp.

"I can't believe no other guard has come yet," she said. The madman down the hall howled, but the other prisoners remained silent.

"That fight was swifter than you think," Ragnar said. "Now let's be away before that one's screams draw the guards down."

"It might be better to face the guards one at a time as they come down," Gyna said. "There were four or five there last I saw. With two dead, we might have a chance to get into the palace."

"No, they can always reinforce and trap us here. I want to be out where we can run if needed."

"On your bad leg?"

Gyna did not wait for the answer. She crept to the stairs and looked up. The light of the torch nearly blinded her. But more orange light showed beyond it. After a long stare, she noticed shadows moving along the ceiling of the guard room. She cursed and returned to Ragnar.

"Someone is up there," she said. The madman howled down the hallway as she thought. Then she realized what to do next.

"Let's get help," she said to Ragnar. "Get that screaming fool out of his cell and force him up the stairs. He'll tie up the guards for us."

Ragnar's shadowed form nodded. "A fine idea. I should've thought of it."

He hobbled down the hall. Gyna watched him vanish into the darkness. He walked like an old man with a broken hip. This was going to be a rough escape, especially if it came to a fight. But Ragnar also seemed strong and he looked confident with the short sword in hand.

She hid beneath the stairs as she heard Ragnar lifting the bar off the madman's cell. Other prisoners began to shout as well.

A voice called down the stairs, not angry but inquiring. The two slain guards were never going to answer. Gyna pulled deeper into the shadows below the stairs. The madman was screaming now and the other prisoners rejoined him in shouting. The voice above grunted a curse. The stairs creaked with the weight of the guard descending. He added his shouted curses to the echoing noise.

When he arrived at the foot of the stairs, Gyna swept out of her hiding place.

She drove the dagger into the Arab's back. Fortuitously the

madman screamed at the same time and drowned out the Arab's dying shriek.

"Three dead," she whispered back to Ragnar, who approached from the darkness. A withered, dark man with no hair followed along, laughing and pointing at the cell doors.

"One more guard to go," Ragnar said. "Let's send this fool up."

The madman was skeletal and naked. His head seemed two sizes too large for his body. When Gyna grabbed his arm he hissed like a snake. But she was not frightened. He had no teeth in the blackness of his mouth. She simply pushed him at the stairs and pointed up with her dagger.

He stared back with big eyes that flashed in the low light. After a pause, he smiled and shouted down the hall to the other prisoners then bounded up the stairs.

The doors began to rattle with the prisoners' hammering at them. Some were the meaty thuds of desperate fists while others were the hollow ringing of their pots against the wood.

"They want to be released," Ragnar said. "Should we?"

"It'd make a fine distraction, but they could give us away just as easily."

She bounded up the stairs behind the madman, who was now running into the room. He disappeared over the top and shrieked. A shout of surprise followed.

She gained the top stair and found the madman wrestling with a guard who had been lying on a pallet. Now the bony, bronze-skinned madman was driving his clawlike fingers into the guard's eyes. He thrashed and his hands flailed against the madman.

"No one else," Ragnar said. "We could've taken this one alone."

"Come," Gyna said. "We need new clothes."

They ransacked the chests around the square chamber while the madman and his victim wrestled atop the bed. Gyna pulled out a white head cover and deep blue robe. It was too long for her, but she wore it nonetheless. She would fool no one looking directly at her, but from the rear she might be overlooked as just another guard.

Ragnar dumped out a chest and found a blue robe, but no head cover. Behind him the madman bit off the tip the guard's nose. He screamed and bucked, clumping both of them onto the wood floor.

"That's too long for you," he said, pointing to Gyna while the life-and-death struggle carried on behind him. "You'll trip."

"You need to hide your hair," she said. "Find a head cover."

Ragnar stepped around the two men struggling on the floor, spreading slick blood beneath their writhing bodies. The last guard's head cover had been folded neatly by his pallet on a table. Ragnar wore it, adjusting the strap while stepping out of the way of the struggling combatants.

"Should we kill them?" he asked.

"Just the Arab," she said. "Send the other ahead to draw away attention."

Shrugging, Ragnar took his short sword to the Arab's throat. He had finally gained position over the bony madman. His eyes were gouged and bloody. But he would have prevailed had Ragnar not reached his blade across the Arab's neck. A quick slash ended the struggle.

He kicked the dying guard aside, then hauled up the madman. He was splashed with blood from the Arab, but was otherwise hale. He laughed and danced when Ragnar got him to his feet.

"I feel like sending him ahead is like burning the palace around us." Ragnar led the man by his arm to the single door, opened it, then shoved him into the dark hall beyond.

"A fire would not be bad," Gyna said. She scrubbed the gore from her face using the bedding of the former guards. "Of course, that madman will draw everyone back here. We need to be quick."

"You've had all the success so far," Ragnar said. "So lead us away."

The rippling orange light shed from brass lamps showed Ragnar to be a handsome man. Capture and imprisonment had worn down his hard edges. But his eyes were still clear and alert and Gyna admired the strong shapes of his neck and shoulders. The head cover shadowed his face, but his light beard was still visible.

She slipped into the corridor which she had recently been dragged through in chains. The air here was already fresher and cooler against her skin. Her bare feet touched cold stone and she slid against the wall where shadow was deepest. Her knee buckled and she feared she would topple. She pressed her back against the hard stone wall.

Ragnar waddled out and limped toward her.

Gods he was slow and unsteady, she thought. Worse than her. She felt some connection to this man for his friendship with Thorfast. But Thorfast might not have threaded that Arab camp. He might be dead. Gyna liked Ragnar enough, but would abandon him if he became a hinderance.

They stared down this hall, where several lamps had gone out but a general light showed farther down. It seemed to stretch endlessly into nothing. She knew it would lead to the first floor of a tower, which would then empty out into the courtyard from where she had been delivered to this prison.

"Where did he go?" Ragnar pressed against her. "Shouldn't he be screaming or something?"

She blinked. "It's like he vanished. Are there rooms along this hall? I don't see any."

Gyna pushed her dagger into the sash that held her robe closed. She had been careful not to cinch it too tight or else reveal her gender. But she had to pull it tighter to keep the dagger in place.

"Hide that sword," she said. "A reflection will give us away. Now stay to the shadows and let me lead."

Ragnar pushed his sword hand beneath his robe and the two shuffled down the long hall. It was much wider than she remembered. But she had been surrounded by guards and everything had felt crowded. In fact, the hall was wide enough for four men to walk abreast.

The stone walls were smooth but joints between stones rubbed against her back as she slid down the row. Her knee buckled once and she had to stop or else scream in pain. The long robe dragged at her feet, and she had to hold it up like a woman crossing a stream.

They were alone in this hall. She knew the captives were screaming below, but their voices did not reach this far. That much was a relief. Though she could not figure where the madman had run. Thus far, she had not found any other exit from this long hall except the door at the end. She could see it now, a flickering lamp set to the left side of it. A circle of thin light illuminated the iron-banded door.

"Where did that bony bastard go?" Ragnar said as he slipped beside her. They both stopped just short of the door. "Did he go through?"

"He must have," Gyna said. "For I do not see him in the shadows and there is no place to hide. But it seems too fast."

She strained to see into the shadowed corners, but nothing stirred. The darkness was not so complete that crouching down in darkness would conceal anyone.

"He went through that door," she said. "He had to have. So there is nothing on the other side or else we'd have heard him."

"The gods are with us after all," Ragnar said. He removed his hand from within his robes to let his sword hang to the floor. "Open it."

Gyna pulled on the door and found it swung easily into the hallway.

Two spear heads lanced out at her. Her honed reflexes saved her from losing her eyes to the weapons that jabbed at her face.

Beyond the door, the madman broke into crazed laughter.

26

The spear points thrust again, driving Gyna back from the door she had opened. She yelped in surprise. The madman beyond the door cackled. She glimpsed him jumping up behind the grim faces of the guards shoving her backward. His eyes were big and lit with maniacal glee.

She slammed the door over the advancing guards. Their spearheads were all that protruded from the door. They shouted in shock and anger as she threw herself against it. Pain shot through her side from her injured ribs. Yet she gritted her teeth and held against the pushback.

"Help me keep this shut," she said to Ragnar.

He fell in beside her, throwing his strong shoulder into the wood beside her.

"What's the point?" he asked. "We're trapped in this hall."

She glanced around as she shoved against the bucking door. Muffled curses and gleeful cackling vibrated though the wood.

The long dark of the hall spread behind her, she hoped had missed some small doorway. Of course she was trapped here.

The spears continued to stab through the gap between door and wall.

"Snap off those spearheads," she said. "Then we fight."

Ragnar nodded. He backed up then threw his full weight on the door as Gyna pressed. The shafts broke against the stone wall. One sharp head clattered to the floor but the other remained fixed on its cracked shaft.

"Now, before they draw new weapons!" Gyna stepped back and drew her dagger. In the same instant, Ragnar stood before her with his short sword.

The door slammed against the wall and two surprised guards fell through with their broken spears in hand. The madman howled in laughter, falling to the ground behind them and out of sight.

Ragnar grabbed the spear shaft that still had a head and pulled it forward. Out of instinct, the guard held onto it and tumbled between him and Gyna.

She stabbed with her dagger, driving it into the guard's armpit. He screamed and Ragnar flung him behind. The next guard fell back, eyes wide with terror. He flung the broken shaft at Ragnar, who batted it away. Yet that delay let him draw his own short sword.

Gyna sprang.

Then crashed to her face behind the door. Her ribs felt as if they had all exploded. The pain was so overwhelming she could not scream. Instead she lay face against the cold stone and blind with white agony. She heard nothing. Felt nothing but burning pain. Each breath was like a saw blade drawing across her chest. Tears leaked from her eyes. Time meant nothing as waves of pain broke over her.

"Are you alive?"

Ragnar's face appeared as he gently flipped her onto her back. She groaned with the pain as her body twisted.

"I tripped on this fucking robe," she said. "What a stupid plan."

Fresh blood had speckled the white of Ragnar's head cover. Yet the dark robes hid most of the blood stains.

"We've come this far," he said. "So the plan is not stupid. But it needs much luck, and we're out of it. I killed the last guard, but that mad fucker ran out into the courtyard screaming for help."

"We saved him," Gyna said, then groaned as Ragnar helped her sit up. "He should've helped us, not betray us."

"He saved himself. Betrayed us to warn the guards, but probably didn't tell them we were armed. He might not be so crazy. Looks like he's going to escape and we're not."

As he spoke, he raised Gyna to her feet. But his leg could not support them both and he staggered back until he bumped against the wall. They stared at each other in silence.

Gyna could hardly straighten her back and Ragnar had to pause against the wall to steady himself. At last he hobbled back to her.

"No more time to waste."

She had to step across the corpse lying in the door. She pointed at the guard's short sword still in his grip. Ragnar bent to fetch it while she gingerly stepped into the room.

Everything was in darkness but for a square door showing a torchlit courtyard. Her heart lifted, for it was night. Time had vanished in the depths of the prison and she had expected full daylight.

Before she could celebrate, she spotted three more guards running across the courtyard toward the open door.

"We're still trapped," she said. "We can't outrun them."

Breathing hurt. She wrapped her free arm around her body.

"Up this ladder." Ragnar pulled her attention to the side of the square room where a ladder rose to an opened trapdoor. "Can't be anyone up there or they'd have joined the fight."

He was already climbing the ladder. Despite his injured leg, he was able to steady himself on the rungs as he climbed.

Gyna thrust the short sword into her sash and put the dagger between her teeth. Then she climbed the ladder behind Ragnar, who had already slipped into the darkness above.

"There's another ladder," he said as she pulled into the room.

"Gods, my side is shattered. That fall almost killed me." She stumbled into the room and again the over-long hem of her robe tangled in her feet.

"Get rid of it, then," he said. "Can't have two of us hopping like rabbits. The door above is shut. I'll go first."

She threw away her head cover and yanked her robes off. Now she had to hold her sword, for her own belt was not heavy enough to bear its weight. She dropped the robes in a pile by the trapdoor in the floor. The guards below entered. Their angry voices echoed through the room. But they had not seen the dead body in the other door.

Yet.

"Go," she hissed. Ragnar began to climb the next ladder up to the top floor. She searched for anything to block the trapdoor they had just come through. This was a storeroom with many sacks and casks stacked against the walls. Empty wooden boxes were strewn about.

She tried to bend over to close the trapdoor behind her. But the shocking pain of her ribs prevented her from even this meager task.

The guards below shouted. Their panic and anger was clear.

"I'm going to open the door," Ragnar said from above. "Be ready."

She started up the ladder, sword in hand, but now with her dagger tucked into her belt.

A small gong sounded below at the moment Ragnar opened the trapdoor.

He shot through the door and disappeared into a wavering yellow light. Surprised shouts greeted him.

Gyna tramped up the ladder after him. Below the gong sounded again, a brassy and loud noise that filled her ears with the sound of death. For what else could await her now?

To have come so close to freedom only to die in the tower. She gritted her teeth against the pain and scrambled after Ragnar.

He was lying on his back, having collapsed again from his leg injury. There was open sky above her. An iron basket burned with bright firelight, throwing the two bowmen on this rooftop into sharp relief. They held short, curved bows in one hand. Their other hands hung free with no other weapon to grab for. Spears lay in a rack far off to their left.

As she pulled up, Ragnar rolled out of her way.

The two guards looked to the spears, their bows useless at such a range.

Pain swirled around Gyna. Sweat poured over her face. The thudding of her heart enhanced the biting agony she felt in her chest.

But she did not hesitate.

Speeding with all her strength, she rushed the two guards. She did not raise her sword. She did not rise from a crouch.

Dropping her sword just before reaching one of them, she then threw her arms around his knees.

She pulled him up, knocking him off balance against the wall, then flung him off the tower.

His scream satisfied her. But she had no chance to enjoy it.

The guard beside her had regained his wits. He kicked at her. The ball of his sandaled foot connected with her side.

In any other time she would have shrugged off such a feeble blow. But in this state, she shrieked with pain and collapsed back. Again she could see nothing while pain ensconced her body. Underneath the burdens of her suffering, she realized to lie still was to die.

Against all suffering, she willed herself to stand and face her enemy. Yet castling up to her feet was slow and painful. When she at last gained her feet, she could hardly stand through the pain.

The guard had rushed to the rack and picked a spear. Ragnar was crawling, also struggling with getting to his feet.

This Arab was thin but broad-shouldered. He glanced at Ragnar, and determined he was no threat while prone. He instead lowered his spear and charged at Gyna.

She had dropped her sword. Reaching for her dagger across her hip, the twist brought staggering pain.

As the Arab plunged his spear at her, she slipped aside and batted down the shaft with a balled fist. She yanked her dagger from her belt.

Then fumbled it. The chime of the iron clinking to the wooden floor was louder than thunder.

She looked into the Arab's wild eyes as he slid past her. If she had held her dagger, he would have died. Instead, she tripped backward from him as he whirled to bring the spear against her again.

Ragnar slammed his body against the Arab. The two crashed against the waist-high tower wall. Gyna's back-step caught on something and she fell. Her head slammed against the heavy floorboards. Sparks of pain filled her vision.

But when it cleared, she glimpsed Ragnar shoving the second archer over the wall to his death. He then collapsed against it and slid down to face her.

They sat opposite each other, heaving and sweating. Gyna smiled.

"I was thinking I'd have to abandon you if you slowed me down."

Ragnar smiled in return. "Yeah, I guessed you to be that kind of woman."

"What does that mean?"

Shouting from below echoed up from the trapdoor. The Arabs were ascending the ladder.

"You're a woman," he said. His smile grew.

He was handsome, Gyna decided. A strange thing to notice as her enemies' shouts grew nearer and fiercer.

"That's not an answer. Well, I didn't leave you. And you didn't leave me."

"Did we have a choice?" Ragnar wiped the sweat from his eyes with one hand. The other cradled his leg against his wounds. She could not see the extent of it beneath his pants, but it must be terrible to drop him like this.

"We had no choice," she said. "But you wouldn't leave me, no matter. I guessed you to be that kind of man."

He laughed easily, as if the threatening curses rising through the opened trapdoor were mere birdsong.

"You are an incredible fighter. Killed seven men before we were caught. And without any weapon to start. It has been an honor to fight at your side. You've humbled me."

Gyna blushed. She did not understand why. She waved off his compliment.

The first guard pulled onto the rooftop. He clenched a long knife between his teeth. Another followed as he scrambled through the trapdoor.

"Will they kill us or capture us?" Gyna asked. Her chest felt as if it were wrapped in hot wire. She reached for her dagger and pain spiked through her ribs. But she would hold a weapon in death. She was a warrior equal to any man. So she would face death as a warrior. Her fingers snatched it into her grip as the first guard reached them.

"We'll know soon enough," Ragnar said.

That was the last Gyna heard from him before pain stole her senses. The Arabs were shouting and screaming. They kicked her flat, kicked her all over while she curled up against the battering. Her side and ribs burned. Soon she went numb from the pain.

They pummeled her with spear butts. She was tied and lowered like a tied pig through the trapdoor. At the bottom of the tower dozens of dark faces waited for her both within the tower and without. She was limp and listless. Her dagger was gone. Every bump and rub she suffered as she was gathered by more guards felt like a nail driving through her sides.

All was chaos as two guards dragged her into the courtyard. Scores of people had answered the alarm. Most were not guards but palace servants and laborers. Her eyes were closing. She had probably been beaten in the face and did not even realize it.

Even if they were to behead her now, which seemed likely, she had no regrets. In fact, as the two men carrying her set her down amid a crowd of curious, dark faces, she smiled.

She had achieved more than she ever expected. True, she had fallen short of her goal. Yet she was never going to find Bjorn or any of the others. It was a fool's errand from the start. As she waited for death on the hard-packed dirt of the courtyard, she accepted the gods had merely wanted to laugh at her. But now they had tired of their sport. Time to send her onward to the next world. Perhaps Odin had a place for her in the feasting hall. Or perhaps not.

She did not care. She had defied every setback to return to Sicily with her ship. Such were the deeds of great heroines, which she counted herself among. Even if she never had learned the fates of her sword brothers.

This was a proud death full of glory.

The crowd parted. A wiry man in a gray robe was upside down in her vision. His high-pitched voice screeched against her ears. She strained to widen her eyes to see him better.

Saleet.

Then Jamil stepped into the bottom of her vision. His arrogant, sneering face hovered over hers as he shook his head.

"I grant that you can withstand a beating. You've killed royal guards, and so Prince Kalim will want to give you a gruesome death.

He'll cut off bits of your flesh and let you watch as he feeds them to wild dogs."

"I will drink mead from your skull, Jamil."

Her voice was wheezing and weak. Jamil barked laughter.

"In another time I might have feared that threat. But not tonight. I will have to secret you from the prince. Your friend can go on and accept the blame for all the dead. It would be more believable to the prince, in any case. You must come with me and my master, Saleet. We have a task for you."

He smiled wickedly.

Gyna let her swollen eyes close.

She welcomed death in any form. Let it come at last.

27

The wood piled over Bjorn's body was rough and full of splinters that pricked his skin and tangled in his hair. The heavy scent of this wood was foreign and irritating to his nose. It was as if mosquitoes bit inside his nostrils. The constant rocking of the cart beneath him had shifted the load as it trundled through the streets of Licata. Now a plank sat uncomfortably against his crotch, causing him to squirm whenever he thought it safe to move.

Yet at each movement greater than a twitch, Ewald would whisper at him through the wall of the cart.

"Don't move so much. There are enemies all around us."

He kept his one eye closed, both to rest it and to keep out splinters and dust from the freshly hewn wood. All around he heard foreign voices. Some shouted. Some laughed. Most voices were simply tired and irritated, in a hurry to move the day along to its conclusion.

He felt the same way.

Norbert was right in believing a Norse ship could not approach Licata directly. Not after their very ship had so recently slipped capture. So they had landed down the coast just long enough to let Bjorn and Ewald disembark. Hamar was full of tears when Bjorn said his farewell.

"Don't be like that," Bjorn had said. "I'll be back with Gyna and a sack of the prince's gold as well."

"Just come back," Hamar said. "We both have too few real friends left in this world."

It was a hard truth, Bjorn thought. But he remembered those two figures racing for the sea during the battle between Arabs and Byzantines. Yngvar and Alasdair had to be alive still. Thorfast was out there.

And Gyna was in a prison cell only a half day away by foot.

"Give us to when the moon is highest in the sky," Bjorn had told Norbert. "Then slip into Licata and set fire to the tower. If we don't have Gyna by then we're not going to have her at all."

"You're certain she is there?" Norbert had asked as his crew prepared to shove the ship back to sea.

"I ain't sure of anything. She's either dead or a captive. I'm expecting Jamil and his wormy friend would want her alive just to learn what she was about. If we don't find her by the time you attack, we will return anyway. Can't help no one if we're dead."

So he and Ewald set out with supplies and silver coins. His arm wound was freshly cleaned out and bound tight. That relieved the pain. He had eaten and drank until his belly stretched. There could be no better preparation for their plan.

"You're too obvious to just walk into the city," Ewald had said once the tower came into view.

They found laborers headed to town with loads of lumber stacked in carts. Bjorn's coin paid for him to hide in one cart and Ewald to act as one of the laborers. Surprisingly, one of the laborers was fair skinned and golden haired like the Saxon. Ewald blended in with even his simple shirt and trousers that matched the laborers. Though none had spoken the other's language, they all understood silver coins. Hand gestures completed the deal.

Now Bjorn was within Licata once more, albeit piled under wood.

After the cart rolled to a stop, the laborers began to unload the carts. Ewald joined in. Finally he lifted away the last of the lumber from Bjorn, relieving him of both irritating scent and pressure. A purple sky shined behind the golden-haired Saxon as he smiled down.

"Well rested?" He extended his hand to Bjorn.

"Wood was crushing my balls. Wasn't my idea of a rest."

Ewald's warm hand gripped Bjorn's forearm. He hauled him upright. Splinters fell away from his face. He was in a small yard in the rear of a square of buildings. The laborers glanced at him as they stacked their piles of wood. A purple-robed man with a shockingly white beard looked surprised. But a few hand waves from a laborer and he ignored Bjorn.

"You kept our weapons safe," Ewald said. "Let's have them and be about our next step in the plan."

Bjorn handed up a short sword to Ewald. He had eschewed his own ax, for nothing would give him away faster than a long-hafted ax. The short sword Norbert had loaned him was well made, but felt too light in his hand. He wanted heft, something to break skulls. He looped the baldric over his shoulder. This would do for tonight's work.

Jumping out of the cart, he felt ready to spring into a fight at the first enemy. Ewald helped him bat splinters out of his shirt.

"Listen, you follow my instructions exactly," Ewald said. "You might be a lord of the battlefield, but we have little use for direct fighting tonight."

"Aye, lord," Bjorn said. "Shall I kiss your foot as well, lord? Anything else my lord needs of his servant?"

"Kiss my foot if I say so," Ewald said while searching his surroundings. "I've learned woodcraft from the best. Though this is a city, and a magnificent one at that, I expect my training will bring us success here as well. So set aside your pride for one night. Heed me and we will have my aunt on the ship before the moon reaches the top of the sky."

"I won't argue with success. Show the way, lord."

In truth, Bjorn was glad to have anyone in charge again. Even if he was a Saxon a good ten years younger than himself. Making so many decisions gave him headaches and ruined his sleep with worries. Ewald would point the way, and Bjorn would destroy any obstacle that needed destroying. Simple and direct, always his preferred way.

They left the laborers, offering a final raised hand in thanks and peace. The laborers returned it with smiles. They were rough men twisted by a hard life under the sun. They likely smuggled criminals around in their carts every day. They did not even glance at Bjorn's sword, which should have earned a call for the guards.

Twilight was upon Licata. In the open, the final light of the day would reveal them as armed foreigners. But the crowded, square buildings of faded and chipped plaster granted them deep shadow to cover their path. The tower that guarded the main entrance to the city jutted into the darkening sky behind.

The paved streets all led up toward the palace with its impossible domes and high walls. It rose like a shining crown above the jumble of buildings imposed before it. Young men ran through the streets with tinder boxes, lighting torches at intersections to aid the city guards in patrolling the night. Other folk were closing down their stores and shuttering the homes. A hammer clanged in the distance where a blacksmith worked past sunset. A child shouted from a room above them as they slid through the alleyways.

"Pardon my saying, lord, but this ain't much craft. We've just been running through shit-filled alleys."

Ewald, who led him through the shadowed maze, turned back with a smile.

"And yet we have met no dead-end or passed where someone might linger and spot us. We draw ever closer to the palace, unseen, and you think it's aimless luck guiding our feet. My skill shows me where other men have traveled before us. We're not the first to want to pass unseen on these streets."

"Well, fuck you." Bjorn kept close to Ewald, who simply laughed at the insult.

Not long after, they came to an end of an alley that dumped out to a street before the side of the palace walls. Ewald bared the exit with his arm.

"The palace of Prince ... What is his name?"

"Prince Kalim," Bjorn said, stopping behind Ewald's arm. "The shit-eating weasel that sent us to slavery for no good reason."

"Aunt Gyna said you despoiled his holy place. Sounds like you deserved it, after all."

"Are you defending him?" Bjorn grabbed Ewald by the shoulder and pulled him up to his one eye. "It was a fucking trap. He wouldn't listen to nothing we had to say. So fuck him. I'll kick his head back to Norway and use it for a shit-pot. You still want to defend him, boy?"

Ewald's proud smile vanished. "Not at all. Let's get to our task. So you can get to kicking heads and shitting on them. Whatever you want."

"That's more like it." He released Ewald and turned his one eye back to the stone walls. Square towers studded the length of it. They were plastered and smooth, defying any hand hold. Without hooks and ropes it could not be scaled. A ladder, while effective, was the same as setting a bonfire for gathering attention.

"You're wondering how I plan to get inside," Ewald said, a smug smile returning to his face.

"And you know my thoughts as well," Bjorn said. "You and your aunt both seem to have the knack of it. I was thinking you planned to walk us through the front gate. But you must have planned something more cunning than that."

Ewald stared at the walls a long while. At last he scratched his head. "Well, I did not have a specific plan. How could I until I saw what we would face?"

"Boy, you better have a plan."

"Don't call me boy," he said, waving his hand airily as he studied the wall. He seemed about to say more, but then clapped his hands together. "But of course! Boy! It will work, at least to get beyond the first wall."

"Spit out that plan." Bjorn was about to call him a boy again, but thought better of antagonizing his only partner. In fairness, Ewald was short but strongly built and certainly a grown man. His whining arrogance just made him seem younger.

"First to find the side gate," Ewald said. "There must be one of those, and I believe I see it."

Bjorn tried to see into the darkness, but a single eye was weak even in the best of light.

"I'll trust that you see it. Ain't going to give myself a headache trying to check you. So what about it?"

"This is a palace of heathens. Godless and horrible men. Right?"

"If you mean they're a lot of dog-fucking bastards, yeah."

"So every sort of sin must be committed behind those walls." Ewald rubbed his beard as he thought. "Well, it would be best if we had a beautiful woman to offer. But I've heard stories of these people of the southlands. There are many man-lovers here, yes?"

"I've not asked," Bjorn said, now scratching his head. "You thinking a quick kiss to the guards will pass us on? That's your plan?"

"No," Ewald said. He stripped off his shirt and handed his sword to Bjorn. "But my guess is young men and women are traded to the guards in that palace. Every bad deed is conducted by side gates. Look at this one. Nothing could look more forlorn and suspicious as this gate. Imagine what happens here?"

"Probably the same gate they took us through to lead us into their trap."

"So, I am tonight's offering. Knock on the gate with me, your helpless captive, to be offered to the heathens inside. We just need them to open the door. Once inside, I expect your big hands will serve to twist off that guard's head. We'll need some proper disguises, at least one, and it can't be splattered with blood."

"This is a poor plan. It cannot be made into any song I'd care to sing."

"That will all come later. As long as we seem to know our business and not be sneaking about, we will be safe. And what danger could they see in two men at the side gate? Let's not waste time."

Once at the gate, Bjorn swung the two short swords to his back and stuffed Ewald's shirt into his pant waist. Their approach to the door was not challenged. It was a simple but heavy door, one not easily broken down but not one meant to withstand a true siege. It kept thieves away, Bjorn guessed. He rapped his knuckles on the door, shouting for attention as if he had business within.

"I doubt anyone will understand us," Ewald said. "But still don't speak anything of our plans while inside."

"I'd not tempt the gods to mischief." Bjorn pounded his fist on the gate again until he heard a voice beyond.

"It's me, bird-shit. Open the fucking door before I kick it atop your empty head."

His confidence wavered when no reply came. Ewald nodded confidently to him. How could he be so certain, Bjorn wondered. Yet in moments a bolt rattled behind the door and it opened wide enough for a suspicious eye to look outside.

Bjorn smiled, then thrust Ewald forward.

"Got this for your master. Don't let us stay out here long."

Ewald lowered his head and tried to look defeated.

The glimmering eye behind the door narrowed and the door closed again.

"They're not buying it,"

"Patience," Ewald said, his head lowered. "I'm sure this is not the first time a slave has been offered at this gate."

The door reopened wider to allow the guard to fill the space. He wore a thick leather vest over his dark blue robes, and a curving sword hung from his hip. He was young with hollow cheeks and eyes as big as a horse's. He pointed with his chin at Ewald, then spoke in his rough language.

With the door opened, Bjorn readied himself to launch through it. But Ewald gently tugged forward in Bjorn's grip. It seemed he wanted to enter the gate.

"Be silent," Bjorn replied. "He's not for you. Let me in."

To his surprise, the guard parted for him to enter with Ewald. It seemed a reckless thing to do. But the instant he stepped beyond the guard he realized the young guard's confidence was not unwarranted.

He pushed Ewald ahead into three other guards who formed a semicircle around the entrance. The young guard shoved the door closed behind him, the wood thumping with heavy finality as it hit the jamb.

Bjorn had two swords at his back, and the young guard would turn to find them in the next breath. The ruse would be over.

Attack now and sort out the plan later, he thought. There could be no other solution.

Ewald looked back to him, eyes wide with surprise at the number of guards who had come to greet them.

"Grab a sword off my back." Bjorn said. "Time for fighting."

28

The room where the guards had dropped Gyna enveloped her in heat and stung her nose with smoke. She opened her swollen eyes long enough to glimpse the orange coals in a soot-stained iron bucket. She heard a rhythmical pumping of air, and realized that above her head someone worked a bellows. Perhaps this was a forge.

Her ribs were tight with pain. Her face throbbed with every beat of her heart. Bare earth was at her back and she realized she stared up at a smoky ceiling. Men moved around her, mumbling in low voices.

But the clear and irritating whine of Saleet was easy to hear above all. She raised her head, but the agony that angle flashed through her torso made her flop back without seeing anything.

"I promised you a cage," Jamil said, sauntering into view. "You will draw out Bjorn and I will finally be rid of all you vermin."

"Bjorn is here?" Speaking hurt her ribs and she held her side against the pain.

"I've already told you as much," he said. "I suppose that beating knocked you senseless. Your lover is near but won't reveal himself. He is not nearly as brave as you suppose. All talk, as it always is with those kind of brutes."

He crouched beside her and smiled. His dry, thin hand caressed her face.

"So you will hang from a cage outside the city. He will learn of you soon enough and come to your rescue. He will not be able to restrain his rage. I can count on him to act out of unthinking fury. Then the two of you shall die. But I cannot have you warn him of the trap."

He smiled and patted her swollen cheek. Gyna's stomach clenched at what Jamil implied.

"It would not do for you to shout a warning to him. So tonight we will remedy this before bolting you into your cage. I will cut out your eyes and your tongue. After all, you just need to hang there and look like something to save. You need neither speak nor see to do that."

"Jamil," she whispered through her pain. "How many men are in this room?"

The old Moor smiled. "Are you worried that you will be defiled first? All the guards have far better choices than an old and shriveled slave. Have no fear."

"Are there seven men here? I cannot keep my eyes open long enough to count."

"There are five men." Jamil smiled indulgently.

"Does that include Saleet?"

"He watches from the door."

"Ah, so really four men."

"This is the gibberish you speak with your last words?" Jamil shook his head.

"Actually, three men. I can't count you as a man, either."

"I am through with this foolishness." Jamil stood from his crouch, his old knees cracking.

"Is one of the three just the smith? So really just two fighting men?"

Jamil did not answer, but instead shuffled over the hard dirt to the man at the bellows. Gyna twisted against the protesting shock of pain that raced along her side. Upside down, she saw Jamil leaning close to a stocky man wearing only brown pants. His body sagged with age and his beard was wild and white. He held iron tongs in both hands.

"Only two men, Jamil. You can't even count, you fool. You're too stupid to find the tongue in my mouth, you old rat."

He sneered down at her but did not answer.

Sweat rolled from her brows into her eyes. She raised her head again and blinked at the two men standing in the door. They also glistened with sweat as they leaned together to commiserate in low voices. Both wore leather jerkins but their swords and daggers were sheathed. One laughed at something the other said. He batted his friend on the shoulder.

It was as if she did not exist. They were probably here just to carry her broken body to whatever cage Jamil and Saleet had prepared for her.

Saleet. Where had he gone? She craned her neck once more, but the wiry Arab was not in the room. Probably too squeamish to witness his vile deeds.

"Jamil, I agree. You've beaten me." She lay flat against the ground, straight on her back. She relaxed her arms and legs. Her breathing slowed and she closed her eyes.

"So at last you will beg for your life?"

"Yes, please, Jamil. Please, don't do this to me. I'll be a good girl from now on. I swear it. I won't warn Bjorn. Can't you just blindfold me and gag my mouth? Why so bloodthirsty?"

It was no effort to sound desperate, for she was. But she had to sell the desperation to Jamil and everyone else in the room. Most importantly, she had to draw him closer.

"I cannot trust you," Jamil said. His haughty, false laugh made Gyna grit her teeth. "And you have the devil's luck. The surest way to ensure you can't see or warn Bjorn is to relieve you of eyes and tongue. It won't take long. And you needn't live long, either. Though live bait always draws the bigger fish."

"Jamil, have you never had a woman? You're just going to cut me up and not take advantage?"

The old Moor gave a long sigh.

She dared a peek at him, tilting her head back. He had drawn a long knife that reflected the coals in the basket. The blacksmith held his tongs, probably to extend her tongue for Jamil's blade. She closed her eyes once more and braced herself for what she had to do next.

"Come on, you old bastard. Is your cock dead? Wait! So that's it! You can't do it. You're a man-lover!"

"You waste your breath," Jamil said standing over her. "Your insults mean nothing to me. I count you no better than a pile of dog shit."

"Is that why you're with Saleet all the time? Did you have to suck his cock to get your freedom?"

"You little whore. I will enjoy cutting out your tongue."

"I mean, it can't be all that big. So really not a struggle for you. But I'm sure he makes you do it every night. Does your neck get sore?"

"You wretched hag!"

She pried open her swollen eyes.

Jamil knelt over her and brandished the dagger at her throat.

"Jamil."

His blood-shot, hazel eyes glared into hers only a nose-length away.

"I've got a surprise for you."

Digging her hand into his crotch, she drove up until she clasped the soft flesh under his robe.

His eyes widened and she yanked hard.

"Men all have this weakness."

She shoved him back as he gasped in pain. Her heart raced and her chest throbbed. But pain would come later.

This was her desperate hour. Her moment where the Three Fates looked at her and decided whether to cut the thread of her life or spin a new story.

The two guards continued to chat, unaware that Gyna had literally seized control of Jamil. She needed that hesitation to rise up.

With a shove and a scream, she pushed Jamil back between her and the doorway where the guards idled. He collapsed on his backside, both hands cupped to his crotch.

Then she was on her feet. The rage of the bear god, though never truly hers, was here to summon. For so many years with Bjorn, she had learned to embrace her anger and frustration and channel it all into battle. All pain, all worry, all fear swept aside before it.

The old man with the iron tongs turned to her. She stepped back from him in the tiny room. He was the key man to disarm and the hardest, for she had no weapon.

Fortunately, the old man went rigid at her seemingly miraculous recovery. Gyna launched at him. She grabbed his wild, white beard into her left hand and pulled his head down. Off balance, she stuck her right foot between his.

He hunched over her and landed atop the forge of yellow coals. His flesh sizzled and filled the room with the pungent stink of seared skin. He screamed and flailed.

Gyna wasted no time. She grabbed the iron tongs that had fallen from the old man's grip as he pushed back from the forge. His face and beard trailed smoke and fire as he reeled back against the wall.

The heft of the warm iron in her hands brought a smile to her face. Wielding the iron tongs like a club, she slammed the burned old man across his head. He crumpled against the wall as he clawed at his burning face.

Her heart roared in her chest. All pain had vanished from her.

She whirled to face Jamil and the two guards.

To her it seemed as if hours had passed. But the guards still leaned together as if only just recognizing their changed fortunes.

Jamil sat before them.

"Never should've left me untied," she screamed as she bounded forward. "You fucking old goat!"

Yet as she swung the iron tongs in both hands, Jamil ducked aside. He rolled into the wall and out of her furious strike. So confident had she been in shattering his proud head, the force of her blow carried her off balance when it struck nothing.

Then her knee betrayed her.

Fury might mask pain. It might tame fear and grow strength. But it cannot mend what is broken.

She felt something pop when she rotated through what should have been Jamil's killing strike. Her knee buckled then she collapsed.

In that instant, all the cushion her fury had granted her drove out of her along with her breath. Agony sparked fresh in her chest, numbing her from neck to waist. Her vision flashed white as she fell upon her side.

Twisting at the final instant, she had avoided crashing on her broken ribs. Yet the impact was enough to debilitate her.

The two guards were finally alert. They were sensible men, unfortunately for Gyna. For they did not instinctively reach for their swords as she had hoped they might. The room was far too small for those weapons. Instead, they had pulled long, straight daggers that gleamed like wolf fangs in their dark hands.

Her hands still gripped the tongs.

A bloom of intense heat against her left temple reminded her of the iron bucket and the hot coals that had been prepared for the iron Jamil would have used to cauterize her eyes and tongue.

Against all pain she twisted around to grab the bucket rim with her tongs.

The first guard was over her.

She flung the bucket at him, raining hot coals over his face and down between his jerkin and flesh. Coals fell on her legs as well. Yet her deerskin pants were tougher than the Arab's cloth. She shook away the burning coals before they could sink into her flesh.

The guard, however, had fallen back against his companion. He batted at his clothes and danced in terror. The room shook with his screams. Even his other companion had suffered burns.

The room smelled of smoldering coals and seared flesh. Gyna backed away, but was shoving against the wall.

Jamil stood, penned in the room by the guard struggling at the door.

Gyna had no more strength to hold up the tongs. She let them thump to the dirt beside her. Pain raged through her body, and though she had defeated two of those arrayed against her, two yet remained.

"You whore!" Jamil waddled over to where the burned guard had dropped his dagger in his panic. The guard still flailed while his companion tried to work him out of the room. But Jamil snatched it from between the guard's feet.

"I'm going to lay you open from crotch to throat!"

She held on to the iron tongs. This was a weapon, was it not? She had no strength to fight even this old fool. She would try.

"I'm ready, you old man."

The moment the two guards fumbled out of the doorway, Jamil leapt at her.

29

Four guards surrounded Bjorn. Three in a semicircle before him and one who had just closed the side gate behind him. He gripped Ewald by the arm and felt his muscle tense. The young Saxon prepared to have their ruse exposed. Bjorn was glad enough to be through the gate.

The three guards regarded them with raised brows, but no outward hostility. Bjorn frowned as if they were stupid.

"Ain't none of you know why we're here?" He shook Ewald as if to emphasize he was tonight's business.

One seemed about to answer.

Then a gong sounded from one of the towers behind the guards.

Bjorn and Ewald both looked to the sky. It was a clear night but the moon was not yet at its highest point. Blue light shined down over the prince's castle, but nothing seemed amiss to Bjorn. Norbert should not have launched his attack yet. But perhaps he had been pressured into it.

He hated making decisions. What would Yngvar do now?

Then a man ran at the group and the four Arabs turned as one toward him.

A wretchedly thin man garbed in foul rags charged the four

Arabs with his arms up like a mad bear. His skeletal face was taut with rage and fresh blood had been splattered across it.

"Now's the time," Bjorn said. "Grab your sword, boy."

The madman leapt atop the first guard, who had barely put a hand to his sword. They both collapsed to the ground. His companions laughed at the madman's ineffectual assault. None paid attention to Bjorn. He snatched the sheathed sword off his shoulder in one smooth draw.

Then he rammed it through the guts of the young guard behind him. He stared up in shock as he slid from the blade to bump against the wall.

Ewald shouted a Saxon battle cry as he pulled his short sword from the sheath on Bjorn's back. It rang free and caught the moonlight as it arced toward the remaining three Arabs.

While the madman raged against his personal foe, Bjorn and Ewald fell into battle with the last two guards. All around them, men raced toward the brassy sound of the gong. Their desperate combat took place in a shadowed, unimportant part of the palace courtyard. The golden domes of the palace shined as a backdrop against their quick skirmish.

Their swords clashed twice before Bjorn and Ewald both stood over two corpses. The madman and the Arab wrestled in the dirt. At last, the Arab drew his dagger and plunged it into the madman's ribs. His shriek should have brought the palace to this spot. But the desperate gong drew streams of men, not all guards, toward the distant tower.

Bjorn kicked the dying madman off the Arab. Then he stamped his foot across the hapless guard's throat. That alone likely killed him, for his back flexed and his hands grabbed Bjorn's ankle. Yet he cut open the ties of the guard's leather jerkin with a deft slice, then stabbed him through his heart. The guard's struggles ceased as blood leaked out around the sword.

"That was easy," Bjorn said. "So I expect the gods to make it harder after this."

Ewald's face was flushed. He wiped off his blade on the hem of a corpse's robe.

"Still we should hide these bodies and hide ourselves. I was hoping for a better disguise, but these will never do."

A crowd of the palace's guards and servants had converged around a tower close to the main gate. Their shouting echoed across the open courtyard. A glance at the walls showed men either racing toward the tower or else leaning forward to see it better.

"We better hide our mess," Ewald said. "Pile these bodies in the shadow behind that cart."

An empty cart rested by the wall where two empty barrels sat beside it. Rotten straw had fallen out of it and the cart seemed unused.

Bjorn worked with Ewald to drag the bodies into the shadows. Each took their own man, leaving trails of blood and tracks in the earth. Such evidence would be obvious by daylight. He trusted to night to hide the signs of battle, at least until they had located Gyna.

They crouched behind the cart and observed the scene by the courtyard tower. The alarm had not been for an attack.

"We could not have asked for a better distraction," Ewald said as he crouched by the wagon wheel. "Someone must have tried to attack the front gate."

"Except that ain't the front gate," Bjorn said. "It's the tower that leads to the prison. I've only seen it twice, but can't forget it. It's the gate to the Mistlands, far as I'm concerned."

"Is that where Aunt Gyna will be held?"

"If she's here, I guess so."

Ewald tapped his finger against the side of the wheel as he considered.

"Well, if she is not here, we can at least find the weak point in this palace. You are going after, Jameet and Samil?"

"You mean Jamil and Saleet," Bjorn said. "They are most certainly here. They wouldn't be in this part of the palace. That little rat likes to rest by the prince's hearth fire."

"So while everyone is busy here, we can try to get deeper into this palace and find your enemies."

Bjorn nodded, though his eye was ever drawn to the chaos at the tower. If Gyna had been turned over to Prince Kalim's men, she would certainly be held in his prison. If she were captured, she would kill herself trying to escape. She loved freedom above all else. It's why they hadn't married yet. Didn't want to be tied to anything or anyone, she had said.

"That mess feels like something Gyna would be in the middle of."

Ewald was already looking toward the gate to the inner courtyard. He turned back to the crowd and shrugged.

"We have this single advantage," he said. "To approach that crowd will risk revealing ourselves. But right now I think we could slip deeper into this place. Maybe even catch your prince. Would you risk losing that chance?"

"Gods, boy, I hate making these choices. The prince is the fattest prize. But his head belongs to more than just me. Thorfast and Gyna want a piece of that skull. And Yngvar and Alasdair live. I know it. We should return together."

"That makes no sense," Ewald said. "There may never be another chance."

"It's not about sense," Bjorn's voice rose and Ewald hushed him with a finger raised to his lips. Bjorn adjusted his words. "You want me to choose. My gut tells me there's something to see by the tower. So let's go."

Ewald nodded without further protest. He motioned Bjorn to say put while he found a path that led through shadow.

Bjorn's knees ached from crouching. He settled on his knees, looking down as he did. When he looked up, his world changed.

Jamil and Saleet had joined the back of the crowd and two guards were with them. They dispersed the crowd with shouts and shoves. As the onlookers peeled away, he saw a stocky man carried between two guards. They dropped him on the dirt.

Behind him, more guards swarmed a figure on the ground.

Jamil and Saleet went unerringly to that figure, ignoring the other.

"Gyna," he whispered. "I'd gamble my only eye that's you there."

Yet he did not know. Still an invisible hand drew him forward, beckoning him to join the crowd with ax swinging and a song of death on his lips.

His palms itched for the ax he left aboard the ship. Norbert's short sword was too light in his grip to give him the confidence to charge such a crowd.

Ewald scrabbled back to him in a low crouch and his voice crackled with excitement.

"That is Aunt Gyna," he said, bumping up to his side. "And another man, a Norseman. He curses his guards in Norse and another language. They must have escaped together."

"A Norseman? Maybe another of our crew?"

He strained to see the man, but a spearman had interposed himself into the view.

"We can't get near Aunt Gyna now," he said. "But that Norseman has only a single guard."

"I'm not here for him," Bjorn growled. "There are three people I want, lined up as if the gods have set them before me. One to hold and two to kill. Let's be about it."

"Now? The entire courtyard is watching. Look, you fetch the Norseman and I will follow Aunt Gyna. I can go wherever they go, but you could never follow."

"I don't care about that man." It took all his strength not to scream out and smash the wagon he crouched behind.

"He must know something and was Gyna's partner. Look, they are already moving."

Bjorn twisted his head back and forth to see both crowds at once. Gyna was lost in the largest crowd. The Norseman was lifted between two men and being dragged toward the tower he had just been pulled from.

"The crowd is breaking up," Ewald said. "We'll be found. They'll definitely find these corpses. The moon is approaching the top of the sky. We cannot delay. Go for the Norseman, I will find my aunt. She is here on my account. It is my duty to save her. You cut the path out of this palace. We will follow whatever soldiers are sent to answer the attack to cover our escape."

Ewald pulled him by the arm and Bjorn followed. Men were ambling toward them. Though none approached the wagon, if one drew near enough, the hidden bodies would be easily discovered. So

Bjorn did not protest as he clung to the walls and moved with speed through the shadow. Ewald's bare torso showed as gray in the dark. Once they were halfway to the tower, he paused to sheath his sword and collect his shirt from Bjorn.

"We part here," he said. "They are taking her to the far end of this courtyard. You only need slip into that door. Sheath your sword, or else a flash of light could betray you. God bless you, Bjorn. When Norbert attacks, we will join at the gates and Gyna will be with me. I swear it."

"Don't bother to come back without her," he said. "If you fail I'll kill you myself."

Though the threat was in earnest, young Ewald smiled and clapped Bjorn's shoulder.

"I've trained with the best. I'll be there and back before you figure out where the front gate is."

Bjorn watched Ewald flicker into shadow and then vanish. The challenge would be to cross the gate where most of the guards clustered in discussion. He had to admit Ewald was right. He could no more sneak past that many guards than a glacier could pass down a stream. But the door to the tower hung open within mere strides.

"Do what you're best at," he said to himself. "Let the younglings have some of the glory, too."

He walked into the tower, careful to look as if he belonged. He was not garbed as the locals, but running or acting fearful would draw eyes. Inside, the scent of blood hung in the air. Light shone through an open door where blood stains marked a deadly fight. He smiled. Gyna was the most dangerous woman he knew and the fresh blood was proof none were fiercer.

Shouts echoed down the hall. He recognized this long stone-walled passage that sloped down to a room where guards watched over the prisoners beneath the palace courtyard.

Now that he was inside, he drew the short sword and stalked down the hall. The shouting came from two Arabs. He raced to the end of the hall. A door hung open.

Inside, low lamplight shone over two Arab guards and the stout

Norseman. One Arab leaned over a dead body while the other held the Norseman by his arm while he slumped to the floor.

They all looked to him.

He swung his short sword like an ax, which was the wrong way to wield such a weapon. The inexpert strike merely slashed the guard on the ground across his face. A painful but ineffective wound. The Arab slipped away with both hands on his face. Bjorn whirled to the one holding the Norseman, and before that fool could draw his own weapon Bjorn ran him through his liver. The Arab went wide-eyed and collapsed against the wall.

"Can you stand?" Bjorn asked the Norseman.

"If I could, I should've been dead by now."

Bjorn stepped over the fallen Norseman. The other Arab had struggled to his feet, but one hand clamped over his right eye and cheek. Bright blood streamed out of it.

"Sorry about that," Bjorn said as he closed the gap. "Let's do it right."

The last man fell, taking Bjorn's short sword with him as he staggered back and tripped over a stool.

"You are Bjorn," the Norseman said from behind.

"Well met," he said. He put his foot on the slain guard's chest and worked his short sword free from the Arab's ribs. Norbert would be furious if he lost the weapon. "Gyna told you about me?"

He turned to find the Norseman pulling himself onto a stool. He draped his strong body over it, but had no strength to do more. His face was bloodied and swollen, otherwise he might have been a handsome man with a strong jaw.

"No, I am but newly met with Gyna. I learned of you from Thorfast. He described you well enough, I can see."

"Thorfast?" Bjorn rushed to the Norseman's side. "How have you come by him? Who are you?"

"I am Ragnar," he said. "Do we have time for stories? I traveled for a time with Thorfast, but he is now gone to the Romans."

"What of the others?" Bjorn grabbed Ragnar's shoulder and shook him. "Yngvar and Alasdair? Any of the old crew?"

Ragnar shook his head. "They are only names to me. But the gods are at work tonight. Let us not waste action while they watch us."

"Your leg is hurt. I have a battle to fight." Bjorn stared down at Ragnar. What had this man done? Had he helped Thorfast or betrayed him? Had he aided Gyna in this escape or had he simply followed? He had yet another decision to make and it drove him mad. When could he return to the happy life of swinging his blade wherever Yngvar or Thorfast pointed?

"Leave me," Ragnar said, lowering his head. "But give me a weapon that I may meet you again in Valhalla. I have survived longer in this land than any of my sword brothers. I am not afraid of death. If I can kill one more enemy before I die, then I shall be happy."

"Take this." Bjorn reached down to the guard slumped against the wall. He drew the dagger still in its sheath and turned its grip toward Ragnar. He accepted it with a grim nod.

"Now climb upon my back. I only need one hand for this child's sword. If I had my ax, I might've left you here. But ain't you lucky? I've got a ship coming and I could use a strong back to row it to freedom. Your arms are unhurt?"

Ragnar smiled. "My arms are the only parts of my body unhurt. Let's go."

With Ragnar on his back, Bjorn returned down the hall.

"You're not as heavy as you look. Ewald has gone to fetch Gyna. We might need to help him. But otherwise we wait for the alarm. My fellows will attack at the docks to draw away attention. We'll meet them down shore then be away."

"Sounds like a fine plan." Ragnar's tired voice was beside Bjorn's left ear. His legs and arms wrapped tight around Bjorn's torso, leaving his sword hand free. He supported Ragnar with his other arm.

"Well, fine plans are like fine crafts. Both break if handled roughly. I'm confident this plan will be a fucking mess. But it's all we could think of."

"Seems to be successful so far."

Bjorn was about to agree when he heard voices and then saw shadows in the doorway at the end of the hall.

"Hold on to that dagger," he said. "I'm not slowing down for anyone."

30

Jamil's face was red with anger and his pale eyes wide with rage. He shrieked as he leapt at Gyna. She had backed up to the wall of the small forge. Heat spilled from it to wash over her on the floor. Coals were scattered everywhere and grew white beards of ash as they cooled.

"Die!" Jamil screamed. The knife he had recovered from the burned guard lifted over his head. His gray robes were covered in dirt. Gyna's handprint showed at his crotch where she had seized him.

Blind with fury, Jamil stepped on a hot coal.

He hopped away. His howls of agony bounced off the walls of the crowded room. In his desperation to avoid another coal he tripped then crashed onto his back. He landed on more coals.

Gyna laughed no matter how badly it pained her ribs.

"You old fool! Look at you! Like a fish on a beach."

He thrashed and flopped over the coals that she had scattered around the room. The knife fell from his hands as he tried to bat away the burning coals. His flesh sizzled and the thick scent of seared skin clogged Gyna's nose.

"Your time is done," she said. Then she turned her eyes toward the smoky ceiling. "And gods grant me this last favor. I will send you fresh blood."

The agony of standing was beyond anything she had ever felt. Her knee, which she thought had popped, still held. Her ribs screamed in pain. But she believed if she did not look at her knee or touch her ribs, the pain could be managed.

The other guards had vanished. She glanced out the door. The small entrance was blocked with a wall that led to the courtyard. She could not see beyond it. Perhaps the guards had gone to fetch help. She turned back to Jamil, who had at last settled against the far wall. He sat beside the dead blacksmith, whose burned face still smoked.

Retrieving the dropped dagger hurt as she bent. Her knee wobbled and her ribs protested. But the gods had granted her wish. The warm leather grip felt comforting in her hand. With careful deliberation, she picked a path through the coals. These had mostly been knocked aside from Jamil's wild thrashing and left a clear path to him.

"I've thought about this for a long time," she said as she stepped forward. She rested the dagger point against her finger and twirled the blade slowly. The edge was not as sharp as she would have kept it, but it was keen enough for murder.

Jamil whimpered, holding his body as if it might fall apart.

"You've been a bad slave," she said. "And there's a punishment for that."

The words seemed to bring him back, for he raised his chin and marshaled his voice.

"You are nothing but a filthy, heathen whore. You will roast in hell while I go on to paradise."

She stood over him now, her two feet set on either side of his legs. His head seemed twice as large for his body at this angle.

"Can't say I'd want to be any place that'd welcome you as a hero. So, Jamil, it's just you, me, and this knife. Want to wipe your tears before I kill you? Or do you care if your severed head is forever like a crying baby?"

Jamil narrowed his eyes at her.

"You arrogant bitch. You really think you've bested me?"

"Looks like—"

He punched her knee.

If it had not been ruined before, now it collapsed and she with it. Bright pain flashed over her eyes. She thought of her ribs and held them tight as she fell. But she struck the packed earth floor and still a shudder of pain crashed through her.

She lay still, moaning and holding her sides.

Jamil's cold hand grabbed her ankle.

"It's my knife now," he said as he clawed the dropped blade back to his hand. She saw him through a red haze of pain. His face glowed with victory as he climbed toward her with the dagger lifted to drive into her heart.

"Your arrogance has undone you." His hand reached up to the back of her calf as he hauled himself closer. "I will rid the world of you, you stinking pile of—"

She kicked back with her good leg, driving her heel into his face. His teeth slammed shut and he fell aside with a groan.

"Didn't even have sense to grab my good leg." She unfolded onto her side, and reached again for the dagger that had traded so many hands.

"This blade is thirsty, Jamil. It calls out for blood. And looks like at last it will drink its fill."

Jamil lay on his side, hand over his face and blood running between his fingers. She had struck him truer than she had thought. Now she summoned the last of her strength. With a roar, she flipped atop him. Her side burned and her knee stabbed pain. But she slid over his prone body.

With her free hand, she grabbed Jamil's hands from his face so she could see the fear in his eyes as he died.

"I'll grant it was a better fight than I thought you could give," she said, her face inches from his. "But in the end, I claim your head."

She allowed no protests, no final words.

The dagger slipped into the yielding flesh of his neck. Jamil's hazel eyes flicked wide, locked with hers. Foamy blood bubbled into his mouth.

"This is revenge for Bjorn, for Yngvar, Thorfast, Alasdair, and all the others you betrayed. But most of all, this is for me."

She dragged the blade across his throat. The hot blood spray on her face relieved all pain from her. It assuaged anger that had smoldered in her heart since the day she had fled upon Fargrim's ship. She sawed at his throat until the old Moor's beard dripped red.

His eyes stared up in terror. His mouth would forever hang open in a scream that had smothered in his own blood.

"I'm taking your head with me," she said. "No matter where I go. I've earned it."

A long knife was no tool for a beheading. But she sawed and cut and pried. Finally she twisted and pulled, oblivious to the world around her. The horrid task consumed her entire mind. In the end, she had dulled and bent her knife, but still prized Jamil's head from his shoulders.

She held it up level with her eyes.

"Well, I won't live to drink from your skull. But it's good to see you like this, Jamil. Too bad no one else did."

"Auntie!"

Gyna turned. Blood, sweat, and pain blurred her eyes. She blinked until she could see clearer.

"Ewald? How—"

But her question died when she saw who accompanied him.

"I caught him sneaking away for help," Ewald said. He shoved the wiry Arab in a gray robe to the floor before her.

"Saleet." She said the name full of hatred.

Saleet did not look to her, but stared at Jamil's head held between her hands.

"There were two guards outside, one was burning. I killed them and caught this one hiding behind barrels. His robes made him seem important. Is he the one you called Jamil?"

She shook her head, staring at Saleet who remained frozen in terror.

"So, little man, do you recognize your servant? Here, give him a kiss."

She pressed the head at Saleet, whose dark skin turned ashen. Only when Jamil's gore-soaked face touched Saleet's did he scream awake from the terror that gripped him.

"Auntie," Ewald said. "Bjorn is here. He has gone to fetch your friend."

She heard but could not stop laughing at Saleet, who now balled up at Ewald's feet like a terrorized puppy.

"We are not safe," he said. "The guards have dispersed, but there are dead bodies all over this palace. An alarm must go—"

The alarm gongs sounded, deep and throbbing peals that began far away and grew ever closer. Ewald grimaced.

"I hope that is Norbert's attack and not an alarm for the palace alone. Come, Auntie."

At last she looked down to her knee. It was swollen to the point of stretching her pant leg. Blood had splattered all across it.

"I can't walk," she said. "My knee is in a bad way."

Ewald clicked his tongue. "I can't take you and this hostage."

"Don't let him go!"

Her sudden shout startled both Ewald and Saleet. She gathered her fingers into Jamil's thin hair and held up the head.

"This is worth more than all the gold in this palace. And this little rat you caught it worth all the gold in the world."

"Well, Auntie, no one is paying gold to us if we're dead. So take my shoulder and we must leave. I'll keep the rat at the end of my sword, but if he runs I cannot chase. I hope he will not realize this."

They had no other choice. Saleet, beaten and stunned into compliance, waited on his knees as Gyna got up to Ewald's shoulder.

"You can at least thank me, Auntie."

"As I remember it, you should thank me. But let's not argue. When I'm healed I'm going to take a switch to your hide for being an arrogant, impatient, little brat."

"Certainly, Auntie. But don't strain yourself. You are an old woman. Now, let's see what bad news awaits us in the courtyard."

"Norbert's attack?" She hobbled along with Ewald.

"A diversion to draw guards out of the palace. We were hoping to sneak out with them. But you are carrying a severed head and are sopping with blood. So I think we need a new plan."

Ewald kicked Saleet, who sat listlessly at their feet. He stood when Ewald flashed his sword at him. Then he stuck the point in Saleet's back.

"Go ahead of us, rat. If you run, I'll cut your spine."

"He doesn't understand any language you speak."

"Everyone speaks the language of fear," Ewald said. "He's obeying for now."

The brass gongs were bright and strong crashes filling the night. Gyna's knee barely held up, but Ewald's support allowed her to hobble. Inside the small hall that shielded the forge door, two guards were piled atop each other. One seemed to merely sleep but the other had his throat laid open. Saleet moaned as he skirted the corpses.

"Good work, boy," Gyna said as they passed over them.

"Thank you," Ewald said. "Do you think you can move faster than this?"

"What are we rushing to? With these alarms sounding, we're only going to meet our deaths. You say Bjorn is out there?"

"Have some cheer, Auntie. You'll have a whole courtyard of enemies to kill."

She laughed. She could have wept. Ewald was a good lad. Arrogant and foolish, but capable. A shame to spend his life like this. But what else would they find in the courtyard but the end of their long struggle?

At last she limped into the courtyard, leaning on Ewald's shoulder who in turn marched Saleet ahead of them at the tip of his sword.

Arabs lined the walls and towers. Soldiers had rushed to the courtyard with long spears leveled. Bright blue pants and flowing shirts showed gray in the moonlight. Yet all through these ranks, servants carried smoking torches aloft. The gongs pulsed out a brassy rhythm, but as more Arabs assembled, these faded out into silence.

All along the walls and tower tops they faced the courtyard. Those in the yard faced Gyna.

"Looks like Norbert is late," Gyna said. "Or not coming."

Ewald had no reply.

Saleet made to run. Gyna flung herself on him, tackling him by the legs.

"He can't be freed," she shouted though her pain. The tackle left her strung out on the ground, but firmly gripping Saleet's thin legs. "He is a hostage. Hold him close, Ewald. Don't worry for me."

Ewald grabbed Saleet by his collar and hauled him up. Gyna crawled on the ground.

"Gyna!"

She raised her head to the voice.

Bjorn emerged from the tower where she had been captured. Blood glistened over his ragged clothes and on the short sword he held in one had. Ragnar clung to his back.

She smiled. Her hands balled up in the dirt.

"Gyna!" Bjorn rushed to her, even as guards closed the circle around them. Ragnar held on with both arms and legs wrapped tightly around Bjorn's torso. "What has happened to you?"

She turned her face to the dirt, suddenly ashamed to look so beaten. This was not how she wanted to find him again. Her face throbbed with pain and the hot flush of embarrassment. She heard Ragnar shout as he was sloughed to the ground.

Bjorn's strong hands turned her over. She looked up to his sole eye, and tears leaked down his cheek.

They stared at each other. She saw or heard nothing more. He was alive and she had found him. Even if it had been too late. They were united now and would never part again. Never.

"You came for me," she said in a hoarse whisper.

"Ain't no other choice, woman. You didn't come for me."

"I tried," she said.

Bjorn's lips quivered, then he laughed. He swept her up into his arms and laughed with all his strength. She did as well. She buried her face in his shoulder, taking in the long absent smell of him, feeling the coarseness of his beard against her cheek.

"Auntie? Can this wait for later? We are surrounded by foes."

She pulled back from Bjorn. The Arabs stood ready on the walls with arrows on their bows. The soldiers in the courtyard surrounded them.

Ewald clutched Saleet to his chest and held his short sword against the wiry man's neck. Saleet trembled and whimpered but did not dare to struggle free.

"Is that Jamil's head?" Bjorn asked. She had dropped it in the dirt when she had leapt at Saleet.

"And I am covered in his blood. We are avenged on him, at least."

"That is why I love you," Bjorn said. "You could've given me no greater gift."

Then a voice on the walls shouted down to them. It was imperious, haughty speech but in a language Gyna did not understand.

She looked up to the gatehouse that led to the inner courtyard. Atop it a man in rich yellow robes and blue head cover looked down through hooded eyes. A red jewel gleamed at his brow. Beside him, another Arab spoke his master's words in Frankish.

"Prince Jamil demands to know who has defiled his house this night. For he would know the names of those whose heads will hang from his palace walls."

Gyna sneered, then looked to Bjorn.

"There's a whole courtyard of enemies to kill. Should we get started?"

31

Gyna wrestled to her feet with Bjorn's help. The guards surrounding them did not flinch. They remained with weapons readied and arrayed in precise ranks. None of them made a noise besides the creak of their leathers or the rattle of their weapons. Their eyes reflected the torches lighting the courtyard, enhancing their fierceness.

"Answer my prince," the Frankish interpreter shouted again.

"Well, he fucking knows who we are or you wouldn't be translating to Frankish," Bjorn said as he helped Gyna stand.

"Auntie, what is going on?" Ewald still held Saleet with sword to his neck.

"Just keep him tight. I think he's the reason we're not dead yet."

"I don't understand either," Ragnar said, still crumpled on the ground. "I'm holding a dagger. So I am prepared to die. Just don't get us captured again."

"Do you want to answer or me?" Bjorn asked. He propped her gently, smiling at her as if they were chatting among friends in a mead hall. "I think you've earned it."

"Give me Jamil's head," she said. "And I'll answer."

Bjorn kicked the head toward her, then picked it up. He gave it to Gyna.

"Stand behind Ewald," she said. "So no one shoots him in the back. We're going to bargain our way out."

"Bargain, eh? I just killed two men with one hand and Ragnar on my back. If I can do that, I can cut us out of here. Norbert has to be nearby. Though the time for his attack has passed."

She leaned on his shoulder as she raised Jamil's head toward Prince Kalim standing over the gate. A pool of yellow torchlight revealed him in all his royalty. The gem at his brow must be worth a jarl's fortune alone. She wished to pluck it from him. But tonight she would be satisfied to get her life back.

"Old man, translate this for your lord. See this head? It is the head of a slave who betrayed me. I am Gyna, this is Bjorn. You know us well. You who led us into a trap rather than pay us the gold we had earned in your service. This is also what happens to a false lord."

She shook the head at the prince. Saleet groaned but Ewald dug his blade harder against the wiry man's neck.

Once the words were interpreted, a ripple of curses flowed through the guards and those on the ground brandished their spears. Yet Prince Kalim raised his palm for silence. Gold glittered around his fingers. From this vantage, he seemed no more than a shadow swathed in yellow silks and gold bands. He spoke at length, then paused for his interpreter.

"I had marked you both as dead. That you live is an unfortunate surprise. But your lives no longer interest me. If I cannot punish you then God, who is almighty, will surely double your suffering. What I am concerned with is the man you hold hostage. He is dear to me."

"I knew it," Gyna said. She shared a wicked smile with Bjorn. "We've got to trade our prize for now. But we will return for him. Thorfast lives, you know."

"As does Yngvar and Alasdair," Bjorn said. "I just know it."

She stared at him in surprise. But Bjorn merely nodded with solemn confirmation of his belief. She shook away the shock and looked back to Prince Jamil.

"How dear is he? I have his life in my hands."

Again once the interpretation was complete, a growl went up from the guards.

"I should remind you that your lives are equally in the balance. You cannot kill him and live. Though I know you may end Saleet with the slightest turn of a wrist. If you think to demand gold of me, you are as foolish as you are daring. Here is my bargain for one who is dear to me and yet caused me so much trouble."

He paused and Gyna thought the prince might leave. But he whispered with his interpreter, who nodded throughout the instructions. At last, he shouted down the offer.

"Your ship prowls the coast but cannot come near. I do not underestimate the threat of your people. For are you not a vengeful race? I will grant you safe passage to the coast and allow you to board your ship then leave my lands. Know that henceforth I will sink every ship of your people that sails within sight of my shore. Every one of your kind reaching my shore shall be put to death where they are found. I shall brook no more chances with your kind. But for tonight, in exchange for Saleet, I will grant you a final peace."

"There's got to be some gold," Bjorn said in a whisper.

Gyna flicked her hand at him. The fool never knows when to stand down.

"We need a cart," she shouted back to the prince. "And you can't have Saleet until we're aboard the ship."

"You have my word," Prince Kalim said through his interpreter. "Release Saleet and you shall be freed."

Both she and Bjorn burst into laughter at the words. She leaned on Bjorn's shoulder, shaking her head. All the shouting and laughter strained her ribs, but she could not help herself.

"I'd kiss a viper before I took your word. You don't know us well, do you? We are all prepared to die. If you cannot meet our demands, which are simple and fair, then we'll kill your man and each take twenty of your best warriors into death with us."

Her words must have been fairly translated, for the guards again shouted and cursed her. Even Saleet offered Ewald a token struggle, muttering something in his harsh language.

"Let it be so," Prince Kalim said. "But if Saleet is even scratched, I will grant you the deaths you are ready to receive. But I will grant it to you in slow measure such that your suffering will be as legend."

Bjorn groaned. "Why do these kings always say the same thing?"

"Because they don't know what else to say when they're defeated." Her heart sped and a smile spread on her face. "We've done it. We're getting back to our ship and sailing away. The gods love us."

"Careless speech, woman. We are not free yet."

Despite Bjorn's fears, the prince's words were honest. His guards provided a cart where Gyna and Ragnar could be transported. A single driver was given to lead the horse that drove the cart. They kept Saleet squeezed between all of them so that he could not escape. Saleet sat with his head bent and his eyes lowered. His face burned red and he mumbled what must have been prayers as their cart rolled out of the palace.

Guards followed them through streets shrouded with gloomy silence. It reminded her of the night she had left the prince's palace thinking nothing was remiss. An ambush had been set for her then. Could one be now?

Yet they rolled out of the city. Each bounce of the cart sent a shock of pain through her ribs. Her knee, now that it was outstretched on the cart bed, throbbed but less painful than when she stood. No one spoke as the column of guards followed. The prince had not accompanied the column. Saleet might be important, but not important enough for the prince to risk himself in the open.

As they rolled toward the shore, she stared at Bjorn. He looked so strong and hale, except for the bandage on his arm. What stories did he have to tell her? What would he think of her stories? Above all, they were united, and she would never part from him again. She had enough separation for a lifetime.

"What are you smirking at?" Bjorn asked. Though his blind side had faced her, he must have still felt her gaze.

"I was wondering what I ever saw in such an ugly man."

Bjorn shrugged. "I wondered the same. Though now that you've had your face reshaped to look like a squid, not sure you'll find many men that'll have you."

She touched her cheek. The brush of her fingertips over the hot skin was painful. She still smiled.

"I guess we're stuck with each other."

"Seems so."

At last they rolled to a stop by the sea. Gyna strained to see into the dark waters.

"Ewald, I can't see through these swollen eyes. Is our ship out there?"

He stood and peered into the distance. "It is there. Though another ship is not too far from it."

"Ragnar, you can speak a language these Arabs understand?"

"I speak Greek, which some should know enough of."

"Tell them we need to signal the ship."

Ragnar propped himself on the cart and shouted in strange words that no one seemed to understand. At last, five Arabs approached and one of their number negotiated with Ragnar. At last he slipped back from the cart side.

"They will signal the ship," he said. "With white cloth. I told them we cannot release Saleet until we are aboard our ship."

Gyna felt as if it took Norbert half the night to approach the shore. Doubtless he had been dueling with the other ship that still followed yet kept a safe distance. At last they came ashore in the shallow waves.

The Arabs demanded Saleet, who had suddenly regained his confidence. He rattled off orders that no one understood. He spoke to Ragnar who shook his head.

"The little bastard thinks I understand him," he said. "I know about twenty Arab words and no one of them are any good,"

"Well if they're curses," Bjorn said. "Heap 'em on the little rat. His usefulness is about done."

The Arabs pressed closer, but Ewald was careful to keep his sword to the wiry man's neck. This silenced his imperious shouting.

Bjorn and Gyna were first aboard the ship.

"Every time I approached the bay these Arabs ran me off. I hoped you would meet us down coast once you realized I could not land." Norbert had explained himself to Bjorn, but when he saw Gyna he offered a genuine smile. "But I see you have had success where I have had none. Well done, and welcome back to your ship."

Gyna waved her hand and hopped to the side to lean on the rails. She watched Saleet struggling with Ewald and Ragnar, who held himself against the hull waiting to board.

"Be careful with that one," she said to the men extending their arms to Ragnar. "He is badly hurt."

At last Ewald handed up Saleet. The Arabs protested with shouts and raised weapons, but Ewald leapt the low sides and was aboard before they could do more.

"Do we sail off with him?" Bjorn asked.

Gyna shook her head.

"We killed Jamil. We'll come back for Saleet. If we hold him or kill him, we'll be chased to the end of the world. No more fighting for now. I cannot take it."

The Arabs had now reached the water. Norbert gave the order to shove off and men jumped into the surf to launch the ship into the waves.

"Ewald, throw the rat Saleet overboard."

"As you say, Auntie."

Saleet flew screaming from the side and crashed into the waves. Norbert's crewmen climbed back aboard at the same moment.

The archers hidden among the ranks of Arabs came forward, their arrows raised. But a sensible captain shouted them down. They might strike Saleet, who flailed in the shallow surf as if he were drowning in a storm.

So Gyna watched the nighted shore slip away. The Arab ship trailing them just out of distance began to follow, but the Arabs raised their white flag again. Whatever their message, the Arab ship fell behind.

She felt a heavy, warm hand on her shoulder.

"We're away," he said. "Now to find Thorfast."

Tears stung her eyes. She could not see Licata through the night, except for the orange points of light that showed where torches lit the darkness.

"I suffered so much. And now we will be joined together again. Truly, the gods have been kind."

Bjorn's warm hands drew her back and she let herself fall against his strong body.

She had won her greatest victory and now would revel in the spoils.

32

After three weeks, the swelling on Gyna's face had subsided. Ewald had braced her knee and bound her ribs. Her nephew had not only learned fieldcraft but how to treat wounds as well.

"You should have been a great warrior," she had told him while they had camped on the shore of an empty island. "When you return home, you will be a great boon to your uncle."

"I'm in no hurry to return," he had said.

"That's good, because we're not going back soon." Gyna patted Ewald's head as if he were a boy, something he hated. She hated being called Auntie, but it had been growing on her.

They sheltered on that rock where the frequent rain provided fresh water and bird eggs and fish provided food. Compared to what she had suffered, the forlorn island felt like a paradise.

Bjorn had shared his incredible stories and she shared hers. Most nights were spent around the fire recounting their challenges. Norbert and his crew could hardly believe any of it, particularly Bjorn's boasts.

"While I carried Ragnar on my back," he said one night over the orange glow of the campfire. "Two men blocked the hall just as we thought to leave the tower. But such was my fury I charged them and slew them in one go. I put my short sword through both of them, like meat on a skewer."

"A short sword's not long enough for that," Gyna said.

"It's true! Ask Ragnar. He saw it."

Ragnar, whose leg and hip wounds were healing every day, simply laughed.

Gyna wished these days might never end. But the rocky island was nowhere to call home. Ships passed in the distance and some day one would venture near enough to threaten them. Jamil's head sat on a pole and rotted. Gulls had picked off most of his flesh so that now he was merely a skull. It stank with rot and drew flies. At last she had to put it in a bag until it could be properly flensed.

The halcyon days immediately following their escape had grown wearisome. The crewmen were surly at having not earned any treasure. Many felt now that Bjorn had been saved, they could return to Frankia. But none dared defy Bjorn, who assumed command in his father's name. The ax he carried across his shoulders helped quell any stronger protests.

"There's gold aplenty here," he said. "Just stay with me a while longer and you'll be rich. If not, you can take my other eye and piss on my head."

So they had travelled to Pozallo, where Ragnar said he would have allies and also find Thorfast.

Yet upon arrival, they found the fortress commander unwilling to meet with them. He had instead sent a representative along with a Frankish slave girl named Valgerd. Gyna thought she was pretty though fragile. She was terrified of them, but said Thorfast and a woman named Sophia had stayed a short time in Pozallo then travelled on. She told them they had gone with traders to the mainland. She had not heard of Yngvar or Alasdair.

"I'd swear they were among these Romans or Byzantines or whatever they call themselves," Bjorn had insisted. "That girl just didn't know."

Their journey to the mainland was short and uneventful. They served as an escort to an empty supply ship. In the first port they landed, they had more luck finding information on the woman,

Sophia. Her father had been a man of some importance. This led them to another port town, where they now had just tied off at a dock. Norbert was low on silver, but still could afford the fee.

"It's not going to be easy to find him," Bjorn said as he worked with Gyna in the prow. The rest of the crew scurried around them at their tasks. The bright day was full of activity along the docks, where dozens of workers carried loads to and from the various ships.

"The woman is the key," Gyna said. "She has a name here. If we find her, we will find him. I am confident of it."

Gyna let Bjorn mumble about the challenge. She rubbed her aching side and adjusted the heavy wrap hidden under her shirt. She was tiring and her knee was throbbing in its wood brace again. Sitting for a while would relieve the pain.

"Hey, who owns this ship? I'll have words with him."

The challenge was sharp and clear above the background of foreign chatter. It was perfectly accented Norse and it made the entire crew stand up from their work and turn toward the dock.

Bjorn shot up straight and stared at Gyna.

They both pushed forward to the rails.

Gyna's tears rose again.

The Norseman waiting on the dock with his hand on the hilt of his sword, ready to kill them all for stealing his ship, was white-haired Thorfast.

His scowl faded. He was naked but for dark pants and soft boots. His body was leaner and thinner than she remembered. But that smile, so charming and yet so devious, came easily to him. It shined through all the hardship he had gathered to himself since coming to this evil land. It cut through Gyna's hardened hide and pierced to her heart. She felt about to collapse from the joy of seeing him alive.

Bjorn leapt over the rails, screaming like a madman, and thumped to the dock. He slammed together with Thorfast and the two swayed and cried together while dock workers stared after them.

"So we've found Thorfast, Auntie?" Ewald offered his shoulder to her. "That was easier than I expected."

"That is him," Ragnar said, laughing. "The bastard looks good. But where's Sophia?"

Gyna took Ewald's offered shoulder and watched Thorfast and Bjorn dancing together, crying like old women. Neither could get out a word before they fell into a new back-slapping embrace and choked on their tears.

At last Bjorn gestured to the ship.

Ragnar hobbled to the edge to extend his hand. Thorfast paused at it, his face bright with astonishment.

"Never thought to see me again?"

Thorfast blinked. He had no answer.

Gyna stood leaning on Ewald. Both her hands were folded over her mouth. The tears flowed down around them.

She had done this. She had brought them all together.

Never had she felt a greater reward. Until this moment, she had never known true satisfaction.

Thorfast paused before her. His eyes flicked to Ewald, but then returned to her. He held his arms wide and she fell into them.

"It is good to see you again." His voice was hoarse and weary.

She simply nodded and pulled tight against him. She wanted to offer a jibe or sharp retort. But she could only sob. Her sword brother was returned to her at last.

After a moment, he gently pulled out of her embrace. Then he gathered Bjorn and her together, and his smile flooded away all the pain she felt.

"I have news," he said. "Yngvar and Alasdair are alive. And I know where they are."

Bjorn punched his fist into his palm. "I knew it. I knew I saw them."

Thorfast nodded. "As did I."

Gyna rubbed away her tears and cleared her throat. She tilted her head back then looked to Bjorn and Thorfast.

"At last, on this day, the Wolves are reborn."

NEWSLETTER

If you would like to know when my next book is released, please sign up for my new release newsletter. You can do this at my website:

http://jerryautieri.wordpress.com/

If you have enjoyed this book and would like to show your support for my writing, consider leaving a review where you purchased this book or on Goodreads, LibraryThing, and other reader sites. I need help from readers like you to get the word out about my books. If you have a moment, please share your thoughts with other readers. I appreciate it!

ALSO BY JERRY AUTIERI

Ulfrik Ormsson's Saga

Historical adventure stories set in 9th Century Europe and brimming with heroic combat. Witness the birth of a unified Norway, travel to the remote Faeroe Islands, then follow the Vikings on a siege of Paris and beyond. Walk in the footsteps of the Vikings and witness history through the eyes of Ulfrik Ormsson.

Fate's Needle

Islands in the Fog

Banners of the Northmen

Shield of Lies

The Storm God's Gift

Return of the Ravens

Sword Brothers

Grimwold and Lethos Trilogy

A sword and sorcery fantasy trilogy with a decidedly Norse flavor.

Deadman's Tide

Children of Urdis

Age of Blood

Copyright © 2019 by Jerry Autieri

All rights reserved.

No part of this book may be reproduced in any form or by any electronic or mechanical means, including information storage and retrieval systems, without written permission from the author, except for the use of brief quotations in a book review.

Printed in Great Britain
by Amazon